ROBERT B. PARKER'S
CHEAP SHOT

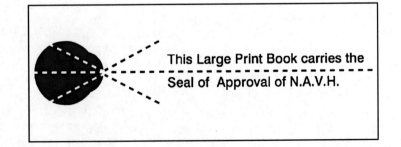

This Large Print Book carries the
Seal of Approval of N.A.V.H.

A SPENSER NOVEL

ROBERT B. PARKER'S CHEAP SHOT

ACE ATKINS

LARGE PRINT PRESS
A part of Gale, Cengage Learning

GALE
CENGAGE Learning·

Farmington Hills, Mich • San Francisco • New York • Waterville, Maine
Meriden, Conn • Mason, Ohio • Chicago

LIBRARY OF CONGRESS CATALOGING-IN-PUBLICATION DATA

Atkins, Ace.
  Robert B. Parker's cheap shot / by Ace Atkins. — Large print edition.
    pages cm. — (A Spenser novel) (Thorndike Press large print core)
    ISBN 978-1-4104-6665-5 (hardcover) — ISBN 1-4104-6665-5 (hardcover)
    1. Spenser (Fictitious character)—Fiction. 2. Private investigators—Massachusetts—Boston—Fiction. 3. Football players—Fiction.
4. Kidnapping—Fiction. 5. Large type books. I. Title.
PS3601.T487R56 2014b
813'.6—dc23   2014010199

ISBN 13: 978-1-59413-831-7 (pbk.)
ISBN 10: 1-59413-831-1 (pbk.)

Published in 2015 by arrangement with G. P. Putnam's Sons, a member of Penguin Group (USA), LLC, a Penguin Random House Company

Printed in the United States of America
  1 2 3 4 5   19 18 17 16 15

For Bob and Joan.
Still here.

Spenser's BOSTON

to Susan's home and office, Linnaean Street, Cambridge

Charles River Dam Bridge

CHARLES STREET

Massachusetts General Hospital

Charles River

ESPLANADE

Longfellow Bridge

CAMBRIDGE STREET

ESPLANADE

Hatch Shell

State Ho

STORROW DRIVE

to State Police, Boston Post Road

BEACON HILL

BEACON STREET

Spenser's apartment

Boston Common

CHARLES STREET

The Taj Boston (formerly the Ritz-Carlton)

Public Garden

ARLINGTON STREET

Swan Boats

MARLBOROUGH STREET

BERKELEY STREET

Four Seasons Hotel and Bristol Lounge

COMMONWEALTH AVENUE

BOYLSTON STREET

Spenser's office

TREMONT STREET

Boston Public Library

Copley Square

Old Boston Police Headquarters

STUART STREET

Grill 23

to Boston Police Headquarters, Roxbury

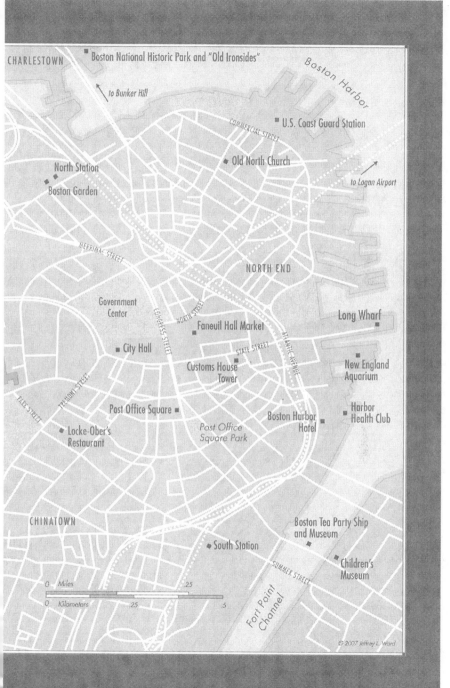

CHARLESTOWN

Boston National Historic Park and "Old Ironsides"

Boston Harbor

to Bunker Hill

COMMERCIAL STREET

U.S. Coast Guard Station

Old North Church

to Logan Airport

North Station

Boston Garden

MERRIMAC STREET

NORTH END

Government Center

CONGRESS STREET

NORTH STREET

Faneuil Hall Market

Long Wharf

City Hall

STATE STREET

ATLANTIC AVENUE

Customs House Tower

New England Aquarium

TREMONT STREET

PARK STREET

Post Office Square

Post Office Square Park

Boston Harbor Hotel

Harbor Health Club

Locke-Ober's Restaurant

CHINATOWN

Boston Tea Party Ship and Museum

South Station

Children's Museum

SUMMER STREET

0   Miles   .25
0   Kilometers   .25   .5

Fort Point Channel

© 2007 Jeffrey L. Ward

1

I had dressed for Chestnut Hill: a button-down tattersall shirt that Susan had bought me, crisp dress khakis, a navy blazer with gold buttons, and a pair of well-broken-in loafers worn without socks. The lack of socks implied a devil-may-care attitude understood by the wealthy. Even though the wealthy individual I was calling on today was a two-hundred-and-sixty-pound NFL linebacker with a twenty-inch neck named Kinjo Heywood. I'd seen Kinjo toss around quarterbacks like rag dolls and doubted that he'd notice the missing socks.

Kinjo's agent had sent a private car for me. A private car was not needed or requested to find Chestnut Hill, but there were some ground rules that had to be discussed on the ride over. I tried to remain attentive and alert as we turned off Route 9 and made our way up and around on Heath Street. The homes were very old and stately, with lots of brick and ivy. The leaves had started to turn loose on the oak branches overhead. As we drove, it all felt like a ticker-tape parade.

"You can't discuss this case with anyone, Mr. Spenser," said Steven Rosen, Kinjo's agent. He was a beefy guy with thick black hair and dark, humorless eyes. He smelled like a quart of Brut aftershave and was dressed in a pin-striped suit with wide lapels and a purple shirt open at the neck.

"Will he sign my bubblegum card?" I said.

"You're trying to be funny," Rosen said, making a sour face. "But Boston is a sports-crazy town and everyone is up in Kinjo's business. If it gets out he's hired a private investigator, this thing will become even more of a pain in the ass."

"Mum's the word."

"And this all may turn out to be nothing."

"Of course."

"And we're straight on the fee offered?"

"No."

"No?"

I told him my standard rate.

"Seriously?"

I nodded modestly. "As you know, a fee separates the pro from the amateur."

"Okay, okay."

The Town Car slowed and we dipped

10

down off the road past a stone fence and toward a very large stone house with two identical white Cadillac Escalades parked outside. Before the driver got out, I opened my door and waited for Rosen to follow.

The air smelled of a good fire burning and crisp autumn sunshine. A brisk wind warned of cold days to follow.

The front door opened. Rosen ushered us toward the brick walkway. He seemed less than enthused with having to clean up the latest mess for his client.

An old woman with copper-colored skin and dressed in a gray maid's uniform led me into the foyer. The foyer led into a great room, where a very large black man was watching an old samurai movie on a very large television. A skinny white woman with enormous breasts and blond hair sat across from him, drinking a red drink in a martini glass. The furniture was all leather and glass and too modern for such an old house.

"What's up, Kinjo?" Rosen said. "My main man."

Kinjo pressed pause on the DVD player. He looked up, surprised that he had guests, and stood up as if he'd been dozing. The woman with the large breasts continued to sip her drink. She wore a white tank top with gold embroidery, gold hoop earrings, and blue jeans so tight they might have been applied by Earl Scheib.

Kinjo was much larger than me. I wasn't used to meeting anyone larger than me except for Hawk. And Hawk stood only a half-inch taller. Kinjo was made of muscle the way a jaguar is all muscle. He moved with a strong confidence, eyes shifting from me to Rosen to his wife with just a flick. He had a mustache and a goatee and kept his hair in long cornrows. He wore a light blue Adidas tracksuit and no shoes. I'd read that he was twenty-seven, a Pro Bowl selection for the last two years, and faster than a cheetah.

"You the detective?" Kinjo said.

"Yep."

"You look like a detective. Or a cop."

"A cop would have worn socks." I pulled up my pant leg.

Kinjo nodded. A frame of the film remained on the large television screen. *Yojimbo.* I nodded toward it.

"Toshiro Mifune."

"I've seen every movie he's made."

"I've always been partial to *Seven Samurai.*"

"My mother named me after the emperor of Japan," he said. "She found it in an encyclopedia, because she wanted me to

12

stand out. That's how I got into these movies and the way of the warrior. Not a lot of black kids in Georgia digging Kurosawa."

"But you played college in Alabama."

"Auburn," Kinjo said. "Don't ever say I played for the Tide."

I smiled. He nodded over his shoulder at the woman with the red drink.

"That's Cristal," he said. "Say hello, Cristal."

She said hello. She was slightly tipsy but did not seem drunk. Her eyes took me in with some humor. "Do you carry a gun?" she said.

I opened my blue blazer and showed the .38 on my hip.

She said, "Wow." I tilted my head modestly.

Rosen seemed impatient with all the small talk. He stood by the housekeeper and pulled an iPhone from his pocket and studied the screen. The maid whispered in his ear. Without looking away from his phone, he said, "Teresa wants to know if anyone would like anything to drink."

I said coffee would be nice. Kinjo turned off the film and we sat in the little grouping. Cristal finished the red drink.

It was one in the afternoon.

"You gonna catch these guys?" Kinjo said.

"Sure."

"And find out why the hell they following me?"

"Why not."

Kinjo looked to super-agent Steve Rosen and Rosen nodded in affirmation. *Goody.*

"So how much do you know?" Kinjo said.

"I know you and your wife were having dinner at Capital Grille by the Chestnut Hill mall and that someone followed you home. And when you tried to take another route, they kept on following you, and you decided to take matters into your own hands by discharging your weapon on Route 9."

Rosen looked up from his iPhone and swallowed.

"Goddamn cowards wouldn't get out of their car, so I tried to get their damn attention."

"That's one way to do it."

"His actions were ill advised," Rosen said. "A cop with the Boston police suggested we talk to you."

"Instead of Mr. Heywood continuing to pursue the matter himself?"

"Stevie said if I shoot one of them, it might mess up my new contract."

"Ah," I said. "And the weapons violation?"

"Mr. Heywood has an attorney to make

that disappear if it doesn't happen again."

"Have you seen the same car again?"

Kinjo leaned forward, elbows on knees, and nodded. "Yesterday. Different car. First time was a new black 4Runner, but it was a green Tahoe yesterday."

"Same men?"

"Couldn't tell," he said. "But when I left Gillette, they rode up real close, I took some turns and they didn't back off until I got home."

"And then what did you do?"

"Got my damn gun, jumped out of my car, and they took off."

Rosen held up his hand and smiled at me. "And the reason we called you, Mr. Spenser. You came highly recommended."

"By whom, may I ask?"

"A detective named Belson."

Rosen nodded. Heywood watched him nod and then nodded, too. I nodded. We looked like a collection of bobbleheads. Cristal stood and went to the kitchen.

"Could this have been just some fans?" I said. "Your face is on several billboards, and often on television."

"These people didn't want no autograph," he said. "This was all business."

"How so?"

Kinjo rubbed his goatee in thought. He

tilted his head and met my eye. "They were real aggressive about it."

"You want protection for you and your wife?" I said.

"I don't need protection," Kinjo said. "They need protection from me. I just want to know who they are and what they want. And I don't want to have to shoot no one. That might make me look bad."

"Always the trouble with shooting people."

He looked to Rosen again. Rosen was too busy texting someone to notice.

"Any enemies? Anyone who would want to do you harm? People you owe money?"

Kinjo shook his head. "I got lots of both. Plenty of enemies and money."

"Mr. Heywood just signed a contract extension worth ten million," Rosen said.

"Makes you a good target."

"Yeah." Kinjo looked down at his hands and then back up at me. "But I think this shit is personal."

"Why would anyone want to hurt you?"

No one said anything. Rosen unfolded his arms and made way for Teresa, who brought in two coffee mugs on a serving tray. Somewhere in the kitchen, I heard a martini shaker. Rosen shifted in his seat. "I'm sure you read up a little on Mr. Heywood before coming over."

I nodded.

"I pissed a few folks off over the years," he said.

"Okay," I said. "Who would most likely want to get back at you?"

Kinjo leaned back into the couch. It was a big white sectional in a U shape. He stared right at me. "How much time you got?"

I shrugged. "I'm paid by the hour," I said. "Take as long as you'd like."

2

"Don't you need a notebook, Spenser?" Rosen said. "You're not writing down any of these women's names."

I tapped at my temple with my index finger.

"You're kidding," Rosen said. "Right?"

"Nope," I said, turning to Kinjo. "Have any of these old girlfriends tried to contact you recently?"

Kinjo shook his head.

"Any asked for more money?"

"Just my ex-wife," he said. "She's always asking for money. I hadn't even gotten done at the press conference when my cell started ringing. Her lawyer knew exactly how much more I'd be owing her."

"If she wants money from you," I said, "seems like she'd want you healthy."

"Yeah, I guess," he said.

Kinjo continued to stroke his mustache and goatee. Behind him was an expansive bank of windows. Beyond the glass, there was an elaborate play fort made of reddish wood and fashioned like something for the U.S. Cavalry. There were four turrets at each corner topped in a lookout point. In the far-left corner, I spotted a young kid, maybe seven or eight, watching us with binoculars.

I lifted a hand and waved.

The child disappeared.

Kinjo peered over his shoulder and then turned back to me. "My kid," he said. "Akira. We work things out with games and my schedule."

"Your ex lives in Mass?"

He nodded. "Akira my heart, man," Kinjo said. "Everything I do is for him. Nicole never liked the name, wanted to name the kid after her uncle George or some shit. But I wanted him to stand out, the way my momma wanted for me. We love anything Japanese. Movies, comics, sushi. How many kids like raw fish?"

Kinjo turned back to see if his son was still watching us. Rosen drank his coffee, waiting for the right moment to cut the conversation short. Cristal Heywood entered the room with another big red drink in a martini glass. I would have guessed a Manhattan, but it was too red, too fruity to be an authentic cocktail. It was the kind of drink that needed the shade of a tiny umbrella.

"Nicole's a fucking nightmare," Cristal said, taking a seat beside Kinjo. She took a quick sip, holding up her hand to continue her thoughts. "I can't even stand being in the same room with her. She talks down to me. Looks at me like I'm trashy or something."

Cristal slurped her cocktail and giggled.

Kinjo gave a hard sideways glance at his wife. Cristal wore a bright pink bra under the white tank top. She giggled again and pulled up a single pink strap.

"Anyone else I should know?" I said.

"Nope."

There was a long silence. Cristal sipped her drink. I held my coffee mug and smiled.

"When can you get started?" Rosen said.

I shrugged. "Are we going to talk about the nightclub shooting in New York?" I said. "Or pretend it didn't happen?"

Rosen looked to Kinjo. Kinjo did not look pleased I subscribed to *Sports Illustrated,* watched ESPN, and that I even knew how to use Google. His jaw clenched and eyes flattened.

"I was acquitted," he said. "I wasn't even there."

I nodded. "But the man's family sued you in civil."

"Digging for money."

"Sure," I said. "But don't you think you might have listed them under the heading of people who would like to do you harm? Probably more than some jilted girlfriends."

"That's bullshit," Cristal said. "Just because Kinjo is tough doesn't mean he's a thug."

"I'm not being hired to investigate that," I said. "But you told me that you believe these men want to do you harm. If you want me to find them, you need to help me with a list. I start with a list and then narrow it down. Unless it's some nuts, and then we just wait till they follow you again."

Kinjo nodded. Cristal swigged a bit more.

"Kinjo needs this thing settled," Rosen said. "Regular season starts in two weeks."

"I understand," I said. "But I need to know if you think these men might be connected to what happened in New York."

"No," Kinjo said. "No fucking way."

"A man was shot to death," I said. "The family blamed you."

"The family knew I was at the club," Kinjo said. "The family wanted money."

"Then who else would you guess?"

He looked to Rosen and then nodded

along with his thoughts. "I swear to you I think it's another player messin' with my head."

"For the Pats?"

"Hell, no," he said. "Not a teammate. Somebody I hurt. They want my ass taken out before the season."

"Who?" I said.

"You better get some paper and a pen," he said. " 'Cause I had a good season last year. People call me dirty. What's my job but to take people out? That doesn't make me a hit man."

"That hatchet piece in *Sports Illustrated* about Kinjo being the NFL bad boy was a lot of crap," Rosen said. "They barely mentioned his recent marriage or relationship with Akira. I thought the piece was completely racist. We will never work with that reporter again."

"So it's messing with your head?" I said. "And to play, you need to be relaxed and loose."

"Yeah, that's right." Kinjo looked up from his hands. He met my eye and nodded. He studied me again, as if I'd reentered the room. "You play?"

"A couple years in college," I said.

"Where?"

I told him.

"That what happened to your nose and around the eyes?"

"Nope," I said. "We had face guards back then. Leather helmets had just gone out of style."

"Fight?"

"Boxing," I said.

"Pro?"

I nodded.

"Boxing?" Cristal said. "Wow? Like Rocky?"

"Yep," I said. "Just like Rocky. I used to have pet turtles and everything."

Rosen rolled his eyes. Kinjo stood and walked to the bank of windows. Akira had moved onto another turret, another wall to be protected from the enemy. He was a skinny kid with short hair and a mischievous smile. A bright red Under Armour sweatshirt swallowed him to the knees.

The child looked at us through the binoculars. When I smiled directly at him, he ran away. A strong wind rustled tree branches overhead. A bright sun shone across the tree fort, creating small pockets and insignificant shadows. Leaves fell and fluttered to the ground.

Cristal made another drink. I finished my coffee and said my good-byes.

I would start tomorrow.

3

I made corn muffins from scratch for Susan.

I had not planned to make corn muffins but had decided today's brisk fall wind called for chili. And to me, chili always seemed lonely without corn muffins. Or perhaps I made them because I had stocked a six-pack of Bohemia in Susan's refrigerator. Truth be told, it was very difficult to know the meal's catalyst. Probably the beer.

I had let myself in shortly before five and took Pearl for a short walk. Susan was in session, so as silently as possible I crept up to the second floor and helped myself to a Bohemia. I had bought the corn meal, flour, eggs, and ingredients for the chili at the Whole Foods on River Street. I drank while I chopped some peppers, garlic, and onions and browned some ground buffalo. Pearl showed a lot of interest in the sizzling buffalo.

I added the peppers, garlic, and onions to

24

the browning meat, and then a couple dashes of the beer. Some chili powder, kosher salt, cumin, and black pepper. More beer. I played some Mel Tormé at a volume low enough not to disrupt psychotherapy. Pearl tilted her head and I scratched her ears.

"Mel Tormé?" Susan said, walking in.

"The velvet frog himself."

" 'Goody Goody' is very odd to hear after talking with a patient who wishes to be impregnated by her husband while conducting an extramarital affair."

"Better odds?"

"She has no desire to be impregnated by her lover."

"Must draw a line in the sand somewhere."

"Yes."

"How hot is too hot?" I said.

"Is this a trick question?"

"Yep," I said.

I turned on the oven and found her lonely mixing bowl and measured the corn meal, flour, salt, baking powder, and sugar, and then added the eggs, butter, and some milk and whisked it all to the proper smoothness. I searched for the muffin tin I had stowed in a secret location. When I added the sautéed mix of meat and onions to a large pot of bubbling tomatoes and beans, Pearl lost interest and trotted over to a window facing Linnaean. The branch of an oak tapped at the glass.

I added more beer with the simmering chili. And a quart of water so as not to waste more beer.

"For fear of sounding too domestic, how was your day, dear?"

"I met with a professional football player named after a Japanese emperor," I said. "His agent hired me to help him."

"Protection?"

"In a roundabout way," I said. "The Patriots organization thinks it's a bad idea if their player shoots or beats up someone."

"So you've been hired to protect the bad guys?"

I nodded. I stirred the chili. I waited to put the corn muffins in the oven. Mel sang "A Stranger in Town."

"The team also wants me to find out who is following Kinjo and why."

"Kinjo."

"Emperor of the gridiron."

I reached into the refrigerator for a bottle of sauvignon blanc. I poured Susan a modest glass.

"Should I know who this is?" she said.

"You should."

"Did you?"

"Of course."

"I thought you only paid attention to baseball and basketball?"

"Sometimes it's on TV," I said. "Sometimes I watch it. I played it once."

"But you prefer baseball."

"I prefer baseball for the skill and nuance," I said. "I'm sure a damn good bit of sportswriters could talk to me about the elegant violence of football. But I like the pace of baseball."

I greased the muffin tin, poured in the batter, and placed the tin into the oven. I finished the beer and opened another.

"How does an investigator, even one of your advanced skill, watch a client and sleuth at the same time?"

"I am hoping the watching will lead to a meeting with the bad guys."

"As it often does."

"And if not," I said, "Z can watch while I sleuth."

"Nice to have an understudy."

I nodded. I set the timer. "Of course, I'm not even sure if there are any bad guys."

"And how is that possible?"

"There is a distinct possibility that his celebrity status is making him a bit paranoid," I said. "He's a famous athlete. Some overzealous fans may just recognize him and see where he lives or what nightclub he prefers."

"Did he seem paranoid to you?"

"You mean did he pace around with some metallic ball in hand and mutter about strawberries?"

"Or something more subtle," she said. "Was he jittery or nervous? Did he seem on edge?"

"Nope."

"Yet he felt threatened."

"Yes," I said. "But he couldn't really define it."

"Hmm."

"What's your diagnosis, Doc?"

"Time will tell?"

"What if he tells me the men following him are little and green and perhaps from another planet?"

"Give him my card," she said. "I have people he should meet."

I turned back to Susan, pulled her in close, and placed a hand against the flat of her back. I tilted my head toward her open bedroom door. I had missed her a great deal when she'd been away teaching that spring.

"Sometimes I think you use simmering for an excuse," she said.

"But it's such a damn good one."

28

4

The next morning, I picked up Kinjo Heywood and drove him to Foxboro.

The Patriots kept their training facilities, offices, and practice fields in and around Gillette. Up the hill from the stadium, a sprawling entertainment complex called Patriot Place had recently opened to make sure every dime stayed within a quarter-mile radius. There were shops, outdoor cafés, and a movie theater. Bass Pro Shops, a Renaissance Hotel, and even Toby Keith's I Love This Bar & Grill made Patriot Place about as unique as a trip to suburban Ohio.

On the south end of the complex, I watched Kinjo go through a series of warm-up drills, stretching and running with the team. They had dressed out in half-pads, helmets, and shorts. It was still early and gray, a misty rain falling. I stood, watching, next to Kinjo's brother, Ray, who was also his business manager.

"They shouldn't practice in the rain," Ray Heywood said. "Somebody is going to get hurt."

"But if you don't practice in the elements, how will you play in them?"

"You sound like Coach Belichick," Ray said. "You see that big metal building behind us? Cost something like twenty million and he's used it maybe two times. Rain, sleet, snow, the players' asses are out here."

"Might ruin Tom Brady's hair."

Ray Heywood laughed.

If Kinjo hadn't introduced me to Ray, I would have never figured them for brothers. Ray Heywood stood a little under six feet and was short-legged and thick around the waist. He had shaved his hair and beard very short and had an earring in his right ear. He wore a pink oxford cloth shirt hanging out over designer jeans and designer sneakers.

"You like working for your brother?"

"I work for him but don't work for him," Ray said. "I just look out for his business affairs."

"So you're his other agent?"

Ray shook his head. "Un-uh," he said. "Kinjo has the same agent he's always had. I only take care of his money while he keeps his mind right. I handle investments, off-season appearances, and endorsement deals. A life in the NFL ain't forever. He's got to make that hard cash now and see how it can grow."

"What did you do before?"

Ray ran a hand over the back of his thick neck and smiled. "Sold cars," he said. "I know what you're thinking. But it was a dealership in Atlanta, and I am very good with money."

I nodded and stuck my hands in the pockets of my A-2 bomber jacket. I wore a navy Lowell Spinners ball cap, since I didn't own anything with an NFL logo. Maybe if I caught the bad guys and forced them to talk, the Pats would comp me a cap.

"You have any theories as to who's been following your brother?" I said.

Ray shook his head.

The misting rain kept on falling. Kinjo had joined up with the other linebackers and was running his feet with great speed over a row of red blocking dummies. When his foot hit the grass after the last dummy, he darted toward his coach, who zinged him the ball. He ran the ball upfield. The coach blew a whistle.

"Kinjo said you think it has something to do with that shooting?"

"Nope," I said. "I just asked him what he

thought."

"Two years ago."

I nodded.

"He didn't have nothing to do with that."

"Have no reason to think he did."

There were maybe twenty or thirty people perched around the aluminum stands where we now sat. The practice was closed to the public, and most looked to be sportswriters or family of the players. A couple news stations for film at eleven.

"He seemed to think it was a player for another team," I said. "Maybe wants to rattle him before the season."

"You read that *SI* piece?"

"Yep."

"Calling him the league's hit man?" Ray said. "That's some bullshit. They had coaches and players saying he took cheap shots. Someone said he wasn't no different from the guys on the Saints who worked for a bounty. What's a linebacker supposed to do to a quarterback? Hug and kiss him?"

"Hardly appropriate."

"You running at a quarterback on a blitz full-out, man," he said. "If he let go of the ball a tenth of a second before, how you supposed to put on the brakes? Kinjo start doing that and he'll fuck up his knees and hips. That story's told by people who never played the game. Most sportswriters hate athletes 'cause they know they'd shit their pants if they ever stepped on the field."

Kinjo and the other linebackers had joined up with the rest of the defense and were going through different alignments. The Patriots, like most pro teams, ran a four-three defense, four down linemen and three linebackers roaming the mid-ground. Kinjo was the middle linebacker, the Mike, who was pretty much the quarterback of the defense. He could rush the passer or drop back and cover a receiver.

I'd seen some highlight film of Kinjo. He had aided many players to early retirement. But I saw nothing dirty about his play. No dirtier than a fighter who had a hell of a right.

"So you gonna follow him to and from practice and see who's tailing him?" Ray said.

"That's the plan."

"What you do if you find out who they are and where they live?"

"Reason with them."

Ray laughed. "You don't look like the kind of man with many reasoning skills."

"I am a man of many talents."

An air horn sounded and Belichick called the entire team together to scrimmage. The hitting was very light on the line and the offense went through a series of plays while the linebackers shot the gaps in the line or went into pass coverage. Passes were thrown and caught, the orchestra of the defense and offense working with speed and efficiency.

As the special teams ran onto the field, a man in a dark suit approached us.

"Oh, shit," Ray said. "This dickhead runs the security for the Pats."

"Lovely."

When the man got closer, Ray stood up and said, "Spenser, this is Jeff Barnes."

We shook hands while the players scrimmaged. The misty rain seemed to make the practice field glow an intense green.

Barnes smiled without warmth, eyes wandering over me. He was a compact man, blue-suited and red-tied, with chiseled features and thick white hair. His lips were thin and his nose hawkish, and he had a superior posture that reminded me of a rooster.

"Nice to meet you," Barnes said, shaking my hand. "Can't say I was excited that Steve Rosen didn't tell me about you."

"Not everyone can sing my praises."

"I'm not familiar with some of the local cops, but I did call up a friend with the FBI," Barnes said, still gripping my hand.

"His remarks weren't kind."

"Are you taking my fingerprints right now?"

Barnes let go of my hand. A smile remained frozen on his face.

"You must be quite a hot dog to draw the ire of the special agent in charge of the city."

I wavered my hand in a so-so gesture.

Barnes's face reddened. His cheek twitched just a bit. The air horn sounded on the field and Belichick called in all the players. Ray stared down at the field where the team had gathered, but Barnes remained splayfooted and cocksure.

"Rosen is a hot-shit agent," he said. "But I can pull you off the tit fast. When you're on this property, I am in charge."

"Yikes."

"What?"

"I said, 'Yikes.' It means my knees won't stop knocking."

"If you see anything, suspect anything, or spot anyone in or around Gillette, you call me first. Connor said you're overly fond of your weapon."

I let that one go and simply shrugged.

"These kids out there don't have normal problems like you and me," he said. "Kinjo is probably being followed by a carload of sorority girls who just want to bang him.

You make a mistake, and this team looks bad and my entire job is in question. You understand?"

"Un-uh. Go back to the sorority girls."

"Christ," Barnes said, shaking his head. He walked away.

I sat back down with Ray. He studied the field and the players fanning out on one knee and listening to the coach talk about their opponent. His chin was lifted as if he hadn't heard a word. Not looking away, Ray said, "Looks like they got the right guy," he said.

"Thanks."

"Don't let that prick get in the way of protecting my brother," he said. "Kinjo's a good man. He never wanted Akira to grow up like we did. It's important to have a father, not just around, but in his life. We never had that. He and that kid go to the zoo, the mall, to movies. Disney World twice a year. That's why the bad stuff hurts Kinjo. Because that ain't him. You can talk shit about him on the field, but anyone who tarnishes who he is as a man, that's about his family honor."

"A Southern man's code?"

"And all that Japanese shit he's into. Man loves his family and he takes care of his people. Look at me. I may be good with money, but I never deserved all this."

I nodded. "You think it's really just a carload of girls?"

"Tell you what," Ray said. "If it is, I'd better be the one you call first."

5

The next day, I followed Kinjo away from Foxboro and into the city. Akira was to spend the weekend with his mother, and both had agreed to meet at the Quincy Market. This was not my decision, only a stroke of luck, as I had not eaten since early that morning. The Pats had not invited me to partake in their training table for carbo-loading or fruit smoothies.

We parked side by side at a garage with a nice view of the North End. I hung back as Kinjo followed the sidewalk with Akira, the son a little moody about the exchange. He wore an oversized Pats jersey with HEY-WOOD written above number 57.

There were a few whispers and sideways glances as they made their way into the market. A couple of people stopped him for an autograph. Akira seemed used to all this. He'd smile up as his father signed a piece of paper or someone's hat. Inside, I bought a turkey sub and sat down with them at a table in the common area under the rotunda.

"Shit," Kinjo said. "Nicole's always late. She can't help it."

I unwrapped the sandwich and offered Akira half. He declined. He said his mother was going to take him to the Five Guys in Medford. As I ate, two unsavory-looking men in leather coats walked from the Faneuil Hall entrance. I watched them move past our table, not a flick of recognition, as they headed toward a pizza vendor.

"You ever shoot anybody?" Akira said.

I looked to Kinjo. Kinjo nodded back.

"Yep."

"Dead?" Akira said.

"As a doornail."

The kid nodded with that, liking what he'd heard. He was smallish, even for eight, with bright eyes and a warm smile.

"Why'd you kill them?" Akira said.

"Akira," Kinjo said. "Hush."

"I just want to know."

"They were very unpleasant people," I said.

"Bad men," Akira said.

"You might say that."

"And they needed to be dead?"

I looked to Kinjo again. He nodded. I

39

looked to the bright-eyed little boy and shrugged. "It's a little more complicated than that."

Akira nodded.

"Akira goes to Beaver Country Day," Kinjo said. "Every student got their own iPad. School where I went in Georgia was just a bunch of trailers. Teachers did the best they could. But they couldn't do much."

I lifted my eyes and nodded at his flat-billed baseball hat. "What's that *R* with the squiggles mean?"

Akira looked at his dad as if I were simple. Kinjo continued to look at the crowded space filled with people eating and talking, coming and going, carrying food from the long food court. I ate more of my sub.

"It's Rocawear," Kinjo said.

"Of course," I said. "Rocawear."

"Jay-Z," Akira said. "He owns it."

"Hat cost a hundred damn dollars," Kinjo said.

"Daddy never ate in a restaurant till he was in high school."

Kinjo shrugged.

"And he had three jobs after school when he wasn't playing ball."

Kinjo grinned. "Actually, just two."

"Shining shoes and loading shelves at the

Piggly Wiggly."

Kinjo nodded and put an arm around his son, pulling him tight. "Akira's gonna work training camp next year. Learn what it's like to make money."

"I don't want to shine shoes."

Kinjo nodded, grabbed Akira's sneaker and dusted off some dirt. Akira laughed, but Kinjo looked away and shook his head. "Okay. Here we go. Here comes trouble."

A woman had walked in from the south end of Quincy Market, splitting the tourists like Moses and the Red Sea. She was diminutive but moved with purpose. Kinjo's former wife was dark-skinned, with short black hair reminiscent of Audrey Hepburn's. She wore a blue-and-white vertical-striped sleeveless blouse and navy pencil skirt. Her heels were brown and tall and her jewelry was simple. As she walked closer I noted a tiny silver necklace with a diamond pendant on her long neck.

She smiled at Akira. She ignored both me and Kinjo. I put down the sub.

"I've been waiting for you outside for fifteen minutes," she said. "What the hell?"

"I told you we'd be inside," Kinjo said. "It's getting cold. Damn."

She turned back to her son. "Don't you have anything else to wear besides football jerseys?"

Akira shrugged. Nicole looked to me. I wrapped up my sub and stood. Her eyes were big and almond-shaped. She had full lips and fine features. I smiled at her. She did not return the gesture.

"Why'd you bring a coach?" she said.

"He ain't a coach," Kinjo said. "He does security."

"And why is he here?" she said.

Kinjo's eyes shifted from me to Akira and back to Nicole. Kinjo offered his palms and said, "He's doing some security work for me." Akira slowly moved away from his father and hugged his mother around the waist. He was content. His mother glared at me.

I smiled some more. My cheeks started to hurt. A young Hispanic man in a do-rag and a skinny young white man with shoulder-length red hair watched us from a long table on the far side of the rotunda. They spoke back and forth, eyes on Kinjo and Nicole. One of them nodded. The Hispanic man continued to watch.

I asked Nicole if she'd like to sit.

She shook her head. Akira unwrapped his arms from her and took his backpack from his father. The kid watched the ground as his parents talked to each other.

"You get straight with the lawyer?" he said. "You see we doing things right?"

Nicole looked at Kinjo, eyes flicking across his face. "Sorry I didn't trust you," she said. "Don't know why that is."

She turned. I smiled at Akira and winked at him. He returned with a weak smile and looked away.

I sat back down. I returned to my sub. The Hispanic man and Eric the Red continued to watch us. They watched Nicole and Akira as they passed, hand in hand. I started to follow, but their gaze hung back on Kinjo. The Hispanic man picked at his teeth with his small finger, eyes unwavering.

"You recognize those two?" I said.

"Where?"

I ate a bit. I motioned slightly with my head.

"Nope."

Eric the Red started to stand. He had a matching mustache and goatee, red hair long and curly.

"So how the Falcons look this week?" I said.

"Okay."

"You okay?"

"She shouldn't talk like that in front of the kid."

"I noted a trace of hostility."

43

"Shit," he said. "She'd be glad if someone did kill me."

Kinjo shook his head. Akira and Nicole had disappeared into the long, narrow space of the mall. The Hispanic man joined Eric the Red, and they walked toward us. The Hispanic man had his hand at hip level. Both eyes were serious and intent. Eric the Red licked his lips. His Celtics T-shirt hung nearly to his knees.

I had one bite to go but steeled myself.

The men approached the table. The Hispanic man reached into his jacket.

Kinjo jumped up fast and threw a right hand at the man's face. I caught his fist in my palm. The man ducked, yelping, "What the fuck?"

A pen fell to the floor. Eric the Red ducked and covered.

Kinjo breathed hard out of his nose. His face twitched.

I let go of Kinjo's fist. My palm smarted as I picked up the pen and handed it to him. "Sorry about that." Kinjo took it and forced a smile. "What's your name, man?"

6

The Pats flew out to Atlanta the next morning. Kinjo was now under the watch of Jeff Barnes. I told Kinjo to give him my best.

As I had a couple days to sleuth, I drove to the Harbor Health Club to search for some company. I found Z and Hawk sparring in Henry's newly expanded boxing room. Hawk and I had taken turns coaching Z that summer.

Z wore cut-off gray sweats, a pair of eighteen-ounce gloves, and leather headgear. Hawk wore a black satin Adidas getup with red stripes, focus mitts, and no headgear. Hawk's head was made of steel and Teflon and shone black and smooth in the harbor's morning light.

Hawk played James Brown on the sound system. He had been telling Z he moved more white than red or black, and he needed rhythm.

"Keep yourself bladed, move, come on,

duck, okay, two, three, two. Slip. Up on that toe. Breathe like you live. Don't breathe to punch. You do that in the ring and you get killed."

I stood next to the heavy bag. The new section of plate glass provided a commanding view of the harbor. The boxing room had more than doubled in size, which, at first, Hawk and I thought came from Henry's undying gratitude. Then we noted the flyers around the gym for kickboxing and something called Punch Fit classes. It didn't matter. We now had two heavy bags, two speed bags, and a big mirrored room to shadow-box and to offer classes to promising young thugs.

"Where's the snap?" Hawk said. "You pushing a punch. Don't push it. Snap that jab out there. Come on in. Make me back the fuck up."

The three-minute timer buzzed. Z was drenched. He winked at me and made his way to the water fountain.

"As a white man, I am deeply offended by your comments on rhythm."

"Only white man could move was Gene Kelly," Hawk said. "Only white man who could move and fight was Hollywood fantasy."

"Besides being part of the Big Brothers

46

program," I said, "what else do you have going on?"

"Besides lookin' good and pleasin' the ladies?"

"Yeah," I said. "Besides that."

Hawk shook his head. "Nothing that interest me."

"I thought I had something," I said. "Good pay, too."

"Fella offered me a job in a grocery store," Hawk said, grinning. *"Said I'd make a crackerjack clerk."*

"Crackerjack," I said.

"What happened to the job?"

"Still on it," I said. "But starting to think it's all in the client's mind."

"Sounds like Susan's kind of work," he said.

"Maybe."

Hawk removed the focus mitts. Without looking at his watch, he told Z to take on the heavy bag. Within two seconds, the buzzer sounded. "So, if it is real," Hawk said, "what's the job?"

"Shooing flies off a man who just may be tougher than you."

Hawk raised his eyebrows. He doubted it.

"Kinjo Heywood," I said. "Pats linebacker."

"Playing a game ain't the same, babe."

47

"No," I said. "It's not."

" 'Course millions of people don't pay to watch us kick the shit out of people, either."

"True."

"They should," Hawk said. "We good at it."

"And Z is getting better."

Hawk shrugged. Z worked on the heavy bag. Despite his injuries from a few months ago, his body had healed and his punches had become even more substantial. The bag hopped and bounced on the heavy chains. Z's breathing was smooth and easy, his muscles bulging from his cut-off sweatshirt. He had cut his long, black hair as short as mine.

"Full-time job for Z to unlearn all your bad habits."

"Thank God you stepped in when you did," I said.

"Another month with you, and he'd be ready for the Ziegfeld Follies."

"Shall I serenade you with 'There's Beauty Everywhere'?"

"How about I teach Z to fight, and you teach all the useless shit you know."

"We each have our calling."

7

Susan and I had dinner at Casablanca. Everything was the same: the polished wood, the gleaming brass rails, the churning ceiling fans, and the colorful murals of Bogart and scenes from Rick's Café. Even Sari, the restaurant's owner, kept his place at a back table and whispered in conspiratorial tones with Catherine Boyle, another loyal customer and one of Susan's friends. I'd never have guessed the restaurant's days were numbered.

"How long?" Susan said.

We stood at the bar. I ordered a Blue Moon ale. Susan ordered a gin martini and waved at Catherine.

"Sari says the end of the year," I said. "He says there will be a big going-away party."

"Hard to envision Brattle Street without Casablanca."

"Or downtown without Locke-Ober."

Susan nodded and smiled a bit. The

bartender served my beer. He started work on Susan's concoction. I did not touch my beer.

She nudged me. "Go ahead, big guy."

"I can wait," I said. "Contrary to popular opinion, I don't salivate at the sound of a cracking bottle top."

"What do you think they'll do with all the murals?" she said. "I'll miss the murals."

"They'll be ripped out with the rest of it," I said. "Progress."

The bartender presented the martini. Susan lifted it in a toast and said, "May it pass us by."

We clicked drinks. Sari nodded and waved to us. We waved back. Susan cocked a hip and leaned into the bar. She wore a pair of very tight dark jeans and a green scoop-necked cashmere sweater. Her shoes were high-heeled and très chic. I bet I could not pronounce their maker.

"Before we're seated," I said. "Do you mind talking shop?"

"Do you know how much you would owe me if you had to pay for my professional services?"

I smiled and tilted my head. "Perhaps I could work it off?"

"Shrinkage for sexual favors?" she said. "A slight ethical dilemma we have discussed many times before."

"This is nothing solid," I said. "Just some general advice."

"On?"

"Paranoia."

"That's a very wide topic," she said. "Aren't you the one that said paranoia was very healthy in your business?"

"I said that?" I said. "My wisdom occasionally astounds me."

Susan rolled her eyes. She toyed with her drink, taking a short sip.

"How might I recognize someone suffering from unhealthy paranoia?" I said. "When people come to me and need help, I often believe them. But what if the only trouble was in their head?"

"Something new with your client?"

I turned beside me to make sure no one was within earshot. I gave a small nod. I took a sip of beer. Sipping beer fueled the thinking. The thinking would lead to the right path.

I shrugged. "A couple of guys approached him at the Quincy Market for an autograph and he nearly ripped their heads off."

"What did you think?"

"Maybe it's contagious. I nearly slugged one of them."

"What stopped you?"

"A Bic pen looks very different than a .44 Magnum."

"How does Kinjo treat you?" Susan said. "Does he confide in you or is he standoffish?"

"Straight ahead."

"Besides people following him," she said, "has he said anything that seems irrational?"

"He thinks it may be another player who wants him hurt."

"Is that plausible?"

"Sure." I smiled. "Anything is plausible in the NFL."

"Lots of money at stake."

"Money, power, ego. Take your pick."

I drank some beer. I thought. I drank some more beer and waited for enlightenment. "Something is off about what he's told me. Something doesn't ring true."

"But he's your client," she said. "You've given your word to help, and you must trust his."

"Yes."

"Could he just want attention?" she said.

"Why would a football hero need more? His picture is on soda cups."

"Maybe he has a head injury," she said. "The man does use his head as a battering ram professionally."

"I was told that would only hone your

52

intellect."

"Yes," Susan said. "Of course."

"Time will tell if someone is trying to kill him," I said. "And I'll try to protect both him and his reputation."

"A noble goal."

"If they don't shoot me in the process."

We clicked drinks. I took a swallow of beer.

"And what will you be having for our last supper?" I said.

"Tapas," she said. "I'm very fond of their deviled eggs and fried green tomatoes."

"Chicken seems fitting to me," I said. "Fries, collard greens, and more beer."

She nodded and turned back to the wide-open space of Casablanca. She looked at the Bogart mural and then up toward the staircase leading down from Brattle Street. "Have you confronted Kinjo with your doubts?"

"Nope."

"But your normal bullshit detector has sounded, you're just not sure why."

"Don't talk too shrinky to me," I said. "All that medical jargon is confusing."

"When does he get back?" Susan said.

"Sunday night after the game."

"Is it football season already?" she said.

"Sort of," I said. "Preseason."

"And you are to guard the Emperor of the

53

Gridiron all season, if that's what it takes?"

"Or until he cracks."

"The unknowing is frustration," she said.

"Speaking from experience?"

She toasted me with the drink. "You better believe it."

8

I had spent the weekend reading up on Kinjo Heywood. Since the bad guys were still theoretical at this point, I needed to learn about potential enemies.

There was a lot written about the night-club shooting in Manhattan. A twenty-two-year-old man named Antonio Lima had died. A couple witnesses said Kinjo and Lima had been fighting earlier. He denied it. The witnesses later recanted. There was a civil suit from the family for wrongful death, but it was quickly dropped. No murder weapon. No physical evidence. If it came down to it, I'd pull the file and make some calls. But at this point, I had nothing to suspect Kinjo's problems and the incident were tied.

I sat parked for an hour outside Gillette until the team bus arrived. It was past midnight by the time Kinjo sat in the passenger seat of my Explorer. We drove north on 95. It was early Monday, with no traffic. The ride was easy and pleasant. I turned down *The Jordan Rich Show* so we might talk.

"Congratulations."

"We won," Kinjo said. "But it was an ugly win."

"Better to win ugly than lose pretty."

"Who said that?"

"Bobby Bowden," I said. "I think."

"His son coached at Auburn," Kinjo said. "Long time before I got there."

"Is that where you met Nicole?"

"Yeah," he said.

"You don't like to talk about her."

"Doesn't matter to me," he said. "Met her freshman year. She got pregnant with Akira sophomore year. We were in love and now we're not."

"She drop out?"

"For a while," he said. "But she finished school. I still got a year to go."

"What's she do now?"

"Works at a bank in Medford," he said. "She's a loan officer."

"Business degree?"

"MBA, too," he said. "I don't know why she wants my money. She don't need it. She knows how to get it."

"Maybe it's on principle."

"Or to prove something to me."

"Or herself."

Kinjo was silent. I had overstepped. My headlights brightened a large swath of the interstate. We rode on an elevated platform over the triple-deckers, boarded-up storefronts, and housing projects.

"You mind me asking what happened?"

"Not much to know," he said. "She caught me fucking another woman."

"Ah," I said. "That will put a damper on a marriage."

"You married?"

"Sort of."

"What's that mean?"

"It means I'm in a monogamous relationship with the love of my life."

"Kids?" Kinjo said.

"Sort of."

"What's a 'sort of' kid?"

"I helped a boy raise himself when he was fifteen," I said. "Now he's family."

"How old is he now?"

"Old enough to be a very successful adult," I said. "He teaches dance in New York. When did we switch roles? Didn't you see *investigator* printed on my business card?"

"I'm just saying it's tough for a man hadn't been married to understand," he said. "I stepped out because she'd given up on me, us, the whole thing. I wasn't out just fucking. I needed someone in my life who needed me."

"Cristal."

"I ain't gonna lie," Kinjo said. "She wasn't the first."

"Did you try and make it work with Nicole?"

"You mean after she found out?"

"Yeah."

"Hard to talk with dishes and glasses flying at your head."

"Imagine so."

Kinjo was silent. Again, I had overstepped. Spenser, master of diplomacy. We drove due north on the empty interstate, my eyes darting up the rearview. All clear. I switched lanes. No boogeymen out tonight.

"I read that piece in *Sports Illustrated*," I said. "I don't see the big deal. What bothered you about it?"

"Man fucked up some of my quotes," he said. "And quoted some quarterbacks who said I took cheap shots."

"Still didn't see anyone mad enough to hurt you."

Kinjo didn't answer. "I didn't like how the man implied that my relationship with Akira was a show," he said. "That reporter hung out with us, and so we did what we always do. Man wrote it in a way like it was an unnatural weekend to be with my boy. That I was an unnatural person trying to play dad."

"Slighted your honor."

"Damn right."

"As did someone trying to follow you and scare you."

"Yeah."

"No insults swallowed down South?"

"Hell, no."

"Not many where I grew up, either."

Kinjo sighed. "Maybe my head is a little messed up right now."

"Maybe someone was following you," I said. "But not to hurt you."

"You weren't there," he said. "You didn't see the look the man had. He was going for a gun and I pulled mine."

"What did he look like?"

Kinjo described him as big, white, and ugly.

"Lots of that going around these days," I said.

"When I was a kid, I always thought it would be cool to be known," he said. "I grew up in this town down in Georgia where most everything had been logged out. Just red clay everywhere. That red clay got

59

all over your clothes and under your fingernails. My mother worked three jobs to take care of me and Ray, wash that mud out our shirts. Year I signed with the NFL, she died of a heart attack. That make any sense to you?"

I shook my head. I drove. I listened. Failed marriage. Check. Abandonment issues. Check. Irrational behavior. You bet. I asked him a few more questions from what I'd read.

"It ain't that nightclub thing, man," he said. "That's all over."

"How do you know?"

"Because they ain't nothing to it."

"Uh-huh."

"Listen, if you're going to help me, you got to believe in me," Kinjo said. "I never shot and killed no one. Someone is trying to do that to me. Someone try to take what I have and I got to step in."

"But for me to work, I need to know all there is to know," I said. "Sometimes something shakes loose that might not make sense to you."

"Like reading an offense?"

"Yeah," I said. "Exactly. I need to step back and see exactly what's developing."

"Okay."

"I read that a couple of your teammates

were there that night."

He nodded.

"Can I speak with them?"

He nodded again. "Sure. Whatever, man."

The highway lights scattered strobed patterns across the interior of the SUV. I got off at the exit for Route 9. A few miles down, we stopped at a red light at the Hammond intersection. There was an all-night CVS pharmacy, a liquor store, and, across the road, the Longwood Cricket Club. Inside the gates were fifty tennis courts for Brahmins to work out their deepest frustrations.

"Ever think of taking up tennis?" I said.

"You kidding me?"

The light turned green. I turned left on Hammond and on into Chestnut Hill.

"Shit, I only moved out here for Akira," he said. "A few of my teammates moved out here. Brady moving out from downtown. I thought, why the hell not? Good schools. Good restaurants. Make his life into something right. He's a good kid. Smart as hell. If I was smart as him, I wouldn't need football."

"Do you want him to play?"

"If he wants to play, I'll help him," Kinjo said. "He don't want to play, that's fine by me. Kid is special. He can draw. He can sing. He can memorize whole songs after hearing them once. Seems like a waste just to do something that's expected."

I nodded. We rolled up onto Heath Street and I turned toward Kinjo's house. I pulled in, killed the engine, and sat there. The engine made hot ticking sounds as I waited for him to get out. But he just sat there, looking at his stone house lit up like a birthday cake in the night. A few leaves twirled down from the oaks.

"Steve Rosen is going to call you tomorrow," he said. "Says whatever was going on isn't going on anymore."

I nodded.

"So he's going to fire you."

"Wouldn't be the first time."

"What do you think?" Kinjo said. "You think you can get these guys?"

" 'Patience is bitter, but its fruit is sweet.' "

"Who said that?"

"Some old Greek guy."

"I'd pay you for as long as it takes, but the front office has spoken to Steve, and now Steve isn't so sure if it's a good thing for you to be hanging around."

"And you have promised to be more selective in the discharging of your weapon."

Kinjo smiled. "Yeah," he said. "Something like that."

"Well, okay," I said. "It's been a pleasure."

I offered my hand and he took it.

We got out of the car, and I walked with him to the back of the Explorer to open the hatch. He reached in and got his travel bag. The front door opened and Akira came running out in blue pajamas and no shoes. He jumped up high into Kinjo's arms and clung tight to Kinjo's body. Kinjo didn't miss a stride, walking with the boy held tight, travel bag in right hand and left hand on the child's back. The kid didn't even see me, his eyes shut tight as Kinjo opened the front door.

I parked down the hill and sat on the house until late. I had been paid for the week and might as well see it through. When nothing menacing appeared, I cranked my car and drove home.

9

"If they were letting you go," Z said, "why follow through watching the house?"

"I was paid until today," I said. "If I didn't follow through, then I might start padding expenses, billing extra hours, charging to drink on the job. The whole thing would get shot to hell."

"The code?"

"Maybe the code," I said. "Or maybe it's valuing my own self-worth."

"But you don't feel guilt about me buying the sandwiches?"

"I bought last time," I said. "And I wish to value your self-worth."

"Sandwiches are very good."

"That they are."

Z had stopped off in Chinatown for an early lunch of Vietnamese bánh mì sandwiches and two hot Vietnamese coffees. Shredded pork, cilantro, jalapeños, and pickled carrots on a baguette. The coffee was milky and strong and sweet.

"If the Vietnamese outnumber the Chinese in Chinatown," I said, "perhaps a name change is due."

"Or you might be overthinking the sandwich."

"Perhaps."

It was brisk and cool. Z wore a black motorcycle jacket over a gray T-shirt with old jeans and cowboy boots, true to his heritage on a Montana rez. His face still showed the scars of a savage beating. The face had mostly healed, but a large swath of skin from his left eye and cheek was mottled with scar tissue. He had spent weeks in the hospital and there had been a lot of rehab. He did not like to discuss it.

"I don't know how much work I'll have," I said.

"Henry got me extra hours at the gym," Z said. "And I got an offer to work as bouncer on Fridays and Saturdays at the Black Rose. Good pay."

"You mind being around the booze?"

"Nope," he said. "I like to be in control. I like to see everything around me."

I ate the rest of my sandwich and sipped the sweet coffee. I swung around in my office chair and planted my feet on a window ledge. The bay window of my second-floor office composed a nice view of Berkeley Street. Shreve, Crump & Low had moved out. I had wished for a good restaurant to replace it but instead got a Bank of America.

"So what does a trained investigator do when business is slow?"

"Live deliberately and front only the essential aspects of life."

"Such as sandwiches."

I nodded and picked up the morning *Globe.* I tossed Z the front page and kept the sports and comics for myself. As he started to read, I furtively reached into my desk for a pair of reading glasses. Once in focus, *Arlo & Janis* were at it again.

The phone rang.

"Spenser? It's Kinjo, I need you quick." His voice sounded tight and high-pitched. I took my feet off the windowsill and cradled the phone to my ear. Z put down the paper and stared at me.

"They got him," he said. "They fucking snatched him, man."

"Who?"

"Whoever was following me took Akira."

I waited a beat, my eyes lifting to Z. He listened with intent.

"Could he be with Nicole?"

"I know when my kid is gone. Cristal was taking him to school and two men with guns jacked her at a red light and took him. Nicole blames me. She's coming over right now."

"Did you call the police?"

"Hell, yes, I called the police," he said. "Spenser, help me. That kid is everything. I don't care what it costs. I don't care. I want these motherfuckers dead."

10

When we arrived, there was a lot of activity on Chestnut Hill. Dozens of cop cars, marked and unmarked, hugged Heath Street in both directions, up and down the winding hill. Z and I parked a good bit away and walked to the top of the Heywood driveway. Two Brookline uniform cops stopped us before we even reached a mailbox.

They asked who we were. I told them and asked who was in charge.

"Captain O'Leary," one cop said.

"Anyone from the staties?"

The cop studied Z's profile and pressed a radio mic on his collar. Some garbled bit of radio noise returned a few seconds later. "Detective Lieutenant Lundquist."

"Tell Lundquist Spenser is here," I said.

"He know you?" the cop said.

"Yeah," I said. "I promise to brighten his day."

"I thought Lundquist was Homicide

under Healy," Z said.

I shrugged. "Nothing gold can stay."

The Brookline cop nodded at me but held up his hand to stop Z. "Only Spenser."

"It's okay," Z said. "While I wait, I can water the horses. Give them oats."

The cops looked at each other in confusion. I followed the sloping drive to the large stone house. At a side door, I was ushered in and taken into a study, where Kinjo Heywood sat holding court in an overstuffed white leather chair. Cristal slumped on a nearby white couch, head in hands, crying. Lundquist sat wide-legged on an ottoman across from Kinjo, taking notes. The house was thick with cops. A few had set up laptop computers on a large dining room table, orange cords running into the wall.

I shook Lundquist's hand.

He was a sturdy man who looked as if he'd just stepped off a farm in the Midwest. He had reddish apple cheeks and clear blue eyes. His red hair had been recently shaved into a crew cut. The clothes were plain: gray slacks, white shirt, and glen plaid sport coat.

"Transfer?" I said.

"Promotion," he said. "Healy signed off on it. Said it was time."

Cristal's sobs developed into wails, face in hands, shoulders shaking. Lundquist looked back at her with mild annoyance.

"I tried to help," she said. "But I froze. God, why did I freeze like that? I stopped at a light and these two men opened the door. They had guns. They said they were going to blow my fucking head off if I moved an inch."

Kinjo looked at the floor. His large hands were clasped in front of him as he took a deep breath.

"They just threw him inside and sped off," she said.

"Yes, ma'am," Lundquist said. "We've been through all this."

"I tried," she said. "I swear to Christ. I really tried to follow them. But they were too fast and I got lost."

Kinjo continued to look at the floor. His jaw muscles flexed. He rubbed his mustache and goatee with nervous energy.

"We're looking for the vehicle," Lundquist said. "Sounds like an old Crown Vic. Dark green. And we'd like you to check out some photo packs. See if you recognize them."

"Sure," Cristal said. "I'll do whatever you want."

In the harsh light, Lundquist's cheeks were reddened and chapped. Small acne scars ran down his cheeks and across his neck. His eyes flicked on mine. "Spenser's been working for you?" Lundquist said.

Kinjo nodded.

"Because you'd been recently followed?" Lundquist said. "And thought someone might want to do you harm?"

"Yeah."

"Any ideas?"

Kinjo looked up at me. I shook my head.

His eyes trailed away and studied the floor. "I thought maybe I'd gone crazy," he said. "Got followed that one time and I pulled a gun. I thought they were on me, not my son. I thought it was somebody wanted to take me out. Something personal. What kind of coward comes for a child? He's a kid, man. He's just a fucking kid."

Cristal cried harder and snuffled some. I did not look back, leaning into the doorjamb, hands in my jacket pockets, letting Lundquist take the lead.

"We have people at the school and in the neighborhood where you stopped," Lundquist said. "We hope someone saw something."

"What time?" I said.

"Nine-one-one call was made about eight-twenty."

"God, he was running late to school," Cristal said. "What will Nicole say?"

Kinjo looked up, eyes sleepy, and looked

at her. "Not your fault," he said. "I should've taken him myself. He's my child. Never thought it was about him. Got my goddamn head up my ass."

"I'm sorry," Cristal said. "I'm so sorry."

The Pats' security chief, Jeff Barnes, walked into the study, looked to Lundquist and then looked to me with clenched jaw. "You, out of here," he said, jerking a thumb. "This has nothing to do with you. Go."

"I called him," Kinjo said. "I want him here."

Barnes wore a tight-fitting blue suit, a crisp white shirt, and no tie. He reeked of aftershave and breath mints and kept on shaking his head, eyes fixed on mine. "Did you bring some Mexican guy with you? Police can't get him to move his car, said he was with you."

"He's Cree Indian," I said. "And yes, he's with me."

"I don't give a flying fuck if he's the king of Siam," Barnes said. "You need to get out of here. This is mine. I'm in charge."

I looked to Lundquist and raised my eyebrows. I had not moved a millimeter from the doorjamb. I felt inside my pocket and found some gum. I took some out and started to chew it. That'll show 'im.

Lundquist stood up and faced Barnes,

hands on hips and dead-eyed. "I'm Detective Lieutenant Brian Lundquist of the Mass state police. And who the hell are you?"

Barnes reached into his tight-fitting coat and pulled out a business card with the Pats logo. Lundquist read it and handed it back to him.

"I'm speaking to Mr. Heywood right now," Lundquist said. "Wait in the next room and we'll talk."

Barnes looked at me and said, "And what about Spenser?"

"He works for Mr. Heywood," Lundquist said. "He can stay as legal representation. And he can also stay because he's not acting like a horse's ass and giving me a migraine. Now wait for me in the next goddamn room, Jeff."

I did not react as Barnes passed me and walked into the kitchen. No reason to be smug.

"You need to stick here," Lundquist said, turning to Kinjo. "I don't want you or your wife to leave. Not for a while. I don't want you to make any calls or talk to anyone that isn't crucial."

"I can't just sit here on my ass and wait for y'all," Kinjo said. "Some shitbags just snatched my child. How can I just sit down here and wait to see what happens?"

"We can connect with both your landline and your cell phone," Lundquist said. "You need to let us know about all your e-mail accounts, Facebook, Twitter, or whatever you use."

"Why?"

"These days, it'll be their easiest way to connect if there's a ransom."

I left the doorjamb and sat down with Kinjo. I realized I had left on my Brooklyn Dodgers cap and removed it. "They want to wait a bit. Make you sweat."

Kinjo nodded. I turned back to Lundquist.

"I'll talk to numb-nuts about the press," Lundquist said. "We don't want this broadcast on sports talk. But, shit, look at the circus outside. How long do you think we can keep a lid on it?"

"Not sure," I said, shrugging. "Maybe five minutes?"

11

I found Z leaning against the hood of my Ford Explorer. He was wearing Oakley sunglasses like an outfielder and staring down the hill to the Heywood mansion. I walked up to meet him.

"I need you to go back to the health club," I said. "Find Hawk. Tell him to hang loose. I may need him, too."

"Is Hawk good at hanging loose?"

"Not very."

"And me?"

"You stick close to Hawk," I said. "I'll call if I need you. Right now I'll stay here and wait."

"What'd they say?"

"Lundquist thinks we're waiting for a ransom," I said. "Staties are wiring the house for a phone call or e-mail messages."

Z nodded.

"Revenge?"

"Don't know," I said. "Some people in

New York that I may have to meet. Other than that, it could really be anything or anyone."

Z nodded. "A man with a ten-million-dollar contract makes for a good target."

"You came close to that life," I said.

"One season away," Z said. "But one season at that level is forever."

"And you'd never have met me," I said. "Potential as a crime buster untapped."

"They okay inside?"

"Nope," I said. "A lot of crying and worrying and general shock. Kinjo is trying to make sense of things while trying to calm down Cristal. Cristal is a mess."

I handed Z the keys to the Explorer.

"How will you get back?"

"I'll get one of the cops to drive me," I said. "It's going to be a long night."

"I hope it is a kidnapping," Z said. "I hope all they want is money. At least that's something."

The first leaves of fall left their branches and twirled about. Smoke drifted from chimneys along the street as the day grew colder. The road was crooked and never-ending down the hill.

12

"Where the hell is my son?" Nicole Heywood said.

The three cops guarding the front door had not been able to restrain her. Nor the maid or Ray Heywood or Detective Lieutenant Lundquist. Even super-agent Steve Rosen could not buffer his client. She was shaking and breathing hard, pumped full of anger and adrenaline.

Kinjo didn't answer. He sat at a long glass kitchen table, head in hand. His head dropped even more upon her entry. The kitchen was very large and lined with white tile, making everything sound hollow. Nicole stood, hands on hips, shaking and ready to pounce on Kinjo or anyone who got in her way. I hung back.

The two detectives in front of laptop computers stared intently at their screens.

Lundquist looked to me. And I back at Lundquist.

"Can we talk outside?" Lundquist said. "We're waiting on a call, ma'am."

"Hell, no," Nicole said. "Tell me. You tell me, Kinjo. I want to hear what happened from his father."

"He's gone," Heywood said. "I told you. Some men took him as he was on his way to school. We don't know why."

"Why the hell would someone take Akira?" she said. "You better tell me right now what's going on. What the hell did you do now? You just handed over your child?"

"Wasn't him," I said. "And they had guns."

She turned to me, folding her arms over her chest, and stared me down. "Who?"

"Doesn't matter," Kinjo said. "They got him. Whoever got him gonna call and I'll pay them and this will all go away."

"Damn right it matters." Nicole put a hand to her mouth and fell to her knees. "Where is that goddamn bitch? I knew she did this. I knew it. What happens when you bring trash into your house."

I helped her to her feet. She squirmed, trying to run for the door, my arms around her. I loosened my grip, and she slammed an elbow in my stomach and ran for the living room, where Cristal sat watching the news. Cristal looked up and cowered as Nicole launched herself from the doorway. She looked like she could tear Cristal to pieces. I finally caught her, wrapping her in a bear hug and sweeping her out of the room. She turned into me and clawed at my face, let out an unholy scream, and seemed to collapse on herself. Kinjo grabbed her and held her close, pleading to her in a soft, intimate voice. "Baby, we're doing all we can. We got to be calm. Think of him."

Lundquist handed me a handkerchief and I dabbed the blood from my face. Rosen helped Nicole to a chair.

The two detectives continued to watch their screens. *Nothing to see here. All is well.*

"Be calm?" Nicole said. She tried to act strong, but there was a breathless fear in her voice. "I try and leave the bank and two cops show up. They won't let me. They want to talk, want to know had I heard from my son. Did I know anyone who would want to do him harm? Was I in a good place with my ex-husband? All the while, nobody telling me anything. Not you. Not the cops. Everyone wants me to calm down. Be cool."

"I got some pills," Rosen said.

"Fuck your pills, Steve," she said.

I stood at the kitchen counter. It was a nice kitchen. Lots of chrome and marble and gleaming stainless steel. The refrigerator would have filled half my apartment. I ran my handkerchief under the faucet and wiped my face.

"At this point, we don't know anything," Lundquist said. "We're treating it as a kidnapping and waiting to hear from the kidnappers. We are tapping both the main line here and Mr. Heywood's two cell phones. We'd like to include your number as well, just in case they reach out to you."

Nicole reached into her purse and threw a cell phone onto the glass table with a thunk. One of the laptop cops picked up the phone and tapped away on his keyboard.

"Why?"

Kinjo did not answer.

"Why?"

Kinjo did not answer.

"I swear to Christ if she did something that caused this," she said. "I swear I'll come after her. I'll kill her."

Lundquist lifted his eyes to me. I showed him the bloody handkerchief and nodded in agreement.

"What if they don't call?" Nicole said.

"They will call," Kinjo said.

"If they want money," Lundquist said, "we'll hear from them."

Nicole turned her eyes to Kinjo. She held the stare until he looked up.

Cristal entered the room. Nicole did not

turn her head, only held up her hand. "If you know what's good for you," she said, "you better get gone."

"I want to help."

"Do I stutter?" she said. "Get."

"You're blaming me?"

"Goddamn right I am," Nicole said. "Funny how you the last one to see him. Nobody else around. You better take your fake tears and fake tits and get out of my damn face."

Without a word, but lots of snuffling, Cristal turned on a tall golden heel and skittered away.

"You'll pay, Kinjo," she said. "You'll pay every cent. Me and you both. Every cent to get him back."

Kinjo nodded. Nicole began to cry. I wanted to place a hand on her shoulder but was concerned she might break it.

"Jesus Christ," she said, moaning. "Jesus Christ."

It was Kinjo who got down on one knee before her and held her hand. He was crying, too. Rosen sat down at the head of the table and started to text.

I walked outside to the back patio. The night had grown chilly. The old play fort looked big and skeletal and quiet as hell in the night. Lundquist came outside and closed the French doors behind him. He lit a cigarette.

"What did you get from that?"

"Consider investing in a catcher's mask?"

"From the exchange?"

I tilted my head. Lundquist burned down the cigarette between his thumb and forefinger.

"Look at the second wife."

"Natural reaction from the first," Lundquist said.

"Maybe."

"You know some things?"

"Probably the same things as you."

"If this goes the way it often goes, I'll be living here for the next week."

"I'll chip in for some deodorant and mouthwash."

"I could send some guys to check out those things we both might know," Lundquist said.

"Or I could go to New York while you check out the second Mrs. Heywood."

Lundquist nodded. He finished the cigarette and flicked the butt.

"Okay," he said. "But call from New York if someone from that nightclub thing looks good."

"Would I ever hold out on you?"

13

"Don't ask me to watch Pearl," Hawk said. "A man of my talent must draw a line."

"Is it the poop scooping that bothers you?"

"You want me to carry a bag of shit in a thousand-dollar jacket?"

Hawk wore a knee-length black leather trench over a designer black T-shirt and jeans. His cowboy boots were made of a crocodile's belly. They were very nice.

"Susan will watch Pearl," I said.

We sat at the counter of one of the five million Dunkin' Donuts in the greater Boston metro area. I drank coffee and worked on an old-fashioned; another one waited on deck. Hawk abstained.

"And Z is sticking with Kinjo if he leaves the house," I said. "His agent requested bodyguard services."

"He ready?"

I nodded.

Hawk nodded.

"But if he needs help —"

Hawk nodded again.

"If the kidnappers call, I'll come straight back."

"No word?" Hawk said.

I shook my head. "Not a syllable."

"How 'bout I gallivant over to Manhattan," Hawk said. "And you stay here?"

"Because I'm the dedicated sleuth," I said. "You're the heavy."

"And the brains and the shooter," Hawk said. "The total package, babe."

"Nice to be you."

Hawk's face showed no emotion. Dull fluorescent light beamed off his bald head. "This one of those deals where we work for free?"

"Nope."

Hawk's mouth moved a millimeter into perhaps a smile.

"Our client happens to be loaded," I said. "You will be compensated for your time and considerable talents."

"Fucked up to take a kid."

"Yep."

"You trust the staties?"

"Lundquist is on it," I said. "Remember Wheaton?"

Hawk was definitely smiling now.

"So you call me out for donuts at midnight

to tell me to stay put?"

"I do not wish to have you gallivanting off to Miami or L.A. or Southeast Asia or wherever else you sometimes go," I said. "Consider the donuts to be a retainer."

Hawk nodded. He reached over for the second donut and headed for the door.

I watched the lights punch the night from his Jaguar and the car slide into the dark.

I finished the coffee and drove back to Marlborough Street to pack.

14

The next morning, I took the eight a.m. Acela to Penn Station. I read the *Globe* and drank coffee as we slowed into New London and raced on to Manhattan.

One of the many advantages of train travel was that I could stash my .38 into my clean underwear along with a couple boxes of ammo. I did not pack much else besides two changes of clothing and a nice blazer in the unlikely event the case called for an elegant meal. I had already left a message for Corsetti, and Corsetti, being Corsetti, would be overjoyed to see me. I told him I had questions on the nightclub shooting from two years ago.

I arrived at Penn Station at eleven-forty-five and took a cab up Eighth Avenue to the Parker Meridien. I unpacked my blazer and underwear. I wore the gun. It went well with my work ensemble of navy T-shirt, A-2 jacket, jeans, and New Balance sneakers.

Fifteen minutes later, I found Eugene Corsetti sitting at his desk, about to attack a forlorn Twinkie. A nameplate stated he was a detective, first grade.

"Jeez, is everyone getting a promotion?"

"Jesus Christ."

"Nope," I said. "Just me."

"Jesus."

"With the promotion, can't you eat any better?"

Corsetti stood, which did little, since he stood only about five-foot-six or -seven. It was more his girth that filled the room. Corsetti was built like a bowling ball.

"I'll buy you lunch."

He dropped the Twinkie in the wastebasket and we shook hands.

"Sure, I remember the case," he said. "Pats player involved in a first-class clusterfuck."

"I need a few more details than that."

"Didn't you pull the file?"

"I got the face sheet and the initial report," I said. "But no transcripts. I need the transcripts."

"Of course you do," he said. "Can we make it quick, sir? You know, I do work other cases between our meetings."

He reached for a satin Yankees warm-up jacket. Despite his questionable wardrobe, we had remained friends for many years.

We walked around the corner to East 45th and a hot dog stand that also served gyros and falafel. I bought us each a dirty-water dog and a Coke.

"May I ask why a hotshot Boston gumshoe is interested in a two-year-old homicide?"

"Background."

"Background?" Corsetti said. "Okay. Sure. Sure. Like I don't read the freakin' papers. Kinjo Heywood?"

He spilled some mustard on his blue satin jacket.

"I can replace that dud with something from Yawkey Way."

"I'd rather set fire to my nuts," he said.

"Dedication."

He dotted away the mustard. I demonstrated the proper way to eat a hot dog, ending up with only some loose onion on my sleeve. I pinged them away with a flick of my index finger.

"Wasn't my case," Corsetti said. "But I did a few interviews for the lead. Not enough to go to the grand jury — .45 shell casings at the scene. We dusted the shit out of a Ford Escape with chrome rims that belonged to the deceased. No prints. No witnesses at the scene. Or at least no witnesses who would talk. No gun. Circumstantial with a capital C."

"What about the victim?" I said. "Antonio Lima?"

"Young guy from some island somewhere."

"Cape Verde."

"If you say so," he said. "I remember cars and faces."

"And Mr. Lima gets into it with Mr. Heywood at Chrome."

"Now, there's a fucking place," Corsetti said. "You been there yet?"

"Next on my list."

"They got women in lingerie and angel wings who bring you cocktails."

I drank some Coke. I finished the dog. "Everyone who brings me a cocktail is an angel."

"I never talked to Kinjo Heywood," he said. "I've seen him on TV and when they play the Jets. He's the toughest linebacker since Dick Butkus or Ray Nitschke. I'll get you his interview transcript if you really want it. But it's probably a hundred pages of him lawyering up."

I nodded. "And the victim?"

"Nice family, bad kid," he said. "What can you say? Moved to the city from somewhere else. Mom's an immigrant with two boys.

Runs a little grocery. Can't believe her son is a gangbanger, even though she's bailed him out of trouble maybe fifteen times."

Corsetti's collared shirt was wide open. Corsetti needed an open collar; his neck was bigger than his head.

"So you have more suspects than Kinjo Heywood?"

"We liked him for it," he said. "An hour or two before the shooting, Heywood and Lima got in a scuffle in the men's room. We had witnesses at one time, but then they flaked. Some bullshit over a broad."

"One of the lingerie angels?"

"How'd you guess?"

"How could he resist?" I said. "You have her interview and a transcript?"

"Gee," Corsetti said. "You think we should've talked to her? Yeah, sure. I'll send it to you and let you know if there's something worthwhile in there. I mean, that's the least I can do for a long-suffering Sox fan."

"New Yorkers are never short on charisma."

We walked back toward the station. Corsetti continued to dab the stain on his jacket. We tried to walk side by side, but being big guys, we would have impeded the sidewalk traffic flow.

"Can I ask you something?" Corsetti said.

"Working out and taking supplements."

"What?"

"You were going to ask how I stayed looking so young and fit."

"No," he said. "The whore. What ever happened to the case with the whore that kept going missing?"

"April Kyle."

"Yeah," Corsetti said. "Kyle."

"Her story did not end well."

He studied my face as we walked. He nodded and didn't ask again.

15

Antonio Lima's mother ran a corner grocery in Yonkers specializing in African and Caribbean food. Besides the spices and rare produce, I could tell no difference in their toilet paper, aspirin, chewing gum, condoms, and coffee. I complimented the clerk on her plantains and star fruit. In turn, she told me Mrs. Lima lived in a walk-up directly above the store.

Mrs. Lima was a stout, light-skinned black woman in a blue flowered housecoat and a scarlet head scarf. When I mentioned Antonio, she started to close the door. "Leave us alone."

"I'm not a reporter or a cop."

"What are you?"

I had many answers but kept quiet and passed my card through the door. It was the one with my name, occupation, and the logo of Saint George and the Dragon.

"What do you want?"

"May I come in?" I said. "I promise not to take long. I need to speak to your son."

"What?"

"Victor," I said. "He may be able to help me."

She closed the door, but as I began to walk away, I heard the chain unlatch.

She let me in and followed me into an open kitchen. Nearby, an older and more wrinkled version of Mrs. Lima sat in an easy chair, watching a newscast in Portuguese from Rio. She wore a similar yellow head scarf and glanced at me once and turned back to the television. The room's walls were made of fading plaster hung with cheap frames of family, popes, and various saints. The sitting room had a view of downtown Yonkers and where the new minor-league baseball stadium was supposed to be built. Two bedrooms and an open kitchen connected. On a chopping board next to the stove a half-sliced onion and quartered lime waited.

"Antonio?"

"I'm very sorry," I said.

"He was a good boy."

I nodded, knowing all victims are good. Even if they had multiple priors of aggravated assault and burglary. A shrine had been set up on a small kitchen table, complete with prayer candles. I recognized the same school photo as the one that ran in the *Times* and *Post*.

"Your son's driver's license shows this address."

"Victor does not want to discuss his brother anymore," she said. "Why do you want to know?"

I could tell her that the man suspected in the murder of her son had hired me. Or I could tell her a blanched version of the truth.

"I'm being paid to find out what happened."

The older woman turned to me and back to the television. I did not speak Portuguese, but there seemed to be a hell of a soccer match last night somewhere. She did not ask why or by whom, and I quickly moved on to the next question.

"I have not spoken to Victor for many weeks," she said. "He works for a moving company in the city. I don't have his address."

"His phone number?"

She looked away and shook her head.

"Any friends or family who'd know? A girlfriend?"

She shook her head some more.

"Has he told you much about that night?"

"He said that football player killed his brother," she said. "He said they were fighting over a woman and that the man and Antonio were very drunk. He said Antonio left this nightclub and the man followed him and shot him in his car."

"What did the police tell you?"

"The police said they had no proof," she said. "But two men were fighting and an hour later one is dead? What do you think?"

"I know your son did business with some dangerous people."

"Lies."

"I still would like to speak to Victor."

She settled into her seat and glanced at the unfinished meal in the kitchen. "He did not see it. He came after. He was with a woman, too. Women, all these women, have caused trouble for my boys for so long."

"Did you know the woman they fought over?"

"No," she said. "But I think she was Cape Verdean. Victor knows her. She is loose and without morals."

"I try my best to stay away from women like that," I said. "Can you please help me? It's very important I talk to him."

"Why? It will change nothing," she said. "This man, the football player, is very rich and very respected and probably paid the police."

"The police said there were no witnesses or evidence."

Mrs. Lima was silent. The newscast spoke of demonstrations in São Paulo. I stayed here any longer and I'd be fluent in Portuguese. The droning voice of newscasters was pretty much the same in any language and filled the silence.

"If Victor calls, will you at least give him my number?" I said. "Let him decide."

"I must get back to preparing dinner."

"Did your son know this man before?" I said. "The man you believe shot him."

"No."

"Was anyone else with your son that night?" I said. "Other friends besides his brother?"

"I don't know," she said. "I don't know. I have prayed a very long time to help with my pain. This brings things back to me. Can we please stop this unless you come here with answers for us? What good will these questions do?"

I took a long breath. I let it out. "There is a child that's gone missing," I said. "The police think the shooting of your son may be connected. The boy is only eight years old."

"Is it not enough to let the killer of my son go free?" she said. "And now you have come to my house with more lies? You insult my one son who lives. These are my boys. My children."

I nodded and stood. I smiled and left my card on the counter.

The old woman watching television never looked up. Mrs. Lima went back to slicing onions.

16

I was sitting in a coffee shop on Washington Street that faced Chrome. I had packed little to go nightclubbing and had to settle for a black button-down shirt and Levi's. I left the two top buttons undone. Perhaps I should have invested in tighter pants or a gold chain. Reviews I read stated I was not the desirable demographic for Chrome. They preferred young and hip as opposed to middle-aged and thuggish.

But there was little else to do. Lundquist said no ransom demands had been sent or contact made. He said Cristal Heywood was a flake but didn't appear to be involved. After my visit with Corsetti, I had spent most of my day running down addresses on Victor Lima. I came up with two associated persons. One led to an empty apartment in Queens. The second led to an angry ex-girlfriend in Brooklyn who had not seen

Victor in two years, well before the shooting.

As I pondered, a homeless guy wandered in and sat down directly across from me. He ordered a cup of hot water and began to unpack several pairs of old socks from a grocery bag. I hoped he didn't need the socks to make tea.

I returned to the transcripts I got from Corsetti, witnesses from that night, including the woman at the center of the scuffle. *Lela Lopes.* But even if she offered me photos, a video confession, and a smoking gun to prove Kinjo was involved, that did not mean the kidnapping was personal.

I wasn't even sure if Lopes still worked at Chrome. Or lived in New York. I could find nothing in a database I sometimes used.

I turned to the muttering homeless man. "Do you know anything about Lela Lopes?"

"Eat me."

" 'The words of the prophets are written on the subway walls.' "

He scowled and sipped his hot water. I watched Chrome through the window. As soon as I had something, I would head back to Boston. This was something. It was all there was right now to help Akira. I could sit in the Heywood house in Chestnut Hill drinking coffee and looking earnest with the staties and offering reassurances to Nicole and Kinjo. Or I could keep moving. Keep moving usually worked for me.

At nine, a very beautiful blonde in a tight black T-shirt opened up the front door to Chrome as honest-to-God velvet ropes were set along the sidewalks. I strolled across Washington to make a personal appearance.

17

Chrome was just as I had imagined. Low lighting, black velvet furniture, billowing white curtains, and lots of candles. The waitresses and bartenders were young and beautiful, while the music was pulsing and nauseating. I drank a cold Heineken at the circular bar until I could tune it out and asked the bartender if Lela Lopes still worked here.

"Lela?" he said. "Are you serving her with papers or something?"

"Why would I be serving her with papers?"

"I don't know," he said. "You just look like that's what you do."

The bartender was in his early twenties, with muscular arms and hair spiked up high. He looked as if he'd just touched a live wire.

"I actually am a special envoy to the Cape Verdean tourist council," I said. "She's been selected to be our newest spokesmodel."

"No shit," he said. "That's fucking awesome."

"Somehow I knew you'd be impressed," I said. "Is she here?"

"She quit in the spring," he said.

"You know someone who keeps in touch?"

"Maybe." He stood there and grinned.

"You mind asking?"

I left a fifty-dollar bill languishing on the wet bar. I recalled when a five-spot would've sufficed.

Spiky disappeared in the billowing white curtains and I continued to sip the beer. I was one of four people inside the bar, which was the size of a Super Target. Three women in short skirts and high heels sat in a velvety grouping, checking their phones. I thought perhaps they were texting about me and offered a smile. They looked back at their screens.

The dance music continued to pump into the empty club. The curtains kept billowing. The candles properly lit shadows. This looked to be the place if you happened to be an NFL rookie with a black American Express card. The drink menu showed cocktails starting at twenty bucks.

"Hellboy knows her," he said. "He'll be right up. You want another drink?"

"Hellboy?" I shook my head and paid with the fifty. I left him ten bucks. I better stay sober for Hellboy.

After a few minutes, a giant appeared from the curtain. He had a bald head and a goatee. I made sure he didn't have but a single eye in the middle of his head. He was dressed as a bouncer, with black pants, black shoes, and a black T-shirt with the word SECURITY across the front.

"Who the fuck are you?"

"You must be Hellboy."

"How do you know?"

"Working hypothesis."

"Huh?"

"An educated guess."

"You want to be smart here or out in the street?"

I stood up. I smiled. "Either way," I said. "But I'm really just looking for Lela Lopes."

He stared me up and down, realizing I was not Mister Rogers and too much trouble to start the night. I smiled to reassure him.

"Depends on who you are."

"I'm a private cop from Boston looking into the shooting from two years ago."

"Fuck that," he said, putting up his hand as if about to turn away.

"Only have a few questions for her."

"Sounds like a pain in the ass," he said. "The guys who own this place, JoJo and Hani, are a class act. They put all their money into this place and now it's about to tank."

The three women who had been surreptitiously eyeing me filed out the front door. Hellboy sighed at the spiky-haired bartender. In defeat, Spiky leaned against the far wall of the bar and poured himself a shot of tequila.

"At first, everyone wanted to see this place," he said. "When we opened, you would have had to give me a blowjob to get in the front door."

"Glad business has cooled a bit."

"Yeah, right," he said. "Now we have to hand out flyers in Times Square to all the loser tourists and businessmen wanting to get laid. We got maybe two, three months, tops. JoJo and Hani will take a bath. Hani is thinking about opening up a strip club in Boca, anyway. That's where he's from."

"Lela," I said. "Sure would like to speak to her."

"I get fired if I talk about that shooting," he said. "People don't even call this place Chrome anymore. You know what they call it?"

"Tarnished?"

"Freakin' Kiss Kiss Bang Bang," he said. He made a firing motion with his hand. "You know?"

"Sure," I said. "But Lela doesn't work here anymore, and so she can't get in trouble. I give you a card and a twenty and all you can do is pass it along."

"I don't know."

One of the waitresses wheeled out a small fan to get the large white curtains to billow more noticeably. The music switched from up-tempo and annoying to pulsing and gut-wrenching. Somewhere above, a bubble machine began to rain on us. I wondered what Lennie Seltzer would think of a bubble machine at the Tennessee Tavern.

"Spenser, huh?" Hellboy said, studying the card in his stubby, muscular fingers. "Sure. Okay. Whatever. I just don't want you messin' with Lela. She's been through enough shit."

I handed him a twenty. I smiled, patted his arm, and thanked him. As an after-thought, as we walked to the door, I said, "Did you break up that fight?"

He nodded. I had noted a bouncer in the report, but he was listed under a real name I could not immediately recall.

"Was it bad?"

He scratched the top of his freshly shaven

throat and tilted his head. "Here's the thing," he said. "All the papers made that guy Kinjo into some kind of nutjob like he was kicking apart that guy's ass. But that's not what happened."

"What did?"

"A bullshit shoving match," he said. "Nobody even spilled a drop."

"Nothing to kill over."

"Just people drunk and stupid."

"You see a lot of that."

Hellboy nodded, looking a bit like Rex Ingram, and reached for the door.

"Open sesame?" I said.

"I get that shit a lot," Hellboy said, grinning. "Okay. Okay. I'll shoot Lela a message."

18

At ten after ten, I received a text from a 917 area code. Someone wanted to meet me at a place called Red Planet in Times Square. I texted back that that sounded dandy and slipped into my jacket and took a cab from the hotel.

When I arrived, Times Square was as garish as usual. Unless you happen to like fifty-foot billboards of superhero movies, all-night shops shilling the latest Japanese gizmos, or Broadway plays based on Disney cartoons. Wide-eyed tourists from Topeka and Cincinnati took pictures with their phones of costumed characters and street performers. One woman walked up and down the avenue in a white string bikini, attempting to play the guitar, with a donation bucket strapped to her hip.

After being jostled and elbowed, I finally asked a cop on horseback where to find the restaurant. He pointed north on Broadway and said it's beneath street level. Soon I found out that the restaurant was beneath me, too. An extraterrestrial-themed burrito restaurant that took lucky "voyagers" into the world under Mars. Naturally, the place was packed.

Aliens with big heads and almond eyes wandered the red and green glowing caverns and passed out tall green cocktails or challenged you to video-game duels or a game of hoops. I studied the menu as I waited, for lack of anything better to do. They offered a Cerberus spicy hot chicken burrito and many Martian microbrews.

Wow.

Maybe I could take Susan here on our next trip. Reservations at the Carlyle, drinks at 21, and dinner on the Red Planet. *How could a woman resist? What would she wear? What would I wear?*

A chubby woman in a short metallic dress took my order. I pointed to the beer choice for fear of saying it out loud. I felt a bit like Han Solo. And, after several minutes, decided that if needed, I would shoot first.

The waitress brought my green beer. No aliens approached me or challenged me to Space Invaders. I checked my inbox. No messages from Lundquist but one from Z:

INT. 10 PARENTS. 2 TEACHERS. NOT ZIP.

As it approached midnight, I knew I had been had. Lela's idea of a decent joke. I left my green beer untouched and stood.

Toward the front of the restaurant, near the bubbling pools, I spotted a black man with braids turn the corner. He caught my eye, looked away, and turned quick for the launch pad door. I paid and followed the man out into Times Square. Victor Lima had changed his hair some since the photo at his mother's house. He now wore tight cornrows. But the eyes and facial features matched. And he was, no doubt, on Lela Lopes's speed dial.

It was a cool night and good for walking. I tugged on my Sox cap, feeling rebellious in hostile territory, and followed Lima across to the Winter Garden and up Broadway north toward Central Park. Lima had yet to look back, figuring I didn't recognize him. I kept twenty yards back. If he suddenly stopped, I would window-shop, turned in profile. Advanced gumshoe techniques. We passed a Duane Reade, a Starbucks, and an outdoor café modeled after spots on the Champs-Élysées.

At 57th Street, Lima stopped and looked back. I was under some scaffolding and did not break stride, only lowered my head. He lifted his hand to hail a cab.

I increased my pace. Two cabs passed him. He stepped back on the curb and started to walk again. I caught him roughly by the elbow.

"In space, no one can hear you scream."

"Get your fucking hands off me, man."

"I can drag you into Central Park and tie you to a tree," I said. "Or we can walk back a few blocks and sit down someplace nice."

Victor Lima tilted his head and thought about it. He didn't speak, only nodded.

"Good choice," I said, and let go of his arm.

We walked a block south and found a place to sit outside the mock-Parisian café. I ordered a cup of coffee. Lima said he didn't want anything.

"Sorry we didn't chat while on Mars."

"I wanted to see who you were," he said. "And what did you want with Lela and shit."

"To find you," I said. "And shit."

"That why you hassled my mother?"

"I only passed along my card."

"What the fuck do you want, man?" he said. "It's over. No one did crap about my brother. You're just making trouble for all of us."

Victor Lima was light-skinned and wore a dark jean jacket over what appeared to be a yellow soccer jersey. His jeans matched his jacket exactly, and the retro-style Jordans on his feet matched the bright yellow of the jersey. He had large, watery eyes and wore a slumped look of exhaustion, like a beaten fighter forced to go one too many rounds. He rubbed his face and leaned back in the café chair.

"You work for Kinjo Heywood?"

I nodded.

"Then screw you, man."

"I don't blame you," I said. "I'm just trying to figure out a few things."

My coffee arrived. It was French press — of course — and I let it steep. A couple at the next table shared some dessert.

"I saw where someone snatched his kid," Victor said. "Man can't stay out of trouble, can he? A straight thug."

So the news had broken.

"Anyone you might know?"

Victor sat up straighter and shot me a sour look. "Are you kidding, man?"

"Just how do you know Heywood killed your brother?" I said.

" 'Cause the police said he did," Victor said. " 'Cause I saw them fighting and heard him say he was going to kill Antonio. 'Cause

111

I know things."

I'd read Victor's statement in the homicide file. "You held something back?" I said.

"His three buddies all lied for him," he said.

"I read there were only two of his team-mates," I said.

"The cops lied," he said. "There were three other football players and the cops took their side. They took their word for everything. They got into it again out on the street."

"Did you see it?"

Victor shot me an unpleasant look.

"Then how do you know?"

I mashed the plunger on the coffee, taking the swirling grounds to the bottom of the glass. I poured some into the cup, added sugar, and this time skipped the cream. I also decided to forgo dessert. It's hard to look like a tough guy with a crème brûlée in front of you.

"Were you inside Chrome when Heywood and Antonio got into it?"

"Yeah."

"Over Lela."

"Sure."

"What happened?"

"Heywood grabbed her ass and asked her to screw him in the bathroom."

"And Antonio took exception to this."

I sipped some coffee. All the world walked by. I wondered if Toulouse-Lautrec ever strong-armed a suspect.

"He's an animal, man," Victor said. "He's the same on the field as off. He likes to hurt people. He got off on killing my brother to make a point. He couldn't stand anyone telling him what to do. How to act like a person."

I put down my coffee. "And now you'd like to see him hurt?"

"Shit, man," he said. "You really think I have his kid?"

I shrugged. "Some would agree you'd have good reason," I said. "And if the kid is not harmed . . ."

Victor rubbed his eyes and shook his head. "I don't ever want to see that man for the rest of my life," he said. "I don't want to be involved with anything to do with him or his family. This is all done."

"How so?"

Victor grinned and shook his head. "Heywood didn't tell you," he said. "Did he?"

I waited.

"Why do you think we dropped the lawsuit, man?" he said. "Heywood paid off my family if we let it go. That's what my mother wanted. What we agreed. We took his dirty money. It's finished. I didn't want to, but my mother thought it was best. I had to agree to her wishes."

I sipped some coffee and kept quiet and still. Two cabs stacked up at the traffic light, held in place by the red light.

"I'd still like to talk to Lela."

"She won't talk to you," he said. "I told her I'd take care of this, and that's just what I did."

Victor stood.

I stood.

"Don't ever come to our home again," Victor said, standing up and walking out to Broadway, where he disappeared around 55th Street. I finished my coffee and walked back to my hotel.

19

Hawk picked me up at the Back Bay Station the next morning in his silver Jag.

"You could have at least held open my door."

"Sure," he said. "I aims to please."

"And surly, too."

"You learn anything?"

"Nope," I said. "Confused as ever."

Hawk drove off, and soon we were heading north on Boylston. He had brought coffee and donuts from Café Dunkin. I had eaten a bagel on the train. This was second breakfast. Maybe I was turning into a hobbit.

"Z at Kinjo's house," Hawk said. "Which is now a three-ring circus."

"Wondered how long it would take."

"Waiting for someone to set up a fucking ice-cream stand."

Hawk wore Chanel shades with a white cashmere turtleneck under a black leather jacket. He handled the Jaguar as if it were an extension of himself, coiled and controlled.

"How's Kinjo?"

"Hasn't slept since you left."

"And his wife?"

"Wife one or wife two?"

"Who's at the house?"

"Wife two," Hawk said. "Z says the woman loving all those cameras on the street. Did her makeup and everything."

"Must be her grief," I said. "And wife one?"

"I sat on her house like you asked," Hawk said. "She doesn't have the boy. And if she did have the boy, she staying put. State police are all over her."

"First to suspect a parent."

Hawk slowed the Jag at the corner of Boylston and Berkeley.

"Not that I minded watching her," Hawk said. "Damn. You meet her?"

"Yep."

"And."

"She scratched the hell out of my face."

Hawk shrugged. "Reached out to some local pros," he said. "Called in some favors."

"And none of our usual suspects are touching kidnapping a kid."

"Nope," Hawk said. "This seem like

amateur hour."

"Anything else?"

"Some nut called in to a radio show last night," he said. "Said he has the kid. Less than credible, but staties checking it out."

The Jag idled at the curb where the new Bank of America was going in. I sampled one of the chocolate frosted to enhance my deductive reasoning. "What did Lundquist say?"

"State cops ain't real fond of me," Hawk said. "Figure they may be giving comfort to the enemy."

"He'd talk to you."

Hawk stayed silent. A tall young woman in tight jeans, a tight black sweater, and tall riding boots strode across our vision. The woman was quite fit. Hawk stayed silent.

"Hmm," Hawk said.

"Hmm," I said. "The office can wait. You mind driving me out to Chestnut Hill?"

"Why not?" Hawk said. "Always wanted to know how the other half lived."

"You can be the other half," I said. "Long as you have money."

"And fame," Hawk said. "Fame helps a brother out."

Hawk knocked the Jag into gear and drove toward Arlington, making his way back toward Huntington and out of the city. He let the window down as we drove under the Mass Pike.

"Which radio show?" I said.

"Paulie and the Gooch," Hawk said. "That sports-talk shit."

"Not a super-fan?"

Hawk did not answer. We didn't speak for a long while as we followed Route 9 into Newton. "So you struck out?"

"Not exactly," I said. "But those most likely to do Kinjo harm are looking less likely. It seems that some key pieces of information regarding the incident were kept private."

"By Kinjo himself."

"Yep."

"How key?"

"His attorney paid off the shooting victim's family so they'd drop the civil case," I said.

"Don't mean it settled."

"Or that Kinjo was guilty," I said.

"But money sure do make this world spin."

20

The back patio of the Heywood house was made of flat stones and littered with dead leaves. I had my second cup of coffee that morning as Kinjo and super-agent Steve Rosen joined me at a wrought-iron table. The inside of the big stone house was filled with Brookline cops and state police. The street at the top of the hill was crowded with news trucks and reporters and rubberneckers standing outside the gates. As we walked down the hill, Hawk again mentioned that an ice-cream stand could really turn a profit.

Kinjo used the flat of his large hand to scrape away the decaying leaves on the patio table. He sat, but Rosen decided to stand. Through the long bank of windows, I could see Hawk sitting with Z and Lundquist.

"How'd it go?" Rosen said. "What did you find?"

"Why didn't you tell me you'd paid off the Lima family?" I said.

"Listen, we asked you to —"

"Shut up," I said to Rosen. "I'm asking Mr. Heywood."

"Don't you ever —" Rosen said.

"Shut up."

Kinjo was worn-out, red-eyed, and beaten. He leaned forward in the chair, elbows on his knees. He was dressed in nothing but workout shorts and a gray T-shirt with the Pats logo. He shook his head. "I didn't want you to think I shot the man."

"Did you?"

"What I'm trying to say —" Rosen said.

I merely held up my hand.

Kinjo never once looked at his agent. He looked at me. "No," he said. "But we didn't want the bad publicity. We wanted it to go away."

"How much did you pay the Limas?"

"Kinjo, you don't have to say a word," Rosen said.

"Half a million."

I nodded.

"A settlement of that type isn't unusual — surely you understand that kind of thing," Rosen said. He had his hands in his pockets and ducked his chin as he spoke.

"Does he ever shut up?" I said.

"I hired you, and I can —"

"Jeez," I said. "That's new. What do you

want, Kinjo?"

Cristal wandered out from the French doors with a pack of cigarettes and a lighter in one hand. Her makeup was fresh, but she hadn't changed out of her light blue silk pajamas or fuzzy slippers. She smiled at everyone as she hunched her shoulders with a little giggle. "Just one, Kinjo," she said. "I promise."

Rosen walked over to her and said something in her ear and they both disappeared back into the house.

"If I am going to keep working on this, you need to tell me everything," I said. "And you need to tell the police everything, too. If I'd known you'd settled with the family, I might've looked elsewhere."

"They think I killed that dude."

I nodded. "What about in Boston," I said. "Has anyone ever tried to offer you money or influence your play?"

"Like for me to shave points and cheat?" he said. "One man can't throw a whole football game."

"But you could affect a point spread."

He looked past me up the hill to the playhouse. Behind the stone wall, smoke rose from his neighbor's chimney. More leaves fell from high branches. "I figured if you thought I'd paid those people off, you

121

wouldn't want to work for me," he said. "But I don't cheat, man. You don't cheat and not make plays and be All-Pro two years in a row."

I caught his eye and stared at him. "Don't lie to me again."

"Akira," Kinjo said. "He has asthma, man. The people who took him don't know. What if they never call? I'm about to crawl out my skin, man."

I nodded. I warmed my hands on the coffee mug. There was much activity through the windows of the house. Hawk, Z, and Lundquist continued to talk in the sectional by Kinjo's large television. Cristal had apparently broken away from Rosen and had taken a spot between Hawk and Z.

"What about the call at the radio station?" I said.

"Paulie and the Gooch," he said. "You know them?"

"I've seen their billboards," I said. "The Sports Monstah. Boston sports all day and all night."

"Police played it for me last night," he said. "Man called in and said he has Kinjo Heywood's child and wanted a payday."

"Anything else?" I said.

Kinjo shook his head. "All I know is they tried to track the call and it came back to a throwaway."

"So maybe it's them?"

"I hope so," Kinjo said. "I don't give a shit what it costs, I want my son back. Without him, I ain't got shit. All this around me? I can live in a trailer like I used to, and it's all the same to me. Something happen to Akira and you better drive me straight to the nuthouse. I can't live."

"I'll talk to Lundquist about that caller," I said. "Maybe pay a visit to Paulie and the Gooch."

Kinjo swallowed. His face was impassive, but he had started to cry. He turned his hulking back to me.

I left him outside in a slight patch of sunlight as I walked inside the glass doors.

21

Paulie and the Gooch talked little else but Boston sports from a two-story brick radio station off the Birmingham Parkway in Brighton. They were hitting their noontime stride when Z and I arrived. Lou from Quincy had taken the duo to task for saying the Red Sox Nation was washed up, blaming fans for lackluster play. Lou said Paulie and the Gooch were the biggest dips in Mass. Reggie from Worcester congratulated the boys for sticking by Tom Brady this season despite inexperienced tight ends and receivers. Reggie said the naysayers would soon eat their words. He actually said they'd eat something else for the five-second delay.

Z and I could hear the broadcast from a stale waiting room outside the studio.

"I never liked to discuss sports," Z said. "I'd rather just play."

"Depends on who's talking." I shrugged. "A Paulie and a Gooch probably don't equal a Frank Deford."

When the show went to a commercial break to advertise a Honda dealership, the producer, Cindy DeLuca, came out to meet us. She was a short woman in jeans, a faded green flannel shirt, and a Bruins hat. From a distance Cindy DeLuca might resemble a fifteen-year-old boy. "How long will this thing take?"

"Quick and painless," I said. "We want to hear the clip."

"Police already heard it."

"I'm not the police."

Cindy scrunched up her nose as if we didn't pass the sniff test. But then she just threw up her hands and shrugged. "Ray Heywood called us," she said. "He said you work for his brother. Ray's a good guy. We need signed jerseys for sick kids? He comes through every time. We need Kinjo to stop by the studio? He's there on time."

Cindy ushered us through a long hall lined with various local awards for charitable events, certificates of big ratings, and framed photos of great moments in Boston sports: Damon's World Series home run against the Cards, the Larry Bird baseline jumper against Portland, Brady celebrating a Super Bowl touchdown against Carolina. We soon found a small closetlike room with an oblong window facing the hall. Paulie and the Gooch wore headphones and were in a heated exchange with someone over why the Bruins blew the Stanley Cup. The caller referred to the radio journalists as a couple of douchebag morons. Both laughed it off right before they cut to a commercial.

"Rotten bastard," Cindy said.

Paulie was thin and bald and wearing a Celtics hoodie zipped to the chin, jeans, and flip-flops. The Gooch was stockier, with a graying goatee, wearing a Dropkick Murphys sweatshirt. Neither had been born anywhere near Boston but had made the smart choice to go native.

We made small talk. I introduced them to Z.

"Wasn't there a football player in California named Sixkill?" Paulie said.

Z shrugged.

"He grew up on a reservation and played fullback," Gooch said. "You know? He was on the cover of *Sports Illustrated*. Great player, but got all fucked up with drugs and got booted before his senior year."

Z remained impassive. He leaned against the door.

Paulie walked over to the console and began to cue up the call. The room was kept very cold and dim. The dials and switches glowed red and green as he worked. "We burned a copy for the cops," Paulie said. "I think it's just a crank. What says the Gooch?"

"Some nutbag."

"If it's good enough for the Gooch," I said.

Gooch smiled and stroked his goatee. "Then again," he said. "Nutbags pay our salaries."

I smiled. "Sometimes mine, too."

The commercial faded into the recorded voice of the hosts taking their next call. The voice had been run through some kind of electric voice changer, making the caller sound somewhere between Barry White and Robby the Robot. *I have Heywood's kid. He's safe and got shit to eat. We got demands and will let Heywood know when we're ready.*

Paulie ran it back and played it again. There was a long silence before the hosts began to speak, and he shut off the recording.

"That's it?" I said.

Paulie and the Gooch nodded. Cindy De-Luca showed up in the window and held up two fingers.

"Caller ID?" I said.

"Sure," Paulie said. "But I thought the state police said it wasn't any good?"

"They can run down where the phone was

bought," I said. "But it's doubtful they'll get a credit card or any video surveillance. They probably bought it from a third party."

"Kinjo's had a rough time lately," Gooch said. "Screwed up his ankle in mini-camp. Looked like he was loafing it in the last two exhibition games. I don't know, it's like his heart isn't in it."

"I don't know," Paulie said. "He's not going to give it all in preseason. To be honest, I was shocked he got selected to the Pro Bowl. I mean, he missed some key tackles in that last game against Atlanta. There's definitely some slipping in his intensity and focus."

The Gooch belched as if to punctuate his colleague's point. There was an open bag of Utz chips by the microphone and two open bottles of Diet Coke.

"I've got Kinjo on my fantasy football team," Gooch said. "Hope this thing doesn't rattle him too bad. Regular season starts next week."

"Yeah," I said. "That would be inconvenient."

Z grinned.

"Shit, I don't mean it like that," Gooch said. "It's just that Kinjo is something special. He keeps it up, even half-ass, and they'll be taking his measurements for a gold coat in Canton. I hate to hear shit like this happening to him right now. It's really messed up."

"You think this kidnapping could be just to rattle his play?"

"During preseason?" Paulie said.

I shrugged. "Anyone else ever call the station mad at him?" I said. "Anyone lately having an extreme hatred for any Pats players?"

The men shrugged in tandem. The Gooch looked to Paulie. Paulie said, "Sometimes people get kind of nuts on Brady or Belichick, like they control it all. But hate? I don't know. I mean, people get pissed. But that's the Boston way. You got to hate your team to love it."

The producer leaned in through the doorway and held up a single finger. Paulie handed me a disc and I thanked him. We all shook hands and headed for the door. The men began to slip their headphones back on.

"You sure you never heard of that guy also named Sixkill?" the Gooch said to Z.

"Nope," Z said. "But who knows? All us Indians look the same."

22

I dropped Z at my office and soon found Logan Wheeler in the weight room inside Gillette. He was squatting what must have equaled a tractor-trailer truck on his shoulders. As he cranked out the reps, deep and slow, he showed little sign of strain. He racked the weight with a small grunt. A coach stood nearby and tracked Wheeler's progress on an iPad.

As more weight was added to an already bending Olympic bar, Ray Heywood stepped up and introduced me to Wheeler. Wheeler had been with Kinjo at Chrome. I'd read his interview on the train back to Boston.

"I don't know what to tell you."

"I work for the Heywoods," I said. "And this isn't about two years ago. It's about now."

"I don't want to talk about it anymore," Wheeler said. "Kinjo didn't do jack shit, man. He's a good guy. When I think about what happened to Akira, I want to throw up."

Ray, dressed in a leather jacket and a scally cap, hung back a little. He told Wheeler that I was cool. I tried my best to look cool as I waited for Wheeler to add some.

"Like I told the police," Wheeler said. "That guy, whatever his name is —"

"Antonio Lima."

"Yeah, Lima," Wheeler said. "He was drunk and tried to start some shit with Kinjo, which was stupid. And then he tried to start some shit with me, which was even more stupid."

Wheeler was six-foot-six and well over three hundred pounds. He had a lot of blond hair and a stubbled beard and wore a gray T-shirt and gray sweatpants. His eyes were brown and tiny in his large head.

"And then?"

"And then nothing," Wheeler said. "The bouncers broke it up and we went back to the Trump. We ordered up some ice cream and cake and laughed about the whole thing. The next thing I know the cops are pounding on our goddamn door, wanting to talk to Kinjo. At first, I thought it was a practical joke."

"Not a good one."

"We all like to screw with each other," Wheeler said. "A couple weeks ago, we had these bumper stickers made up for the rookies. They said *Small Penis On Board.* The dummies didn't notice until people started honking at them and laughing. It was funny as shit."

The Pats' weight room was part of the many chambers inside the stadium. There were rooms for watching film, for meetings with the position coaches, for holding press conferences, a training table, and a locker room nearly as large as the field itself. This room was even larger, with old-fashioned weights and several rubberized mats to work speed, agility, and coordination. A three-hundred-pound man with agility and quickness was a scary prospect. I thought about the other player interview I'd read.

"What about Robey?" I said. "Do you keep in touch?"

Wheeler shrugged. "It's been a while."

"And he was traded to Miami?"

"Yeah."

"You have his number?"

Wheeler nodded. Ray stood next to us. The weight coach looked impatient, waiting for Wheeler to attack the next set. I stepped back and watched Wheeler knock out eight reps. There was more weight this time. He grunted a little.

"You want to try that?" I said to Ray.

"Shit," Ray said. "You?"

"I value my knees too much."

Wheeler racked the bar. He walked over to a table for a water bottle. He drank down a quart and turned back to me. He wiped his bearded face with the back of his hand. One of his sizable knees had a scar on it that looked like a zipper.

"What's not clear," I said, "and the reason I wanted to speak to you, is who else was there?"

"Like you said," Wheeler said. "Me, Kinjo, and Robey."

"Some witnesses said there was another football player there," I said. "A third man out with Kinjo that night."

There was a slight flick of his eyes to Ray, waiting for direction. Ray didn't change expression or say anything. After a second, he nodded at Wheeler to continue.

"That's not right," Wheeler said. "I'll give you Robey's cell when I'm done here. You ask him."

"And he left Chrome with you, too?"

"Yeah, man. What are you getting at?"

"Just trying to clear up a few things," I said. "Was he involved with the fight?"

"There was no fight," Wheeler said. "Robey was off with some girl. That Antonio guy pushed at Kinjo. Kinjo was ready to clock him and then the bouncers came up. I told him to cool off and get the hell out of there. We're not stupid. It was all just some bullshit. How were we to know that guy was some thug? He obviously had his own problems that got himself killed. Kinjo was only talking to that girl."

"His brother said Kinjo had inappropriately touched her."

"Is that the reason she'd hopped up in his lap?" Wheeler said. "Kinjo doesn't treat women like that. Why would he? Women can't leave him alone."

Ray nodded in agreement. Wheeler gulped down more water and looked at us with small, sad eyes. "You find out who took Akira," he said. "Okay? God help the son of a bitch who did this. There isn't a player on this team who wouldn't kill for that kid."

"Strong words."

Wheeler nodded. "Don't play with the meaning. You know what I mean. Kinjo is my goddamned brother."

Ray and I walked out of the weight room and into the long concrete hall.

"What do you think?" I said.

"I think this is a waste of time," he said.

"Kinjo paid the family because he was being eaten alive by the press. The family knows he wasn't involved. They wanted money. Kinjo didn't want to lose endorsement deals."

"Okay." I nodded. "How much do you know about Cristal?"

Ray grinned. He shook his head. "Too much."

"You think she knows more?" I said.

"Let me ask you this," he said. "You think Cristal is mentally capable of pulling something like this?"

"I understand her background's a bit sketchy."

"She ain't a virtuous woman," he said. "But she ain't evil, either. This isn't an inside job, man. Not exactly a secret that Kinjo is now a ten-million-dollar man. Lots of bad folks out there who hate seeing a black man in the catbird seat. How the hell you narrow that down?"

I nodded.

"That man being killed in New York has always been the stuff of whispers and lies," Ray said. "Don't let it cloud what's really happening."

I held Ray's eye for a while. He nodded with extreme certainty, adjusted his cap, and then led the way out of the labyrinth under Gillette.

23

"Play it again, Sam?" I said to Susan.

"How'd I know that was coming?"

"That's not really the line, but it sounds better than 'Play it, Sam. Play 'As Time Goes By.' "

"Do you want to hear 'As Time Goes By,' or do you still want my professional opinion?"

We sat outside on Susan's small wooden deck, drinking and listening to the phantom caller from a portable CD player. Susan drank a glass of Barolo while I worked on an Amstel. There was a pizza ordered and a quick meal planned before I'd drive back to Chestnut Hill. Being able to combine official work and time with Susan Silverman is always a perk of the job.

I played the message again. And then, to punctuate the question, raised my eyebrows.

Susan closed her eyes in thought. After taking a sip of the wine, she nodded. "I hear sexual repression, some Oedipal mother issues, and maybe some hypochondria mixed with erectile dysfunction."

"Zowie." I raised my brows again. "Really?"

"God, no," Susan said. "Do you really expect a clue from a five-second threat as read by a computer?"

"Cops call it a synthetic computerized voice changer."

"Can you even tell if it's a man or woman?"

"I would hope you could tell me."

"Erectile dysfunction would imply man," Susan said.

"So, right."

"Has this been the only contact with the kidnappers?" Susan said. "Or should I say alleged contact?"

"We believe," I said, sipping the Amstel. "You take what you can get."

"And the only thing Akira's parents can do is sit around and wait," she said.

"Separately," I said. "They've been divorced for two years."

"And there's a new wife?"

I explained about Cristal Heywood and the little I'd learned from Lundquist and Ray. I told her Cristal had bragged earlier in the day to Z about how the kidnapping increased her Twitter followers.

"Did Nicole really try and attack her?"

"She did more than try," I said. I pointed to the scratch on my cheek.

"Wow," she said. "Not exactly the reaction of a parent who'd be in on the kidnapping."

"No," I said. "The state police ruled her out pretty quickly. As did I."

"So why's Hawk still following her?"

"Kinjo's paying us to watch her."

"Which she doesn't know?"

I nodded and grinned. "I think Hawk is a bit smitten."

Now was the moment for Susan to raise her eyebrows. The doorbell rang and Pearl launched into attack mode. Susan stood, placed her wine on the table, and turned to the door. "Smitten?" she said. "That word has never been used to describe Hawk."

"Scary, isn't it?"

Susan nodded and walked downstairs to grab the pizza. She returned in a few seconds with a pizza box and Pearl trotting enthusiastically behind her.

"She has a nose for wild game and anchovies," I said.

Susan opened the box at the kitchen island and grabbed some good plates from the cupboards. We ate standing up at the island. Pearl sat at our feet, studying how we worked on each slice, waiting for one morsel to drop.

"Perhaps you should be watching Cristal instead?"

"Lundquist has it," I said. "Even a super-sleuth like me can only follow so many leads."

"You know much about wife two?"

I shrugged.

"And that's why you will check her out, even if she comes up clean."

"Being of a suspicious and doubtful nature has served me well."

"I just hope whoever has Akira calls soon," she said.

I nodded.

"The unknowing is the worst," Susan said. "A parent's mind will go to terrible places."

"If it's just money," I said. "The kidnappers just want Kinjo to sweat a bit. And to throw off the cops."

"And once they're paid in full?" Susan said. She picked at the pizza, taking in little nibbles in a distinctly Susan Silverman way. Pearl seemed frustrated and annoyed by this. Gobbling was the appropriate course of action.

"Do you really want to know?" I said. I drank some beer and reached for another slice of pizza.

Susan waited, noticing something in my face with her large brown eyes. She wore a thin silver chain around her neck.

"There is a fifty-fifty shot whether they get the kid back. Even if they pay."

"A brutal perspective," she said.

"But true."

"Cops say the same?"

"Cops know the same," I said. "Only the child can identify who took him."

"Are you going to tell the family this?" Susan said.

"Not my job."

"I think you should tell them."

"They have hope right now," I said. "And knowing the odds will only take that away. We'll talk when the time is right. When we know more about the people who took him."

"Any other theory besides just greed?" Susan said.

"I thought I had one," I said. "That's why I went to New York."

"And now?"

"I'm not so sure," I said, shaking my head. I told her about the Limas and my conversation with Kinjo's teammates. I had spoken to Robey in Miami an hour earlier and came up with identical answers as those of Logan Wheeler. There was a scuffle, it was broken up, and they went back to the Trump.

141

I mentioned to Susan that I had confronted Kinjo about the payoff to the family.

"And what do we know about Akira?" she said.

"I only met him briefly," I said. "Smart. Curious. Seems to idolize his father. Had a lot of astute questions about my chosen profession."

"And scared to death."

I nodded.

"He's old enough to know exactly what is going on and is probably wondering if he'll live through it. Can you imagine being that age and contemplating death? Or wondering if you'll ever see your parents again? We create these safe, warm places for children. Despite a divorce or animosity with the parents, his world is probably a good one."

"And so we wait."

I checked my phone again.

Susan moved in next to me. I put down my pizza and my beer and wrapped my arm around her. She rested her head on my shoulder. Her curly hair was very shiny and black. She smelled like lavender and the lightest trace of perfume mixed with lovely sweat.

"Call if you need me," Susan said.

I pulled her in closer and kissed the top of

her head. As I did, I saw her drop a pepperoni slice for Pearl.

24

The Heywood house was jumping later that night. Food had been catered, bushels of flowers unloaded, and two big coffee urns set up in the kitchen. Cops drink a lot of coffee. Grief-stricken people need flowers and food.

Lundquist and I waited in a sitting room that faced the driveway. From there, we could see reporters milling under camera lights. The room had white carpet and white leather furniture and a very large oil painting of Kinjo in his college uniform, delivering a bone-jarring tackle on a quarterback.

"You think someone might want to paint me in action?" I said.

Lundquist shook his head. "Sarcasm is hard to capture on canvas."

Across the hall, I could hear the scanner for Brookline PD, which had set up roadblocks around the house. The Heywoods' neighbors had not been pleased with the influx of traffic and gawkers. I'd been there for two hours and had spoken to Kinjo and talked to two Brookline cops about a man they had detained but later let go. The man apparently had a knack for showing up at crime scenes and confessing. Not only to being the Boston Strangler but also to shooting Lincoln.

"What'd you think of the guy who called in to *Paulie and the Gooch?*" Lundquist said.

"Don't know," I said. "Depends on if he or she follows up."

"Very PC of you to think our kidnapper may be female."

"But probably a guy," I said.

"Most often is."

Lundquist removed his sport coat and loosened his red tie. There was reddish-blond stubble on his face and dark circles under his eyes.

"How long have you been here?" I said.

"Two days straight," he said. "I slept for two hours earlier in a guest room."

"Can you go home?"

"Not until we hear something," he said. "I want to be here when the call comes through."

I nodded. I watched a grouping of reporters on a hill. A large bloom of light encircled a male reporter as he stood with his back to

Kinjo's house. Every few seconds he would gesture down the hill and then turn back to the camera. Except for some dotted points lighting a brick walkway, everything was stark black. The reporter turned and pointed a final time, holding the pose. The bloom of light extinguished, and it was dark again up the hill.

"Susan thinks we should tell Kinjo the odds."

"You want to have that conversation?"

"He should know," I said.

"I don't want to tell him anything until we even understand what we've got."

"Agreed," I said. "But what do we have? A trophy wife with a sordid past? A family who believes Kinjo is guilty but took cash instead of court?"

"I guess we're dealing with pros."

"How many pros leave a victim behind?"

"There have been some."

"But not a child old enough to ID them."

Lundquist's head sagged. He patted his shirt pocket for some cigarettes and came out with a crumpled pack of Marlboros and a Zippo. He stood and stretched. He walked to the door, and as he rounded the corner, he nearly ran into Steve Rosen and Jeff Barnes.

"Spenser," Rosen said. "You got a few

minutes?"

"For you, Steve?" I said. "Always."

Lundquist hung back for a second over the men's shoulders. He looked at me, shook his head, and headed for the front door.

Rosen grinned, exposing his eyeteeth in a way that did not make me feel comfortable. Jeff Barnes followed him.

Barnes looked as if he'd just started his day. His flawless double-breasted gray suit matched his flawless gray hair. He was clean-shaven and bright-eyed, and if he'd been maybe six inches taller, he might've even pulled off the glare he was giving me.

"We appreciate all you've done," Rosen said. He kept grinning, and I wished he'd stop.

"Sure."

"And this has nothing to do with you going to New York on your own."

"Of course not."

"But this whole thing has been shot to hell," Rosen said. "This isn't what we hired you for, and with the police involved . . . we think . . ."

I tilted my head. "That we need to see other people?"

Barnes stepped up at the same line as Rosen. He had been standing a few paces back, and I had been waiting for him to hit his mark. "Do you have to be so goddamn glib, Spenser?" Barnes said. "Do you even understand what is at stake here?"

I stood up. I smiled. "Glib?" I said. "I assure you my words are fraught with meaning."

"This thing is way above your head," Barnes said. I was pretty sure he was standing on his tiptoes when he said it. I looked down at his feet to see if he'd let his heels touch the ground. "You what? Work divorce cases? Maybe payroll theft?"

"Wow," I said. "You do your research, Barnes. You have me pegged. Peepholes R Us."

"I wouldn't hire you to take tickets at Gillette," he said. "This is professional business. We don't have time for amateurs."

"Now that you've thoroughly deflated my ego," I said. "Why don't you sit down and shut up."

"Excuse me?" Barnes said.

Rosen took three steps back. Barnes approached me. He was maybe a foot in front of me, nose to nose, or, more accurately, nose to chest.

"I can squat down if you like," I said. "It would make it easier to stare me down."

"I don't have time for this bullshit," he

said. "What Mr. Rosen is telling you is that you are fired. You'll be paid for your time, but it's time to pack up and head back to wherever you crawled out from."

"I'm still waiting."

"For what?"

"For you to sit down and shut up," I said. "Rosen. Call in Kinjo. If he wants me to leave, I'll leave."

"He wants you to leave," Rosen said.

"Okay," I said. "Have him tell me. And I will."

"He's asleep," Rosen said. "He's broken down. Don't make it worse."

"I'll wait."

"I hired you," Rosen said. "And I handle his affairs."

I shot a look at Rosen and held it. He swallowed and disappeared from the room.

Barnes laughed out of his nose. "You came just as advertised, Spenser."

"By your friend with the Feds?"

"Yep."

"Surprised he had time to call you with all the payoffs he's been taking in Southie."

"Keep talking," Barnes said. "Wouldn't take much from him to pull your license."

"Eek."

Z had wandered in, replacing Rosen, and stood wide in the doorway. He crossed his arms over his chest and nodded to me.

"This isn't over," Barnes said. "Not by a fucking long shot."

"Z, have you met my friend, Jeff Barnes?" I said. "Million-dollar personality."

"Don't bother coming back," Barnes said. "I'll notify the police."

"And witty, too," Z said. His dark face showed no emotion. Black eyes steady on Barnes.

I winked at Barnes as I followed Z into the hallway and down into the big kitchen. It was late and the kitchen was empty. Coffee mugs and empty plates crusted with food littered the room. I checked the time and poured some more coffee.

"Have you talked much to the brother?" Z said.

I took a sip. "Some."

"And?"

"And something isn't right."

"Two hours ago, we were outside talking, and Ray Heywood left pretty quick," Z said. "He was inside the house for maybe an hour, talking with Kinjo. An hour ago, he passed me on the road and did not speak."

"Rude."

"His face was sweating and he was out of breath."

"He's overweight and not in good shape."

150

"I followed him."

I put down the coffee.

"He drove to a bar in Newton, stayed five minutes, and sped out of the lot."

"And where is he now?"

"I put a GPS tracker on his car," Z said. "Looks like he's in Boston. What was that about, anyway?"

I nodded. "Mutt and Jeff wanted to put us on waivers."

"They say why?"

"Strongly suggested they were handling matters," I said.

"Looks like Ray Heywood is deep into whatever it is tonight."

25

Nearing midnight, we caught up with Ray Heywood in his silver Mercedes SUV. He'd stopped off at his brownstone apartment in the South End for a few minutes, and we thought perhaps he'd turned in for the night. But thirty minutes later, he was heading up Mass Ave and turning onto Boylston toward downtown. I drove my Explorer with Z riding shotgun. Z tracked the car from his phone.

"I almost feel like that's cheating," I said.

"Is there an honest way to tail someone?"

"Maybe not more honest," I said. "But sporting."

I hung back five cars. Ray's tall Mercedes was easy to spot as it slowed and turned down into the Prudential Center parking garage.

We followed him down into the concrete cavern. I drove past Ray and let Z out before finding a slot two sections over. The garage was silent except for the electric buzzing of fluorescent lamps. Every step, every car door echoed loudly deep beneath Pru Center. Z and I waited until he took the elevator to the street level and followed. Out of the elevators, we rounded the corner and watched Heywood take an escalator up to the shopping plaza. Z and I walked together through the empty mall under the darkened skylights, past the Legal Seafood and the food court, all the kiosks in the center of the mall draped with black cloth. Ray never looked back, heels clacking on the marble floors as he punched the button to the express elevators headed to the fifty-second floor.

"Top of the Hub," I said.

"What's that?"

"An overpriced bar with a great view."

"Maybe he wants a drink?" Z said.

"Or was told to meet someone."

We took the next elevator up the second-tallest building in the city. The elevator rocketed up and soon slowed. When we stepped out, Ray Heywood was standing with his back to us at the hostess stand. I studied the artwork on the walls and glanced back in time to see Ray turning to the right, toward the long bar and the jazz club. A trio had started up before a huge bay window with a view of the city, the water-front, Logan, and if you looked hard enough, London Bridge and the Eiffel Tower.

"Nice," Z said.

"You should see the bathrooms," I said. "They put ice in the urinals."

Z seemed properly impressed. We both took a seat at the bar, not within sight of Ray, but Ray had to pass us to leave. I had removed my Spinners cap. Z took off his coat and ordered a Coke. I had a Harpoon on draft in an effort to support local commerce.

"You want to walk back there?" Z said. "Or me?"

"He knows us both."

I drank some beer and shrugged. I walked back to the jazz club and glanced inside. Ray Heywood was seated near the northern windows. He said something to a waitress and then looked down at his cell phone. The trio played "Skylark."

I walked back to the barstool.

Z looked up from his Coke.

" 'Skylark,' " I said. "In case you were wondering."

Z nodded.

"Melancholy."

"Music of the night," I said.

We did not speak for a long while, occasionally turning back to the bar and waiting for Ray to return. I had been here recently with Susan and Rachel Wallace. We had heard the food had improved a great deal and had heard right. I'd had the spicy lobster soup, followed by scallops as big as a fist. I thought for a long while about what Susan had ordered but came up with nothing in my memory but a garden salad and a gimlet.

After ten minutes, I got up again and looked for Ray. He was still sitting and looking at his cell phone, pressing some keys. The waitress had brought him a tall drink over ice. The trio had moved on to " 'Round Midnight."

I walked back to the barstool.

" ' 'Round Midnight.' "

Z nodded. "Good to know."

"I like to pass on my cultural knowledge with tough-guy talents."

I pointed at his empty Coke glass. "As long as you're driving," he said.

I had not seen Z take a drink since the beating. He did not seem to mind me having a beer but often seemed uncomfortable at the sight of me with whiskey. I sipped the one beer but laid down a nice tip for the bartender so she would not think we were just mooching off the view. Through the shelves of booze bottles, the nightlights of Boston flickered and pulsed in the blackness. Perspective.

"Kid's out there somewhere," Z said.

"Yep."

"Coming up on three days and nothing."

"We'll find him."

"Now what?" Z said.

"Don't know."

"Why don't we just sit down with Ray?" Z said.

"We could," I said. "But might scare whoever he's meeting. If he's meeting one of the kidnappers."

Z nodded.

"Should we call Hawk?"

I shook my head. "Break glass only when necessary," I said.

We listened to the music and sipped our drinks. Just another couple of businessmen out for a good time in ol' Beantown. Z had only recently been able to pass after cutting off his ponytail. If I had my nose fixed, I might be considered midlevel management material.

At one a.m., Ray walked from the club toward the restroom. I followed him inside and saddled up beside him at the urinal. Over the urinals were historic photos of the city. Mine showed a group of mustached men in front of a horse-drawn fire wagon.

"How about that version of 'Skylark'?" I said.

Ray turned to me. "Shit."

"I thought it was pretty good."

"What the fuck you doing here, Spenser?" he said. "Shit. I'm supposed to meet someone."

"That's why I didn't approach you in the lounge."

"This is nothing to fuck around with," he said, stepping away. "Besides, I thought you were through with this."

"According to super-agent Steve Rosen?"

Ray nodded and stepped over to the sink to wash his hands. The bathrooms were very cramped on the fifty-second floor.

"Who contacted you?" I said.

"Don't know."

"But it's the kidnapper?" I said.

"That's what they say."

"When did they call?" I said.

"Didn't call," Ray said. "They fucking sent a message to Kinjo's Facebook page."

"Now everyone knows?"

"I'm the administrator," he said. "It was a personal message."

I had no idea what he was talking about. "What did it say?"

"Man," Ray said, turning off the sink and reaching for a towel. "I don't think I should be talking to you."

"What did they say?"

"If I tell you, they'll get rid of me next."

"Did Kinjo want me gone or Rosen?"

Ray was quiet. He was a rotund man, and the two of us filled the small bathroom. His sky-blue silk dress shirt was stained at the armpits.

"Rosen," Ray said. "Kinjo's ass is knocked out. They gave him some sleeping pills so he could rest."

"Then I'm still on the job."

Ray walked back to the sink and splashed some water on his face. He wiped his eyes and turned back to me. "Doesn't matter," he said. "They didn't show."

I nodded.

"They told me to go to this fucking bar in Newton and so I go to fucking Newton. I get there and the bartender asks if I'm Ray Heywood. I was like the only one in this shithole and said yes. He hands me the phone, and same weird-ass voice as called *Paulie and the Gooch* come on and tell me to go to the Top of the Hub and wait. So I wait, and not shit so far."

"Wait some more," I said. "Z and I are at the bar."

Ray ran a hand over his face. He was breathing hard out of his nose as he thought, and finally nodded. "Okay."

I grabbed his arm, and he looked me in the eye. "If someone sits with you, we'll see them. If you get a message to go somewhere else, just nod at us on the way out. I have a blue Explorer and will follow you out of the garage."

Ray grabbed my shoulder. "They said if we told the cops, they'd kill Akira," he said. "I just told Rosen and he and Jeff Barnes thought I should go alone. You know, find out the terms."

I nodded. Ray left, and I stayed in the bathroom for a minute before leaving.

I sat back at the bar.

Z did not say anything, just stared at the wide expanse of the Boston night. Lights twinkled and pulsed. *Over the shadows and the rain. To a blossom-covered lane.*

"Waiting on demands."

Z nodded. Fifteen minutes later, Ray walked past us and gave a slight nod.

We followed him in the next elevator and out of the Pru Center garage onto Boylston. I called Hawk on the way.

26

An hour later, Z and I sat down across from Ray Heywood and Hawk at the South Street Diner. The restaurant was open twenty-four hours, which made it attractive at two in the morning. It also made it attractive to many drunken kids leaving the bars around Faneuil Hall. There was a lot of noise and boisterous laughing, which was a bit incongruous to our talk of kidnapping and ransom demands. Said demands being left on the windshield of Ray Heywood's Mercedes while we were all listening to "Skylark" up at the Top of the Hub.

As soon as we both drove out of the parking garage, Ray had called. We drove a fair bit around Chinatown to make sure he was not being followed. Z had recommended South Street because it was near the Harbor Health Club and was a favorite of Henry Cimoli's. Not that Henry's taste in food was stellar.

We all drank coffee. Hawk ordered a southwestern omelet with hash browns and a side of bacon. He ate while we spoke. His presence seemed to make Ray nervous. Which was only natural. Hawk made any normal person nervous.

"You're someone," Ray said. "I know you."

"I am someone," Hawk said. "But you don't know me."

"You were an athlete, a ballplayer or something."

"Before your time."

"But I know you."

Hawk shook his head. "You are mistaken, friend." With that, Ray turned back to me.

"Do you think they saw you?" Ray said.

I shook my head.

"How can you be sure?"

"Because we were careful you didn't see us," I said. "And they don't know us."

A waitress refilled our cups. Hawk finished the omelet and pushed the plate away, dabbing his lips with his napkin. Z sipped black coffee and listened to the talk.

"Where?" Hawk said.

I looked to Ray. "South Station at six a.m."

Ray nodded.

"You got the note?" Hawk said.

Z reached into his leather jacket for the

note and handed it across. Hawk read it and handed it back.

"Staties gonna be pissed," Hawk said.

"Yep," I said. "We should tell Lundquist."

Heywood looked at both of us as if we needed to be fitted for straitjackets. "Didn't you read the fucking note?" he said. "No cops or the kid is dead."

"We read the note," Hawk said.

Ray closed his mouth.

"I would have thought they'd ask for more money," I said.

"You don't think a hundred grand is a lot of money?" Ray said.

Z looked up and spoke. "Not when the victim is worth twenty million."

"Kinjo's gonna get the cash."

"Who'd he tell?" I said.

"His agent."

"Terrific," I said. Z still wore his black leather jacket, hands around a thick ceramic coffee mug. Hawk had neatly hung up his trench coat by the booth. His black T-shirt seemed painted onto his body. His forearms corded with muscle and vein. Z studied Ray as he spoke, offering no emotion or reaction. His right hand tapped slightly on the mug.

"What does Kinjo want?" I said.

"He doesn't want the police to know."

"We ain't the police," Hawk said.

"He doesn't know," Ray said, lowering his head and leaning in among the rattling noise to whisper. "This his goddamn kid, man. You don't mess around with that. I think he just wants to bring the cash, get Akira, and get done with this."

I nodded.

"But that shit ain't gonna happen," Ray said. "Is it?"

I shook my head.

"They gonna try and kill him anyway."

"It happens," I said. "But I'd prefer to change the script."

"How?"

"Three of us can even the odds."

"And do what?"

"Make sure Akira is returned safe," I said.

Z drank some coffee. It had started to rain out on South Street and the streetlamps glowed stark and bright white along the pavement. Hawk watched the rain from the booth. He was quiet but completely in tune with every word that was being said. One of the drunk kids dropped a glass of water off a table, crashing to the ground.

Ray recoiled. Hawk didn't so much as turn his head.

"I can call Kinjo," Ray said. "But I can't promise nothing. It's his kid. His decision."

"Just how does he figure to leave the house with a hundred grand without the dozens of police camped out at his house knowing?" I said.

"Y'all just haven't known my brother long enough. But he can do anything he puts his mind to."

Ray stood up and walked outside under the diner overhang to make the call. I looked to Z. Hawk was still very interested in the rain.

"What will Lundquist do if we're involved and don't tell him?" Z said.

"I'll be number one with a bullet on the staties' shit list."

"That bad?" Z said.

"Spenser tops many shit lists 'round here," Hawk said. "Where he feels at home."

Outside, Ray's thick shadow bent over as he spoke into the phone. The streetlights turned the falling rain into sharp gold pellets hitting the asphalt. Gutters collected the runoff and rolled down the dry concrete.

Hawk turned from the window and smiled. "A woman would be mighty grateful to the man who saved her child."

"Sure," I said.

"Hmm," Hawk said.

"I told Susan that you were smitten with Nicole Heywood," I said. "Was I correct?"

"*Smitten* too nice a word for what I got," Hawk said.

27

Kinjo Heywood walked into the Harbor Health Club at four-thirty a.m. and tossed a large workout bag on a weight bench. Hawk had loaded up a curl bar as we waited and repped out with forty-five plates. He had not broken a sweat or showed any labored breathing on his twentieth curl. As he set down the bar, he nodded to Kinjo. Kinjo shook all of our hands. Ray Heywood had gone back to Chestnut Hill.

"I told the police I was headed to the stadium," Kinjo said.

"What about Barnes?" I said.

"Fuck Barnes."

"What about Steve Rosen?" I said.

"Rosen got the cash for me," Kinjo said. "He works for Team Heywood, not the Pats. What we got? Come on, let's go."

Z and I had taken a nice leisurely stroll around South Station and came back with diagrams sketched on sheets of yellow legal paper. Kinjo was to show up at the Au Bon Pain in the center of South Station and take a seat. Someone would soon join him, pick up the bag, and leave, presumably by bus, subway, train, taxi, or car. There were many options at South Station, which made it convenient for a drop.

"I'll cover the platform," I said. "Z can wait at the escalator down to the T and Silver Line. Hawk is our utility outfielder, covering the taxi stand and exits onto Atlantic."

"These motherfuckers didn't say how or when I'd get my kid back," Kinjo said.

"It's a one-way conversation," I said.

"What if this dude tells me Akira isn't there?" Kinjo said. "That he'll get me later or some shit."

"Your son won't be there," I said. "They'll make sure they get the money and then figure out their next move."

"What would you do?" Kinjo said. "If it were your kid? You want me to be cool about all this. Trust them?"

"Nope."

I looked to Hawk. Hawk had selected a leather jump rope and used it to stretch out his shoulders. He shot a glance at me before jumping a little rope by the mirrored wall. Hawk was not proficient at being idle unless necessary.

Z sat, elbows on knees, on a bench loaded with the sack of money. I stood with Kinjo. Most of the lights were off in the gym and the air purifier made gentle humming sounds. I had enough coffee at the diner to overcaffeinate a rhino.

"You don't trust anyone," I said.

"Then what the hell do you do?" Kinjo said.

"We follow him," I said. "I wouldn't want this guy out of my sight until you have Akira in yours."

Kinjo nodded. "What else?"

"We could put a tracker with the money," I said. "But I think they'll check it pretty quickly. The device would get tossed and could definitely piss them off, too. We follow the courier."

"Where'd you park?" Z said.

"At the Aquarium, like y'all said."

Z nodded and stood up, going out to the street to check to see if anyone had tailed Kinjo. Hawk finished jumping rope and walked over to where he'd hung up his holster and coat. He slid into the leather, holstering his .44 Magnum, and then fit his leather trench over it. He turned his head slightly, his neck giving an audible pop.

"Won't be long before Barnes calls the

police," Kinjo said. "Let them know I never made it to the stadium."

I checked my watch. "Won't take that long."

"Can you both promise me something?" Kinjo said.

I nodded. Hawk nodded.

"You snatch up this man and get him to a place where I can whip his ass," Kinjo said. "All I need is five minutes and a quiet room. I'll come to terms, I promise."

"No problem with that, man," Hawk said. "But Spenser and I have years of experience reasoning with people."

"You gonna try and talk it out?" Kinjo said.

Hawk shook his head.

"If this person shows up," I said, "we'll find out where he's taking the money and to whom. He'll talk."

"How can you be so sure?"

Hawk smiled. I nodded my head modestly.

"Y'all stay so cool," Kinjo said, shaking his head. "I feel like I'm going to come out of my skin."

"You just show up with that bag," I said. "We'll handle the rest."

He nodded. And then he got up on shaky legs and walked back to the gym bathroom.

A toilet flushed and we heard him throw up.

28

South Station was busy at five minutes until six. Kinjo was already seated at the table by the Au Bon Pain as I perused a copy of *Radio My Way* by Ron Della Chiesa at Barbara's Bookstore. I could see Kinjo from where I stood, my elbow resting atop a bookshelf, the brim of my ball cap low in my eyes. In the opposite direction, through the mire of travelers and commuters, Z lingered by the escalators down into the T station. If we had wanted to detain the courier, the number of MTBA cops milling about would have made the task difficult.

The loudspeakers announced train departures from various tracks. The big train board clicked and whirred with the latest updates. Early gray light flooded high windows as the station pulsed with brisk energy. I had just got to a profile on Ruby Braff when I saw a thick-necked guy with bleached-blond hair step up to Kinjo's table and lean in to speak.

There wasn't any reason to think this was our guy. Our guy had a knack for not showing. And this could be one of Kinjo's many fans. Working a kidnapping exchange was more difficult with a guy who's been on the cover of *Sports Illustrated* and *ESPN* magazine. But the guy lingered at the table, and Kinjo's body language indicated something other than a casual chat with a fan. His body was tense, leaning into the table. The bleached blond snatched the bag and walked toward the open-air bookstore.

Kinjo stood, walking in a daze into the crowd, lifting his chin at the man but not pointing and calling attention as we had discussed.

The man was tall, maybe six-three, broad-shouldered, and wearing an old-fashioned buffalo-check mackinaw with blue jeans and work boots. I got a good look at him as he passed me. Early thirties, chiseled face, thin lips, pale blue eyes. The hair was a color not found in nature. He had the workout bag tossed over his shoulder and wore a smug grin as he strutted through the crowd. I called Hawk on my cell.

The man headed toward a chocolate shop and a bank of ATMs. Z picked him up at the escalator. I told Hawk he was headed to the front doors that met at the corner of Atlantic and Summer.

I increased my pace, passing the escalator and the ATMs and catching Z as the guy crossed over Summer, dodging traffic. Horns blared and cars swerved around him as he made his way to the Federal Reserve Plaza. He began to jog through the open plaza as Hawk braked in front of us at the curb.

I jumped in. Z ran back to his car parked at the station.

Hawk's car was not familiar to me.

"Trading up?" I said.

"Yeah," Hawk said. "Every black man wants a ten-year-old Olds with bad brakes."

"Borrowed?"

"Something like that."

Hawk zipped down Atlantic and slowed as we passed the guy jogging toward Congress. Hawk pulled to the curb, motor idling, until we saw him run across Congress to a burgundy SUV and jump in. We accelerated from the curb past the Tea Party museum and north along the waterfront.

I called Kinjo and told him to head home. He tried to argue the point, but I'd already hung up.

Atlantic became Commercial, and soon we were in the narrow brick buildings of the North End. They'd spotted us. The SUV took a very hard left, squealing tires, onto Hanover as Hawk hit the accelerator.

"No use in pussyfooting," Hawk said.

"Nope."

"They tryin' to get over the bridge," Hawk said.

"Makes sense."

"Tell Z to wait there."

I called Z and told him to go ahead and drive over to Charlestown.

"Should've figured them for Charlestown," Hawk said.

"Or Roxbury or Dorchester or Southie," I said. "We mustn't generalize a hood's home turf."

"Charlestown got more criminals per capita."

"Per capita?" I said.

"I heard it on the television once," he said. "Don't know what it means."

We raced down Hanover toward the statue of Paul Revere. The burgundy SUV squealed right up onto Charter Street. We followed.

"Yep," Hawk said.

"You sure?"

"Mmm-hmm."

"Then back off," I said. "Let Z take it."

"You trust him?" Hawk said.

"He was trained by us," I said.

Hawk took his foot off the accelerator. We passed the crooked headstones of Copps Hill burying ground where Charter came into the curve at Commercial. At the corner of Prince, we waited and watched the SUV run through a red light and race onto the Charlestown Bridge.

I called Z again.

"Good to have three of us," Hawk said. "Knew the kid would come in handy."

"Especially now that you pissed off Vinnie," Hawk said.

"That was inevitable."

"Inevitable that he's gonna take over Gino Fish's territory and we all be screwed."

"You think?" I said.

Hawk nodded. We idled at the stoplight. A car behind us honked its horn. We turned left onto Commercial and took our time driving over the river into Charlestown.

"You call Vinnie about this?" I said.

" 'Cause you can't?"

I nodded.

"He got his own troubles," Hawk said. "New crew moving into Eastie on account of that casino being built."

"Shocking," I said.

"Mmm-hmm."

We made it over the bridge and drove

175

slowly along the old Navy Yard where the *Constitution* lay anchored. Actually, it wasn't anchored. The proper term was *berthed.* Or maybe it was moored.

Hawk parked along a row of old brick buildings once in official use by the shipyards. Some of them had been turned into luxury condos and restaurants. Others lay dormant. The street was empty. It had started to rain again.

Hawk leaned back into his seat. We sat there maybe ten minutes when my phone rang.

"Charlestown," Z said. "Ludlow and Mead. I parked next to the basketball court. There's two of them. Just went into a triple-decker."

Hawk started the borrowed car and headed out of the Navy Yard.

29

"Kid been gone three days," Hawk said.

"Yep."

"Kid lucky his dad is Kinjo Heywood."

"Or unlucky," I said. "His dad was Joe Blow and nobody would be interested in holding him for ransom."

Hawk nodded. The rain created a pleasant patter on the hood of the Oldsmobile. Every ten minutes or so, he'd hit the wipers and clear our view of the triple-decker. It wasn't a bad house, as Charlestown was not the Charlestown of old. Fresh blue paint, good roof, no broken windows. Of course, every-thing looks better in the rain.

"You know how many black children go missing every year?"

"No," I said.

"Unless you blond with blue eyes, you don't make the evening news."

"Are you trying to say this country still is plagued by racial issues?"

"Nope," he said. "I am simply stating a fact."

The last sentence lapsed into Hawk's James Mason accent. I wondered if Hawk had ever watched any James Mason movies to practice. I did not ask. Some things were better not to know.

"Z's done well," Hawk said.

"He's genetically programmed to track," I said.

"What's a thick-necked Irishman programmed for?"

"Sitting in the pub and bitching about affirmative action."

"Ha," Hawk said.

We had been sitting on the house for five hours and no one had walked in or out. Z had parked his dark green Mustang on the far corner, facing the opposite direction. If our courier or alleged kidnappers decided to leave, we were covered.

"She invited me in for coffee yesterday," Hawk said.

"Who?" I knew but wanted him to say it.

"Nicole."

"Ah."

"Said if I was just going to be loitering, might as well be loitering in her living room."

"Makes sense."

"Mm-hm."

Hawk leaned back into the seat. He crossed his massive arms across his chest. I don't know if his eyes were closed or not. He wore a dark pair of sunglasses that made knowing impossible.

"And," I said.

"And what?"

"How was the coffee?"

Hawk's mouth curled a bit. "Excellent," he said. "She talked a lot about Akira, mostly. Loves the boy, hates the father. Hates the stepmother even more. All that."

"Hate is a strong emotion."

Hawk nodded. The rain fell harder and there was a long, lingering thunder that rattled the windshield.

"Kid had a hard time with the divorce," Hawk said. "Keeps on trying ways to get them back together. Think he the one made the trouble."

"Which is not happening."

"Kinjo seems to have a wandering dick."

I nodded. "That often complicates a relationship."

"Kid will want Kinjo to stick around when he drops him off," Hawk said. "Kid's only eight but starts talking about old times with the family. Trying to bring up good memories. Momma says he's become nervous."

"And now this."

"No kid should be a part of this."

A black Dodge Charger passed us, heading up Mead, and parked in front of an empty playground. A middle-aged white guy with a scruffy beard walked across the street to the triple-decker we'd been watching all morning. He wore an oversized gray hoodie with the Bruins logo. He looked as put together as an unmade bed.

"See that?" Hawk said.

Gray hoodie had an automatic wedged in a belt behind his back.

"Inconspicuous."

The man walked up into the triple-decker without knocking or waiting for the front door to open. We sat in the car for another five minutes, waiting, and no one came out.

"We could call the state police," I said. "And notify them of recent activity."

"Might create a circus."

"Or they might send in a SWAT."

"And try and negotiate."

I nodded. "Negotiation was not part of the plan."

The front door opened and our old pal Blondie stepped out with a spray-tanned gorilla in a pink shirt. They both seemed unfazed by the rain. The gorilla, who we presumed to be the courier's driver, stepped back in the house and then returned a few moments later.

The gorilla wore the tight clothing of a gym rat and seemed to have a hard time walking. With some effort, he crawled into the Charger, cranked it, and turned down Ludlow.

"Just the two now?"

"Only one way to find out," I said.

" 'Course they could be holed up with the Wild Bunch."

I shook my head. Hawk turned to me. He nodded and opened the driver's door. Across the street, Z did the same and met us at the corner. We walked separately down the neighborhood street, Hawk and Z breaking off toward an alley behind the house. I walked up to the front door and rang the bell. The cloudy skies and light rain made Charlestown gray and slick and pleasant.

30

Blondie, the courier, answered the door.

"Avon calling," I said. "We have a wonderful assortment of styling products, sir."

"What the fuck?"

"Don't be angry," I said. "We can do something about those roots."

He started to close the door. I wedged my steel-toed Red Wing into the threshold. I aimed my .38 into his stomach. "How about you invite me inside," I said. "I have so much to show you."

"Hey," he said, very loud.

"Keep it down," I said. "This is a very special offer. Just for you."

He tried to pull a gun. I punched him in the gut and took it away from him and marched him backward into the narrow hallway.

The antique floors had been stained very dark and recently sealed. The walls were Sheetrocked and newly painted. The rest of the house was empty besides a card table, some folding chairs, and a big green Celtics flag that said *Believe in Boston.*

I told Blondie to sit down.

Z and Hawk walked Hoodie into the room. His Bruins sweatshirt was covered in blood and he was holding his nose. Hawk did not tell him to sit. But he sat anyway. His hood was up, which made him look monkish and ridiculous for a man of his age.

"Money is in the kitchen," Hawk said.

Z walked upstairs, gun drawn, and came back. He shook his head. "No kid," he said. "Lots of dope." Z headed into the kitchen and quickly returned, tossing the workout bag stuffed with Kinjo's money onto the wooden floor.

"Where's Akira?" I said.

"Who?" Blondie said.

Hoodie just shook his head and said, "Shit."

I hit Blondie very hard in the mouth with an overhand right. He toppled from the chair and ended up on all fours. I kicked him hard in the gut and he fell onto his back. Hawk made a *tsk-tsk* gesture.

"My teeth," Blondie said. "You knocked out my front teeth."

"Do make it hard to whistle," Hawk said.

I said, "Maybe the tooth fairy will come

183

through."

Blondie poised to get back on his feet. Hoodie stayed seated, wide-eyed and watching all three of us. Hawk had the man's gun on his waist now. Hoodie just shook his head, attentive yet confused at what he was seeing. Z stood by the card table, arms folded across his chest.

"How about you?" I said to Hoodie.

"We ain't got the kid," Hoodie said. "We ain't got the kid. Never fucking had the kid."

He blurted it out as if he needed to push all the air from his lungs. Blondie got to his feet. He shook his head with great disappointment for his partner. Hoodie held on to his bleeding nose.

"Where'd your buddy go?" Z said.

"Getting some food," Hoodie said. "You know, to celebrate."

Z got down on one knee and pulled out bundles of cash in the bag. When he noted it was all there, he nodded at me.

"Did you ever have the kid?" I said.

No one said a word. Blondie spit on the ground and shook his head. He had a large gap where his two front teeth used to be. His mouth was very bloody. He stayed silent. Hoodie shook his head.

"I'm not convinced," I said, turning to Hawk. "You?"

184

Hawk stepped up to Hoodie. Hoodie flinched and covered his head. Between his face and the front of his shirt he was a real mess. "Come on. Come on."

Hawk feinted at him. Hoodie flinched and recoiled. Hawk stepped back.

"Shit," Hawk said. "These boys aren't worth the trouble."

"Yep."

There was a knock at the door. Z pushed Blondie into the seat next to his friend. I put a finger to my lips, only the sound of ragged breathing in the room and the soft clicking of rain against the glass. I looked through the peephole, pulled my S&W, and cracked open the door. I motioned to the juiced-up gorilla in the pink T-shirt who was using both hands to carry a box of Dunkin' Donuts and a tray of coffees.

"Put it on the table."

"What the fuck, man," the gorilla said. "What the fuck?"

I took a nifty little .32 auto out of the front of his pants. I looked at Hawk.

"Little gun," Hawk said. He held his .44 in his right hand.

Z pulled out another chair, gripped the man's shoulder, and tried to force him to sit with his bleeding friends. Gorilla lunged at Z, and Z hit him very hard in the gut.

Gorilla bent at the waist and tried to suck in a lot of air that wouldn't come. He reached for his knees and Z knocked him on his ass.

Soon the trio sat before us in the folding chairs.

"I have an idea," I said, pointing at each of them. "You cover your eyes, you cover your ears, and you cover your mouth."

"We ain't got the kid," Hoodie said.

"We heard about it on the news," Blondie said. "We figured it wouldn't hurt no one. That nigger's got a lot of money."

Hawk whipped his head around and studied Blondie. He reached out and snatched a big handful of bleached hair. "Come again?"

"I don't mean nothin' by it," Blondie said. "But the guy is a millionaire. He signed a freakin' ten-million deal. So we get some. We'd never take a fucking kid."

"Perfect," I said.

Z walked over to the table and opened the donut box. Half glazed and half chocolate. He handed a coffee to me and one to Hawk. There were little packets of sugar and cream containers in a bag. I added some to the coffee.

"Silver lining to everything," Z said.

I nodded. "How much dope is upstairs?"

"Not Tony Montana," Z said. "But dealing near a playground won't look good in court."

I shook my head with disappointment at the morons in front of me. Z hoisted Kinjo's cash up on his shoulder and made for the back door. I dialed Quirk and told him we had something the department might want to see. The juiced-up gorilla opened his mouth as if about to speak. But he seemed to think better of it and stayed quiet.

"What the hell?" Quirk said.

"Just pass along this address to the drug unit," I said. "Consider it a gift."

31

That evening, I returned to Chestnut Hill with Susan Silverman.

I had to tell Kinjo and Nicole that they'd been conned, and that, in fact, after four days, no one had contacted the family about Akira. He was simply missing.

"Will they talk with me?" Susan said.

"Worth a shot," I said.

"Did the state police provide their own therapist?"

"Yes," I said.

"And how did that go?"

"Not well," I said. "Nicole Heywood unleashed a torrent of expletives."

"And why will I do better?"

"Besides you being a hot Jewess with a taut, athletic body?"

"Yes."

"Because, Suze, you're damn good at this stuff."

"You're right," she said. "I am."

I had to park nearly a half-mile away because of the news crews and onlookers, sports fanatics and nutcases. Not to mention the probable assortment of Hare Krishnas, Moonies, and those who follow Glenn Beck.

Susan and I hiked up Heath Street, Susan with little effort. I with a little effort. Of course I had been up all night and had to talk some sense into some faux-kidnappers.

The cops all knew me. Even the press who didn't know me greeted me on sight. Some kid across from the Heywoods had set up a lemonade stand. The hand-painted sign read a portion of the proceeds would go for a welcome-home party for Akira.

A young cop opened the front door and we walked into silence.

The large house was even more of a mess than before. Anytime you have that many cops in a mansion with free food, the results would be ugly. Lots of paper plates and foam coffee cups. More laptop computers on the glass table. More cops milling about outside. More phone lines trailing through the center of the house. Four televisions brought into the family room tuned to two news channels and two ESPN channels.

Kinjo was nowhere to be found. Lundquist looked up from where he sat with a couple of detectives. He looked less than enthused to see me.

I shook his hand. He greeted Susan warmly.

"Figured she might help a little."

"This morning has put me in a tight spot, Spenser." His eyes wandered over my face as he shook his head. "Made me look bad."

"Ray Heywood was going to do it on his own," I said. "We just lent some support."

"Should have called us."

I felt Susan's hand on my back. I nodded to Lundquist.

"Didn't turn out to be much, anyway," I said. "Maybe the worst Charlestown crew ever assembled."

"That would be quite an accomplishment."

Lundquist smiled and turned. His pock-marked face was chapped and raw from a recent shaving. His dress shirt and dress pants were rumpled. Everything about him said cop.

Kinjo and Nicole sat waiting for us in Akira's bedroom. The rain had stopped and a bright gold light flowed through the curtains and across the spotless white carpet. His walls were covered with over-sized posters of superheroes, fast cars, and athletes; I noted one of them was his father.

In the corner of a room sat a fish tank that had grown dirty with algae since the last time I'd been there.

Nicole wore a navy Auburn sweatshirt and jeans. No makeup. Kinjo wore the same standard-issue Pats workout clothes and no shoes. They both looked as tired and emotionally raw as expected.

"This is Susan Silverman," I said. "She's a psychologist I work with on many occasions."

"No," Nicole said. "Not now. Get her out of here."

"Susan isn't like anyone else you've spoken with, Nicole," I said. "If she helps you, you can help me find your son."

Susan smiled that brilliant, disarming Susan Silverman smile. She could have won over Stalin to capitalism. Nicole gave her a second glance. Kinjo didn't show much of anything, waiting to hear what I knew.

"I'm here," Susan said. "If you want to talk. I am not about to offer any meaningless platitudes or give you a fucking pep talk. Okay?"

"Would you believe she has a Ph.D. from Harvard?" I said.

Nicole gave a slight nod. It was not a smile but seemed to be a gesture of acceptance. Susan gently shut the door with a small click and stood close.

"It was a phony," I said.

Kinjo nodded.

"Some drug dealers heard about it on the sports talk and wanted to bleed you a little."

"Evil."

"Yep."

"What did you do to them?" Kinjo said.

"We tied them up with zip cords near their stash of coke and called the cops."

Kinjo nodded. I took a seat on the bed next to Nicole. Kinjo sat at a child's table in a chair made for a five-year-old. Nicole started to cry. Susan did not move. She simply observed and waited. Nicole cried even more.

"That's the second crank," Kinjo said.

"First one wasn't much of a crank," I said. "He claimed to have killed Lincoln and Mama Cass."

"Nothing," Kinjo said. "How can you and all these cops be looking all over Massachusetts and not find anything? What about the Crown Vic they used, men in masks? Someone saw something."

"No one seemed to have seen them except for Cristal."

Nicole's eyes lifted to me and then Susan. Her chin shook a bit. And then she clenched her jaw. "You want to find my son, check her out. But check her out for real, not just let her press up against you and bat her eyelashes. All I know about that woman is that she came to you because you smell like sweat, grass, and money. Am I wrong?"

"Shut up," Kinjo said.

"Am I wrong?" she said. "She's a gold digger, and I wouldn't put it past her to want a big, nice cut before she leaves your dumb black ass."

"She's my goddamn wife," Kinjo said.

"Yeah." Nicole was crying but blurted out a bit of a laugh. "I forgot." She stood up and wiped her eyes. Even dressed down the way she was, she looked regal and put together. Her brown eyes and red mouth were very large. Her short haircut was as hip and trendy as next week. Her attitude reminded me of another woman I knew.

None of us spoke for a few minutes. The cops shuffled and talked and answered phones in the great room down the hall. After a while, Kinjo looked up from his hands. "Is he dead?"

"You can't think like that," I said.

"Why?" Nicole said. "Why do this and ask for no money? Cristal hates Akira. She hates that he doesn't love her and never accepted her for anything but what she is."

Kinjo jumped up from the small table and

193

kicked it over. He clenched and unclenched his hands, then walked over to the wall and put a nice-sized hole in the Sheetrock.

Susan stood and touched his arm. "You can tear each other apart later," she said. "But right now, you need to keep clear-headed. Keep thinking. Whoever did this wants exactly what's happening. They are smart enough to want to keep you unbalanced."

Kinjo rushed from the room and left the door wide open.

"Where else should you look?" Nicole said, wiping her eyes. "Right?"

I nodded.

"Do you know anything about Cristal?" Nicole said. "Why should we take her word?"

"Point taken," I said.

"Would you like to get away from this for a while?" Susan said. "Catch some air? Just to breathe a little."

Nicole took a short breath and held it, as if she changed her mind. "Yes," she said. "That would be a nice change."

Susan smiled warmly. Nicole wiped her face with the back of her hand.

I nodded at Susan as she turned to leave Akira's room. Susan winked back at me.

32

Bright and early the next morning, I paid a social call to my office on the assumption that even offices get lonely. I also had to pay my monthly rent for fear my desk, file cabinets, and framed Vermeer prints might end up on the curb. After urgent checks were written and sealed in envelopes, I congratulated myself with the accomplishment and set my feet at the edge of my desk.

As I gloated, I leaned back in my chair and pondered all that I didn't know about Cristal Heywood. Which was substantial. Susan and I thought Nicole's concerns were grounded, Nicole being more forthcoming with Susan than she had been with me. Susan said she'd thought of me as just another one of Kinjo's yes-men. Susan assured her that agreeing with my employers was not always in my nature.

I listened to the Mr. Coffee trickle on top of my file cabinets. The bay window was slightly open, letting in a cool fall breeze. The sounds of cars, jackhammers, and an occasional siren as comforting to me as a wolf's cry is to an Eskimo. I planned on running a basic criminal background check on Cristal through the state and AutoTrack of her prior addresses, relationships, debts. Nicole told Susan that Cristal never wanted Akira around and found him a barrier to her running Kinjo completely.

Of course, ex-wives were seldom complimentary of their successors.

It took me about ten minutes to accomplish on the Internet what used to take me a day on foot. I was reading through Cristal Heywood, formerly known as Cristal Jablonski, when a familiar face appeared in my doorway.

I looked up from my laptop. Tom Connor, special agent in charge of Boston's FBI office, walked into my office and took a seat in front of my desk.

"To what do I owe this dishonor?"

"You fucked up, Spenser," Connor said. "Again."

I leaned back in my chair. I could not wait for him to explain.

"This kidnapping of the Heywood boy," he said. "You can't just fucking go at it without working with law enforcement. Are you nuts? I don't know what kind of shit you got hanging over Lundquist's head, but the same deal don't apply to me."

"So the Feds are taking over."

"Goddamn right."

"With you gallantly leading the investigation."

Connor nodded with a lot of pride. He was a fat, florid guy with a big helmet of black hair. He always dressed like he'd just escaped the Men's Wearhouse. Shiny double-breasted suits and bright-colored ties. His hands were thick and chubby, and on his left hand was an honest-to-God pinkie ring.

"Whew," I said. "We're safe now."

"I don't want you around Heywood, I don't want you at the house, and I don't want you near a part of this. A fucking kid's life is at stake. Leave it to the pros."

"And you being so good with looking after kids," I said. "Why don't we call up Gerry Broz and see if maybe he can help."

"Eat shit."

"For a federal employee, your elocution is excellent."

"As soon as I got a call from Jeff Barnes, I knew you'd fuck it up," he said. "I just knew it. It's your fault your pal Lundquist got shitcanned. You running around South Station playing cop? Then that freak show you beat up in Charlestown? It all landed on Lundquist's desk like a steaming turd. I don't need that shit."

"That's not up to you," I said. "I don't work for the Pats and I don't need your approval. I work for Kinjo Heywood."

"I spoke to his agent this morning," Connor said. "He wants you gone."

"I don't work for his agent, either."

"Fuck me."

Connor adjusted himself in my client chair. His face looked as if he'd just sucked a lemon. The Mr. Coffee had stopped brewing. I got up, poured a cup, and added a little sugar and milk. I sat back down. I set my feet on the desk. Connor and I sat and stared at each other. He was not an attractive man.

"Aren't you gonna offer me some coffee?" he said.

"Nope."

"I want you clear of this, Spenser," he said. "This is a federal case now. Your involvement will only get his kid killed. If you get in our way, I will have you arrested and put you in lockdown until the kid is home. Be as smart as you think you are."

I nodded. "Did you hear from the kidnappers?"

"I'm not talking to you."

"So you got something?"

"Jeez," Connor said. He stood up, turned his back, and made his way to my open door.

"It's been nearly a week, and the family has heard nothing," I said. "How many cases start off in radio silence?"

"I can promise you I've worked a lot more of these than you."

"Well, I am flattered that you drove yourself all the way from Government Center on your lunch break to say hello."

"I'm telling you to get lost," Connor said. "It's not a request. I want you clear of my case."

"Your predecessor was a much more pleasant guy."

"Epstein is long gone, Spenser," Connor said. "Get used to it. This is my fucking city. And I don't need you fucking up the case all over again."

"I'll think about it," I said.

"Nope," he said. "It's over."

He walked from my office. I heard his cheap, shiny shoes clacking on the halls to the bank of elevators. I drank some coffee and looked out across Berkeley Street and listened to the wind whistle against my building. It would blow every few minutes, almost signaling winter, and then would stop for a long while.

I shrugged and started a file on Cristal.

33

Kinjo called four hours later and asked me if I'd meet him at Foxboro.

When he'd called, I'd been working out with Hawk. Hawk decided to come along, too. If Kinjo did fire me, Hawk said he'd comfort me in my time of need.

We met Kinjo at a restaurant up the steps from the stadium in Patriot Place, since I knew Jeff Barnes would be less than ecstatic to see me so close to Gillette. Kinjo sat in a back booth at a big sports bar, drinking ice water and checking his phone. Hawk also drank some water with lemon. I had a draft beer.

"Y'all can't stop," Kinjo said.

I nodded.

"Barnes got onto me last night," he said. "He sat down with me, Ray, and Mr. Rosen, and said that it was in the best interest of Akira and the organization if you were fired. He said the state police were backing off, too, and this was going to be a federal case. But shit, man. I haven't seen one FBI agent yet."

"I have," I said. "I may have to fumigate my office."

"Just 'cause the Feds are on it doesn't mean I want y'all to back off," he said. "Wasn't your fault that those shitbirds were trying to con me. What if they'd been real and they'd taken the money and then tried to kill Akira? Y'all found out who they were, where they lived, and took care of business. That's what I want. I don't need more talk. I need people to be at the ready when the word comes down."

"Still nothing?"

Kinjo looked down at the phone in his hand. His knuckles had been bloodied in practice. "I look at this screen nearly every second since he's been gone. I'll pay them. I'll do whatever it takes. Why won't they try me? Why won't they reach out?"

I shook my head.

"I give you my word that I'll tell you everything," Kinjo said. "I'll tell you any-thing you want to know. Not telling you about paying off those people in New York was a mistake. That won't happen. I don't give a damn what you think about me. You can think I'm a son of a bitch as long as you trust me."

Hawk drank some ice water. He wiped away the table's condensation with a cocktail napkin, not saying a word since we sat down. There were ten customers in the bar that probably could hold six hundred. The staff was young and female and attractive. The bartender was dressed as a referee, complete with whistle around her neck.

"How did you and Cristal meet?" I said.

"Oh, shit," Kinjo said. "Nicole got you onto this?"

"Nope," I said. "But in the absence of anything else, it can't hurt. How did you two meet?"

"How else? At a bar."

"What bar," I said. "When."

"Bar here in Boston," he said. "Two years ago. Place called Camelot."

Hawk looked up. "Gentlemen's establishment."

"Yeah," Kinjo said. "Strip club."

"And she was a, uh, dancer?" I said.

"Shit, no," Kinjo said. "I don't date strippers. She was a waitress. Said she liked to watch me play and had been a fan going back to when she was a kid. She even knew who Andre Tippett was. He was my hero when I was a kid. I wanted to be just like him."

I drank some beer. There were at least twenty televisions on the bar, turned to various iterations of ESPN and the local news. "Speaking of the old days, did you ever meet a guy named Kevin Murphy?" I said.

"Her ex?"

I nodded. I had made this connection before working out.

"I knew who he was," Kinjo said. "Yeah. Came up to her apartment one time when I was there. He never did that shit again."

"Did you know what he did?"

"He was a stupid punk," Kinjo said.

"He was busted in December for using underage girls in dirty movies," I said. "Arrested several times with drugs, intent to sell. Guy like that has to be connected."

"So Cristal made some mistakes," Kinjo said. "She's got no reason to mess with my family. She loves Akira. And he loves her. Hell, during the season she with him more than me."

"It would've been nice to know the connection," I said. "Maybe Murphy saw an opportunity?"

"State police never asked me about him."

"Some of the state police are not as dogged as me."

The waitress reappeared and asked if we wanted anything to eat. Hawk said he wanted a grilled chicken salad, dressing on the side. I was good with the beer. If I were to eat, I'd decided on the burger. Never order a salad at a bar.

"I don't know," Kinjo said.

"It's worth checking out," I said.

Kinjo nodded. I finished the beer. A couple in matching Pats sweatshirts walked in the front door and made their way to the bar. The man and the bartender chatted like old friends, the bartender leaning across and nodding over to our table. The man and the woman stared openmouthed at Kinjo.

"People are always talking about me," Kinjo said.

"Who?"

"Sportswriters and shit," he said. "There's this one dude with a blog who called me heartless because I've gone back to practice. How's this any of his fucking business? How can he understand?"

"Can't," Hawk said. "Same way he can't understand what it's like to play."

"Other people saying the same thing," Kinjo said. "Those guys Paulie and the Gooch? They were on me last night about going back and practicing. Front office let it be known I'll play this Sunday. What else can I do? I don't have nothing else. I got to believe he's going to be all right. I got to have a place to put all that anger. Hitting brings me level. I got to be level."

Hawk nodded.

I asked for a second beer. Second beers keep me level.

"My mind goes places," Kinjo said. "My heart feels torn to shreds. He's everything. I don't care who you hurt. I don't care what Cristal thinks. You think maybe her ex got something going, check him out. But y'all don't leave. This morning, Detective Lundquist and his people started to pack up their show. They been living with me and then I walk in and get breakfast and they're closing up their computers and shit. Say they still working leads but they aren't in control. Feds taking over. I don't know these people. Or trust them."

"Maybe for good reason," I said.

Kinjo lifted his eyebrows, not considering I'd think he was right.

"Their special agent in charge and I have a history."

"Does that bother you?"

"Nope."

Kinjo shook his head. He stared straight ahead and then wiped his wet eyes. He pounded the table with his fist so hard, Hawk's ice water spilled across the table. Hawk stood before the water dripped into his lap. The waitress came over and quickly cleared the table. My beer was unharmed.

"Be cool," Hawk said.

Kinjo nodded.

"Do what you need to do to keep your mind right," Hawk said. "We'll find your boy."

"How?"

"We always do."

I shrugged and nodded. "I'm with him."

"Even on nothing?" Kinjo said.

"Yep."

"As long as it takes?" Kinjo said.

Hawk and I nodded.

"You know what y'all are?" Kinjo said, staring at Hawk. "You're Ronin. You, him, and that big Indian guy. Don't answer to nobody. Am I right? You understand what I'm saying?"

"I left my sword at the office."

"I'm serious." Kinjo's gaze did not waver. "Y'all are samurai with no master, doing what's got to be done. Roaming the earth, taking care of business without any rules."

"Mostly greater Boston," I said. "And I have rules."

The waitress brought Hawk fresh water. He took a sip, ice rattling, and set the glass back on the table. Hawk stared at Kinjo a long while and tilted his head to the side. "He do. But I write my own."

34

"How do you manage to so artfully piss off those you work with?" Susan said.

"Gumption," I said. "Determination."

We were in bed, wrapped up in the sheets, listening to a cold rain tap against my apartment window. Pearl had given up scratching at the door and returned to her place on my new leather couch. We had already had supper; four mini-apple pies baked in the oven.

"From what you've told me about Connor, he is an absolute shit heel," Susan said.

"True."

"And dirty."

"True."

"But you don't think his dirtiness will interfere with the investigation?"

"I think his low IQ and lack of talent will interfere."

"So you and Hawk remain."

"And Z," I said. "Don't forget Z."

"The Three Caballeros."

"Which one am I?"

"Why, the fucking duck, of course."

Susan propped herself up on one elbow, and was bathed in a slice of light from outside Marlborough Street. The air smelled of baking apples and cinnamon.

"Kinjo feels a lot of guilt for returning to practice," I said.

"If it works for him, it works."

"Sure."

"But you find it odd."

"I don't find it odd, but apparently he's taking the heat from the piranhas who now pass as so-called sports journalists."

"You're not suspecting him?" she said. "For acting indifferent?"

"No," I said. "Not at all. He's broken up very badly. He's as eaten up and sick with worry as is possible in a man. He walked away from us before the drop yesterday and vomited in the bathroom."

"But you're asking if it's healthy?" Susan said. "Or therapeutic?"

I nodded. My eyes lingered on Susan's chest. She smiled and settled onto her back, pillow under her head, her body half covered, and stared at the ceiling.

"Doesn't it help you to work out, pound out frustrations on a heavy bag, whatever it takes for a release?"

"And other things."

"But violent exercise, too."

"Even playing in a game this Sunday?"

"If it works for him," Susan said. "Screw the bloggers and nuts on the radios."

"That's the same advice I gave him," I said. "Should I charge him an extra hundred bucks?"

"I charge one-fifty."

I resettled against the pillow, reached over to the nightstand, grabbed my watch, and checked how long the pies had been in the oven. We had another five minutes. I turned my head to her. Her curly head lay on her pillow. We stared at each other, smiling.

"Did Nicole tell you anything specifically about why she disliked Cristal?" I said.

"She said she's a terrible parent."

"In what way?"

"Absent," Susan said. "She said that Akira runs wild at their house while Cristal has cocktails with friends or watches television or posts pithy comments about Kinjo on her Twitter feed."

"Kinjo said Nicole is jealous."

"I'm sure she is," Susan said. "But which woman would you trust?"

"But why might she want Akira out of the picture?" I said. "What's in it for her?"

Susan blinked. Her large brown eyes turned slightly upward in thought. "There are bad stepparents," she said. "And then there are bad stepparents."

"If the child is dead," I said. The words so horrible they seemed to resonate long after I said them in the silent room.

"Is that what you're now thinking?"

"Five days without contact," I said. "Doesn't look good."

"And you suspect Cristal?"

"She is, as the cops like to say these days, a person of interest," I said. "Before she met Kinjo, she bedded down with a known pornographer and drug dealer in Dorchester."

"Women do like bad boys."

"Is that me?"

"Except for baking," Susan said, lifting herself out of the bed and striding across my bedroom, completely naked, to my closet. "Baking puts you into a category unto your own."

" 'She walks in beauty, like the night,' " I said.

Much to my disappointment, she fitted herself into an old navy terry-cloth robe. "Does Lord Byron stock ice cream?" she said.

"I made that, too."

"Of course you did."

35

My mental Rolodex of thugs had ebbed and flowed over my years of business. The old Italian and Irish crews I'd known seemed to have mostly disappeared or gone to that big house in the sky. Over the last decade, there seemed to be a lot of ethnic crime around Boston: Ukrainians and Albanians, Chinese, and lots of Vietnamese. Fast Eddie Lee had a stronger and stronger grip on the city. Gino Fish still did a nice bit of business about town, as Tony Marcus kept his eyes on much of the working ladies. I had removed Joe Broz from my Rolodex after his recent demise and had added his son's name in light pencil.

Gerry Broz had owned a pretty posh sports bar in Southie. Sports bars being a cultural obsession in Boston almost like the coffeehouses of Vienna. But Gerry's bar, Playmates, had gone into bankruptcy, and he'd decided to start a tropical-fish distributorship in Coolidge Corner, down the street from the old movie house.

It was still raining that morning as Z and I walked into the large brick warehouse.

Gerry looked up from vacuuming out a fish tank as large as my apartment.

He was wearing a custom T-shirt reading *Broz Tropical Equipment and Supplies,* old khaki pants, and knee-high rubber boots. His mouth hung open when he recognized me.

"Fuck me," he said. "Out. Get out."

"Gerry Broz, wow," I said. "You work here?"

Broz put down the vacuum and turned off the pump. He wiped his wet hands on his khakis and stared at us.

"I'm in the market for two clown fish and some information on dirty deeds in Dorchester," I said.

"Good luck with that," Broz said. "I'm out of the life."

"Sure you are," Z said.

"Who the fuck are you?" Gerry said. "Do I fucking know you, kid?"

"Sorry, Gerry," I said. "Gerry, this is Zebulon Sixkill. My associate. He's named after Zebulon Pike. Of Pike's Peak fame."

"I don't give two shits," Gerry said. "I'm out of the life. You come around and harass me and talk about dirty shit and I'll call the cops. I pay fucking taxes."

"Fish," I said. "Really?"

"I always been into fish, Spenser," he said.

I tilted my head. He had me there.

"All I need is some direction," I said. "You know a guy named Kevin Murphy?"

Gerry roamed his hand over his pudgy face. "Sure," he said. "I'll get right on it. Weren't you the same guy who wanted to turn over my dad on his deathbed? Yeah, I'd love to help you."

"Did I?"

"But you would have," he said. "You forced me getting into a lot of shit that wasn't my fucking business."

Z wandered off along a row of fish tanks stacked five high. The warehouse was dim, but the aquariums were brightly lit with all manner of colorful fish. I couldn't name any of them if a marine biologist put a gun to my head.

"What if I said I'll owe you one?"

Broz dumped the vacuum and the hose in a stainless-steel work sink. He rinsed out the sludge and looked to be thinking. Of course, it was very hard to tell if Gerry Broz was thinking, as he did it so infrequently.

Z walked up the metal framework that balanced all the aquariums. He pushed at it lightly, as if testing its strength. Pushing with his arms and shoulders, leaning into it and stretching out his back. The metal and glass made the slightest cracking sounds.

"Hey," Gerry said. "Hey."

"A favor?" I said.

Z let go. He smiled and placed his hands back into his leather jacket.

"A favor," I said. "Anytime. Within reason."

Gerry shot an unpleasant look at Z. Z grinned back at him.

"Murphy," I said. "Kevin."

"Yeah, I know him," Gerry said. "What do you want to know?"

"He used to be the main squeeze of a woman who is now married to my client," I said. "I want to know if he'd be the kind of guy who might expand from making dirty pictures."

"Into what?"

"Kidnapping," I said. "Maybe murder. All kinds of good stuff."

"Murphy is a fucking punk," Gerry said. He scratched his neck and patted his pockets for a cigarette. He fished one out and lit it. "Man, I don't know. He's got a pretty decent deal going on, thinks he's the Bob Guccione of the Internet. These young guys kill me with their macho bullshit."

"Where?" I said.

"Why don't you ask your cop pals?"

"I did."

"And?"

"Couldn't help."

"Me, either," he said. "Don't know."

"But can you find out?"

"That's it?" he said.

"That's it."

"A favor?"

"To be named later," I said.

Gerry squinted at us as he smoked. He stared hard at Z, to whom he had taken an instant dislike, and let out a long stream of smoke. "What are you? You sure ain't from around here."

"Cree Indian from Montana," Z said.

"He's running with you and Hawk?"

I nodded. There was a lot of noise from the pumps in the large, enclosed space. Gerry nodded and took another drag. "You putting together one of those Village People tribute bands? You guys would be great."

"Keep thinking, Gerry," I said. "That's what you're good at."

"Okay," he said. "Where can I get you?"

I told him my number. Twice.

36

Kevin Murphy made art above a corner store just south of Adams and just north of an elevated train trestle in Fields Corner. The convenience store windows were covered in posters for Keno and Mega Millions tickets, while the neighboring storefronts were covered over in plywood. Z and I sat across the street eating Chinese takeout from what may have been the very best Chinese restaurant in all of Dorchester.

There wasn't much to do. Or see. In the last hour, we watched one guy, who was not Murphy, walk upstairs and turn on the lights above the store. I ate chicken fried rice direct from the carton. Elegant. After we finished, Z took the trash, tossed it into a barrel down the way, and wandered back to the car with his hands in his pockets.

"Fine meal," I said.

"Maybe we should've eaten the carton?"

"Probably," I said.

"More nutrition," he said.

"Hot sauce," I said. "Hot sauce makes everything palatable."

I leaned back into the seat of the Explorer and stretched out my legs. Z remained silent. He was nearly as chatty as Hawk.

I turned on the radio and found *Paulie & the Gooch.* The guys were engaged in a heated debate about Kinjo Heywood. *And if the call was real, which we have no reason to believe he is, should in fact Kinjo play in tomorrow's game? Next caller.*

I turned up the volume. Z turned away from the window and listened.

Hey, it's Bobby from Dedham. You don't think that guy's real. Holy crap. That sounded like business to me. If I were Kinjo, I wouldn't do crap until my kid was safe. But you know, I'm not Kinjo. He loves his teammates and the Pats and is doing the best he can. I think he'll play his heart out every moment until his kid is safe. Like he said, he's sick with worry and it helps. I think he's a freakin' hero.

Paulie and the Gooch chewed on that for a bit and then teased the listeners by replaying the call-in from earlier. A muted voice announced he, or she, was the real kidnapper of the Heywood kid and they'd be announcing demands during Sunday's game. The veteran broadcasters did not discuss.

They instead ran a commercial for penis-enlargement pills being shilled by the former head coach of the Cowboys.

I turned down the volume.

"During the game?" Z said.

"Probably doesn't want Kinjo at the drop."

"If there is a drop," Z said. "Could be electronic."

"Could be," I said. "Real money makes it easier on us."

Z nodded. "How long you want to stick with this Murphy guy?"

"Long as it takes to see his routine," I said.

"And to annoy the shit out of him."

"Yes," I said. "That is my most successful tactic."

A Hispanic man walked past us, carrying a grocery bag in one arm and a small boy in the other. He didn't even glance at us as he balanced the load in his arm. He wore blue coveralls covered in dirt, the legs too long and frayed at the bottom. The ragged material dragged the ground over his work boots. I turned up the radio again.

I think Heywood is a liability to the Pats. I think he needs to quit being selfish and sit out until this thing with his kid is over. It's a distraction for everyone in the organization. He's a great player and I feel sorry about his kid. But are you telling me this don't have something to do with his off-field stuff? You know? You wait and see, this whole mess has something to do with the way the man lives his life.

"Wisdom of the masses," I said.

"Fickle," Z said. "College alumni are worse. Pro teams have fans. Alumni who give money think they own you."

"And know more about the sport than you," I said.

Z craned his neck and stared up at the lights burning over the corner store. "Probably same in the porn business," Z said. "Murphy makes the movies and sometimes stars in them, too."

"Performance pressure," I said.

"His whole business is online. You get a membership to watch girls get interviewed by Murphy and then do the deed."

"So the casting couch is his show?"

"Murphy goes by the name Mr. X. He never shows his face but is very proud of his equipment," Z said. "It all takes place on his couch. Sometimes on his desk."

"Few sets."

"Most of the girls don't look eighteen," Z said. "Reminded me of when I was in L.A. Girls looked stoned. Need the money for food."

"Hmm," I said.

"He likes to make the girls hurt," Z said. "He likes to demean them."

The mindless chatter of *Paulie & the Gooch* filled the car. Wind blew grit and loose flyers across the road. Rain tapped absently on the windshield.

"If I see him, perhaps he should hurt, too."

"So many shitbags," I said. "So little time."

Z nodded.

"You see any girls who might have been Cristal?" I said.

"No," he said. "But he had maybe four hundred, five hundred films."

Our prayers are with the entire Heywood family and with the brave men and women of law enforcement looking for Akira. The Gooch and I both have spent a lot of time with the Heywood family, including Akira, and I promise our listeners that there is no more devoted father than Kinjo Heywood. If anyone out there knows anything about these kidnappers or where they might have this child, you can call a special hotline we've set up through the Sports Monstah network.

"No prayers for us?" Z said.

I shook my head.

"Damn."

The lights continued to burn on the

second floor above the corner store. A half-hour later, Hawk called. We spoke all of ten seconds and then I hung up.

"I'm needed," I said.

"Trouble?"

"Nicole is trying to force Cristal to talk," I said. "I'll drop you at your car."

"And I'll circle back here."

"Murphy may not even be up there," I said. "May be a waste of time."

"It's such a lovely night in Dorchester," Z said. "I'll wait and see."

37

Hawk had been keeping Nicole and Cristal Heywood company in the women's bathroom of a Cheesecake Factory off Route 9. A short line had started at the bathroom door and the restaurant manager said she was about to call the cops. I smiled at her, all but saying the cops had arrived. I knocked and Hawk let me in. He leaned against the dimly lit sinks and tilted his head toward a nearby stall.

"Won't leave till she gets the answer she wants," Hawk said.

"And won't leave with you?" I said.

Hawk shook his head. "Woman got a gun," he said. "She says she know how to use it."

"Persuasive," I said.

I heard muffled crying from inside the stall. I knocked on the door and announced my arrival.

There was no answer.

"Nicole," I said.

Hawk shrugged.

"What stopped you from just ripping the door off the hinges and snatching away the gun?" I said.

"Kind of interested to see what Cristal has to say," Hawk said.

"Can't wait much longer," I said. "I don't think the Cheesecake Factory likes to have armed patrons."

Hawk nodded. I knocked again.

"Someone called in to *Paulie and the Gooch* tonight," I said. "They said they'd announce their demands on Sunday."

I heard a sniffle and a cough. There was a low wailing sound coming from the stall. "This won't wait until Sunday," Nicole said. "This bitch knows what happened to my son."

"I don't, I swear to God, I swear to God. Please."

"If you don't walk out with me in five seconds," I said, "you'll be arrested. That call tonight may be legit. Let's not have anything to muddle plans."

"She lost him," Nicole said. "She's trash. She knows."

I looked to Hawk. He turned his neck from side to side, relaxing his muscles. He checked his watch. "Tick, tock," he said.

226

"Maybe," I said.

"I'm not leaving until she tells me what she knows," Nicole said.

"I don't know anything. I swear to God. Spenser, please help me. She's crazy. She has a gun. She says she's going to kill me."

There was more crying coming from the stall. This time it sounded like both women. One of them was even more feral and harsh. I tried the door. It was locked. I knocked softly. Hawk stared straight ahead and waited.

"You'll want to hear the call, Nicole. We need your help. We need you."

"What about her?" Nicole said. "She's lying. I know it."

"We've been checking her out. Just like you said."

"And she's a part of this," Nicole said. "Right?"

"Don't know," I said. "But I need you to allow me to do my job."

More crying. More wailing. The door lock snicked open. Cristal rushed out. Nicole lay in a fetal position by the toilet. A small automatic poked out from her purse. She was crying very loudly now. Hawk walked out of the restroom with Cristal. I helped Nicole to her feet.

"Not like this," I said, whispering.

"She knows," Nicole said. "The bitch knows."

"Maybe," I said. "But we won't find out like this."

Nicole cried hard. I held her close. With my free hand, I reached for the purse and extracted the gun, placing it in my hip pocket. We walked together out of the bathroom with as much dignity as was allowed at a Cheesecake Factory. People stared. Employees glared.

In the parking lot, Hawk stood by his Jaguar. "Nicole followed Cristal," he said. "Didn't know I was following her."

"I just wanted a fucking drink," Cristal said. "We were out of booze at the house. I just wanted a fucking drink."

I nodded to Hawk. Hawk helped Nicole toward the passenger side of the Jaguar. She had a deferential air toward him as they walked side by side.

"I'll get you a drink," I said. "And drive you back to your house."

"I can't take it there anymore," Cristal said. "It's like being in some kind of crypt. God. No one talking. Everyone crying and whispering."

Hawk's Jag started up and motored fast out of the parking lot. Lights refracted off his windshield and obscured their faces as they passed.

"She would have killed me," Cristal said, watching them go. Her face was a mess of makeup. I found a handkerchief in my glove box and handed it to her. "She's gone absolutely crazy. She hates me. She really thinks I took her son."

I had nothing to say.

"Did they really call?" she said. "Or did you just say that so she'd leave me alone?"

"There was a caller," I said. "Tomorrow. I guess we'll find out."

38

The Washington Square Tavern in Brookline stayed open late. They also served Harpoon Maple Wheat on draft and small plates of very good food. Although I felt bad for Z, I knew he wouldn't want me to suffer.

The bar was big and warm, low light, with dark wood and colorful liquor bottles around a large beveled mirror. I ordered the beer and a tequila with lime for Cristal. While the bartender poured, Cristal glanced at her reflection and quickly looked away. "Oh, God."

"Me or you?" I said.

"Me," she said.

On the ride over, she'd dabbed on some makeup, smoky eye shadow and pink lips that went with her jewelry. She wore three necklaces and four rings. The wedding ring glowed pink and was roughly the size of a golf ball. She had on an aqua halter dress that showed off a wealth of cleavage and a lot of leg. Her legs were long and spray-tanned, impressive on a pair of high-heeled gold Roman sandals.

The bartender set down her tequila. She drained half of it in one gulp.

I sipped the Harpoon.

"My nerves are shot," she said.

"If it's any consolation," I said, "I don't think Nicole would have shot you."

"How the hell do you know?"

"Crime-fighter intuition," I said, tapping at my temple.

I drank some beer. I considered Hawk's plan to see how things would evolve. At the very least, Nicole had proven herself to be a very good bad cop. The tequila might prove to be an even better cop.

"How could I have stopped them?" she said. "They blocked in my car. They put a gun in my face and took Akira."

"You've had a lot of guns pointed at you lately."

"Damn right," she said. She drained the rest of the tequila. I lifted my index finger to the bartender. He salted the glass and poured her another, topped with a lime slice.

"She would've done the same," Cristal said. "Nicole wouldn't have let herself get shot."

I nodded.

"I couldn't have done anything."

I sipped some beer.

"Why does she hate me?"

I shrugged.

"I mean, I've made some mistakes in my life," she said. "But this is not my fault."

"What can you tell me about your relationship with Kevin Murphy?"

"Oh, fuck," she said.

"Yeah," I said.

"Holy fuck," she said.

"He was your boyfriend."

"You're doing it," she said, drink held high. "You're on her side."

"I'm on Akira's side."

"Let me tell you something," she said.

"Sure."

She continued to hold the tequila high. She held the pose, as if it was something she'd seen once in a movie. "My life before Kinjo is none of your damn business."

I nodded. I took another sip. Seeing that I sipped, she sipped. Cooperation. Cars zoomed by freely along Washington Street. As I waited for her statement to sink in, I ordered the house charcuterie plate with seasonal pickles.

"You understand?"

I nodded. Cristal stared at herself in the

bar window. She shook her head, disgusted. "I look like a fucking raccoon."

I was pretty sure raccoons did not have purple eyes. But I kept my mouth shut as she excused herself and I sat at the bar. Even at nearly midnight, the bar did a healthy business. Lots of couples talking among candlelight. Young professionals discussing matters of the young and professional. Cristal reemerged from the ladies' room at the same time my charcuterie arrived from the kitchen.

"Why didn't you tell me I was a mess?"

"I hadn't noticed." She looked exactly the same as before but smelled of more cologne. It was not an unpleasant fragrance, only too much of it.

"We were talking about Kevin Murphy," I said, adding some prosciutto to a slice of bread.

"No," she said. "You were talking about Kevin Murphy."

She gulped down the rest of the second double tequila. Cristal subtly turned the glass upside down and stared at the bartender until he took the empty glass.

"If Kevin is involved," I said, "it doesn't mean you are involved."

"Kevin is not involved."

I chewed my food. I swallowed and raised

my eyebrows. Doing both at the same time took some skill.

"Why not?" Cristal said. "Because he's a fucking dumbass. He loves doing what he does. He's not about money, he's into making himself famous."

"As Mr. X?"

"Have you seen that shit?"

I shook my head. I tried a seasonal pickle. It went well with the prosciutto. "But my associate combed the archives."

"Looking for me?"

I nodded.

"You won't find it," she said, ripping her third drink from the bartender's hand. "That was from like four years ago. It's old news."

"Did Kinjo see it?"

"Hell, yes," she said. "That's how we met. He saw me in a movie and wanted to meet me. Fell in love with my body."

"He told me he met you at a club in Chelsea."

"He came to the club to watch me dance," she said. "All the Pats hung out there. Some Bruins, too. I used to be into hockey players. But they're all Canadian and crazy. You know, for a hotshot private detective, you really don't know jack shit."

I shrugged and tried a nice slice of hard

cheese as consolation.

"Kinjo said you were only a waitress."

"I did that, too," she said. "I only made four movies, anyway. Kinjo has seen them. Sometimes I catch him watching them when he's not watching that Japanese stuff."

"Doesn't bother him?" I said.

"He said it would bother him if I was with a man, but since it's just with girls, he's cool with it."

"Ah," I said. "And what about Mr. X?"

"Kevin didn't start doing Mr. X until I was gone," she said. "Back then, we used to have this fake sorority house where we made up stories. Pillow fights and all that crap. Sold a ton on DVD."

I nodded. "Kind of a homemade Linda Lovelace."

She looked confused and drank even more. I worked on the charcuterie plate. I offered a bite, but she turned up her nose. She seemed immune to her cocktails, talking without a noticeable change.

"So, your ex-boyfriend is a self-made pornographer and has several prior arrests."

"Those arrests were nothing," she said. "Drugs and all that. I think he beat up some girl one time because she laughed at his thingy."

"Not impressive."

"Hardly," she said. She picked up one of my pickles and held it up as exhibit A. "I heard he uses a double for close shots."

"When's the last time you talked to him?" I said.

She looked up and tapped at her chin. Many of her movements were like that, practiced for effect. "A year?"

"Has he ever threatened you?" I said.

"Nope."

"Has he ever come to your home?"

"Nope."

"Has he ever approached Kinjo?"

"He tried," she said. "But he got his ass kicked."

"Has he ever asked you for money?" I said.

She again made the practiced tilt of the head. She tapped at her chin. And then she nodded. "Yeah."

"How much?"

"He wanted fifty grand or said he'd make a big thing about my movies," she said. "He wanted to package it like *The Players' Wives Club* or some shit."

"And what?"

"Kinjo and I laughed at him," she said. "I think it just kind of fell through. Who cares if people know I did porn? You think I'm the only NFL wife with a sex tape? Big deal."

236

I nodded. I pushed the plate away, although there was still some sausage and cheese left. I watched more cars pass by the big window facing the intersection of Washington and Beacon. I lifted my chin and tapped at it. I liked it.

"I think I'd very much like to talk to Kevin."

"Are you not even listening to me?" she said. She stood up, mad, straight, and tall in her Roman sandals. She pointed hard at my chest.

Three drinks with no effect. If I had three double tequilas, I'd be singing José Feliciano tunes.

We all have our talents.

I paid the tab and drove her home.

39

I returned to relieve Z at four-thirty that morning.

To show my gratitude, I brought him two corn muffins and a large cup of coffee.

As I crawled into his Mustang, he peered into the bag and then up at me. "No donuts?"

"You're an Indian," I said. "Your people love corn."

"For the record," he said, "I prefer a Boston cream."

"You're officially off duty," I said. "Get some sleep."

"What about you?" he said. He reached into the bag for a corn muffin.

"Be good to switch it up," I said. "New man. New vehicle. The spice of life."

"I don't think they're paying attention to us," Z said, nodding up to the second-floor window above the store. "I think they're in production."

"You spot Murphy?"

"Yep," he said. "Came upstairs about an hour ago with a big white guy with a crew cut. Maybe thirty minutes ago, a young girl in a raincoat and rubber boots walked up the stairwell and knocked on the door. Big guy came out a little later and walked out to a van. Brought up C-stands and lighting rigs."

"Hooray for Hollywood," I said.

Z nodded. He drank some coffee and ate some of the corn muffin. We watched the upstairs window. The blinds were closed, with light burning bright behind them. I told him about the great Cheesecake Factory standoff and my later conversation with Cristal Heywood.

"Three tequilas?" he said.

"Yep."

Z nodded as he listened. "What else do we know about Murphy?"

"Besides him being a creep?"

"Besides that."

"He's dealt drugs, sold stolen televisions, and got caught carrying a pistol without a permit. He has twice been convicted of domestic violence and once been charged with having sex with a minor."

"How minor?" Z said.

"Does it matter?" I said.

239

Z shook his head. "I'll head back to the gym, get cleaned up, and get some breakfast."

"Sleep," I said. "Get some rest. This might be a very long day."

"And this creep?"

"I'll stick here," I said. "See if I detect anything interesting."

"Maybe he'll bring in some farm animals," he said. "Maybe a chicken or a donkey."

"That would be interesting for Dorchester."

Z gave me a look as if he wasn't too sure. I got out and walked back to the Explorer. He started the Mustang and headed north. I got in behind the wheel, where I'd left my own coffee, and watched the street for what seemed like a very long time.

A rusted train trestle loomed behind me and the storefronts stretched north toward Fields Corner. Along Dot Ave, some minor improvements had been made, a few new iron streetlamps lit up the road, a few trees had been planted. There were also plenty of places to cash your paycheck early, get your hair and nails done, and go for some Vietnamese or a slice of pizza.

The only vehicle close to the trestle was an old moving van parked in front of an insurance company. The rear door had been secured with a big padlock.

I sipped the coffee and sat in stillness. A cop passed me patrolling south, not even slowing. Two Asian kids wearing leather jackets and carrying brown bags of beer walked past the Explorer. They craned their heads to see inside and I gave them a polite two-finger wave. They kept walking and did not offer me any beer.

If I stayed here long enough, I'd get to see Murphy and his pals. And if I got to see Murphy and his pals, I still had nothing. I wondered if Lundquist had spoken to Murphy. I could call him and ask, but after the exchange at South Station and the entry of Connor and the Feds, he might not be so glad to hear from me. I probably could accomplish just as much sitting at my desk. But sitting at my desk did not offer such a fantastic view of Dorchester, and sitting at my desk wouldn't tell me about the movements of Kevin Murphy and associates known and unknown.

Or maybe Murphy had turned over a new leaf and was working to help young wayward girls. Maybe he was up above the storefront right now taping a public service announcement about how to watch out for strangers and believe in yourself. Maybe Murphy was a complete turd but not the turd I was looking for. I still didn't like the loose ends and what-ifs of the New York shooting. A payoff was temporary, but revenge was forever. I had the feeling that every person I'd spoken to about the murder was lying.

I still wanted to talk to Lela Lopes. I still needed to find out if there was a third man with Kinjo that night.

At first light, the big guy with the crew cut walked out onto the stairwell and smoked a cigarette. After a few minutes, another man joined him. I assumed it was Kevin Murphy, as Z had seen only one more guy. I didn't have any binoculars with me but in my backseat had a Nikon with a pretty good zoom lens. I reached for it and zoomed in.

If it was Murphy, he in no way resembled the NBA player. This Kevin Murphy was white, pudgy, and very pale. He was shirtless, with a paunchy stomach that hung over his designer jeans. He had a wide, freckled face, jug ears, and brown hair swept back, with longish sideburns and a little tuft of hair below his lip. There was a big tattoo of some kind of animal on his back. It was hard to imagine anyone paying to see him naked.

He talked with the big guy. They pounded

fists and he walked inside. Back to the salt mines.

The big guy flicked his cigarette away and walked down to the street and crossed over to the moving van. He climbed in, started the van, and disappeared for nearly an hour. When he returned and parked in the same spot by the insurance company, he had upgraded to a black Toyota 4Runner. At first I made no connection. But the car was dealership new and very out of place with the neighborhood. I took another sip of coffee and a few moments to recall Kinjo saying he'd been initially followed by a black Toyota 4Runner. This was not the same as saying you'd been followed by a silver 1921 Pierce-Arrow.

Still, it was a connection, however common.

The big guy crossed back over Dot Ave, lit a cigarette as he did so, and had finished it as he'd tramped up the steps and walked back inside.

I called Kinjo Heywood. He sounded as if he'd been asleep. But answered on the first ring.

"What was the car that followed you the first time?"

"Spenser?"

"Yep."

"Whew," Kinjo said. "Oh, man. It was a Toyota, I think."

"I need you to think more," I said. "What color?"

I recalled. But I wanted him to recall, too. "Black," he said. "New."

"And the guy you pulled a gun on?"

"Man, we been through this before," he said. "What's up?"

"The driver," I said. "What did he look like?"

"I don't know," he said. "White guy. Kinda fat and had a haircut like he'd been in the Army or something. What's up?"

40

At six a.m., Hawk joined me.

We walked up to the convenience store in early light and then bounded up the steps. At the metal door, Hawk tested the doorknob, nodded, and we moved quickly inside without knocking.

We both carried our guns of choice. Hawk with his .44. I carried the Smith & Wesson auto I saved for special occasions.

Kevin Murphy was seated on a black leather couch in white-hot stage lights. A woman kneeled between his legs, practicing method acting.

The big guy ran the camera. When we entered, he stepped away from the camera, just a digital on a tripod, and said, "What the fuck, man?"

The girl discontinued performing Shakespeare in the Park and got to her feet. She had on a red G-string. The room was large and open, an old storage area with a wood floor and exposed brick walls. There were old desks and old chairs stacked against the far wall.

"You must be Moose," I said to the big guy.

"And this motherfucker is Jughead," Hawk said. "All ears, no brains."

"What the fuck?" Murphy said. He was completely naked, wearing only what looked like a platinum bicycle chain around his neck.

"Moose already asked that," I said.

Hawk stepped over to a chair and tossed the girl a pink robe. She was blond, petite, in her mid-twenties. She slid into the robe without a word.

"Archie know about you and Betty?" I said.

"If you aren't cops," Murphy said. "You two are dead."

"Kevin, please sit down and shut up," I said. "And please cover yourself before I get sick."

I found a wadded-up pair of jeans and threw them at him.

"We don't have any money here," Murphy said. "Whoever sent you fucked up. We don't keep cash laying around."

"Why were you following Kinjo Heywood?" I said.

"What?" Murphy said. He wore a cocky, big-mouth grin until Hawk slapped him hard across the face.

Moose took a step forward. I simply shook my head. He stayed in place by the girl.

"I never followed him."

"Mr. Heywood pulled a gun on Moose," I said. "You recall that, Moose?"

Moose looked to Murphy, his mouth hanging open. He turned back to me, trying to tighten his jaw and appear mean. The girl wrapped her arms around herself and bit her lower lip. Her mascara had run down her eyes and her forehead was shiny with sweat.

"So, yes," I said.

"Where's the kid?" Hawk said.

"What?"

Hawk slapped Murphy across the face and then punched him in the gut. Murphy fell to his knees. Hawk gripped a lot of his greasy hair and tilted his chin upward. "Where's the kid?"

Moose and the girl stared, openmouthed. Moose probably always had an open mouth. He looked as if you'd need a shovel to find his IQ.

"So the fuck what?" Murphy said from his knees. "So the fuck what if I was following my old girlfriend? That doesn't mean jack shit."

"It means jack shit when her stepson is missing a week later."

"I don't know nothing about that."

"You never turn on the TV, the radio, or look at your phone?" I said. "Yes, Kevin. You're the only one in Boston that hasn't heard the news."

"I didn't take the kid."

"But you followed Cristal," I said.

"That's between me and Cristal."

Hawk lifted a hand. Murphy flinched.

Hawk stepped back and smiled.

"It looks like you have a first-class operation here, Kevin," I said. "The glamour is overwhelming. Cecil B. DeMille of Dot Ave."

He pushed up off his knees and stood. We let him. "I make more money in one day than you probably do all year," Murphy said.

"Probably," I said. "But then again, if I had talent the size of a gherkin, I wouldn't want to broadcast it."

The distraught girl snorted. Kevin's face turned bright red. He rubbed at the tuft of hair under his chin and sucked in his gut.

"You want me to throw 'em out, Kev?" Moose said.

"Yeah, you do that, Moose," I said.

"Anytime," Hawk said.

Moose wiped his face and nodded at us. His toughness had dissipated.

We all stood together in a tightly knit group under the hot stage lights. Kevin nodded to the camera. "It's all there, dumbasses," he said. "Trespassing, harassment. I'll own Kinjo Heywood's fucking black ass."

"And a bigot, too."

Hawk took a short breath and exhaled. Bored, he held the .44 at belt level.

"And now destruction of property," I said. I walked over to the tripod and ripped out the SIM card from the camera. If it had been the old days, I would have ripped the film from the camera and torn the strips from the canister. Pulling a SIM card had less gravitas.

"That's a night's worth of work," Murphy said. "Do you know what this means?"

"I have spared many perverts the horror of seeing you naked?" I said. "Perhaps I have inspired them to recant and shut down the computer for the night."

"I'm a star."

Hawk laughed.

Moose put an arm around the young actress. She tilted her eyes up at him and tore away her shoulder. She did not seem impressed with the studio security.

"I don't know why you're even here," Murphy said. "Two state cops came to see me a couple days ago. I told them the same thing. You come to me and fuck with me? That doesn't change that I don't know anything about Kinjo's kid."

"Why were you following them?" I said.

"Cristal owes me money."

"For what?"

Murphy put a finger to the side of his nose and sniffed.

"Recent?" I said.

"Oh, yes," he said.

"If you're holding the kid," I said, "it's better to deal with us than the Feds. Kinjo might even make you a deal to walk away."

"Do you not speak English?" Murphy said, scratching his neck. "I make flicks and do my thing. I don't steal kids."

"Man got to have ethics," Hawk said.

"Yep."

"I don't have the kid," Murphy said. "You see him around anywhere? You want to follow me for a while? Go check under my bed at the house? Ask my neighbors? Go ahead. You won't find shit. I'm just trying to do my thing."

I walked in close to Kevin Murphy. He smelled like someone had knocked over a piña colada in a locker room. His pupils were dilated to the size of quarters.

"If you're connected, Kev," I said. "You better hope the Feds get to you first."

His shapeless, doughy chest had been shaved, as had his arms. Only the silly patch under his chin remained. It quivered a bit as he tried to stare me down.

I looked to the girl.

"You want to stay?"

She stared at us for a moment and then nodded. We took their movie but left.

41

I took Susan to Gillette Stadium that afternoon. As she strolled across the parking lot in a form-fitting navy sweater, jeans, and riding boots, I decided she looked too good for the super-fans in their oversized jerseys and painted faces. Her designer sunglasses were on top of her head and she wore a light scarf around her neck. The brisk wind smelled of hot wings and kielbasa. Susan preferred neither. I, on the other hand, appreciated both.

"Would you like me to buy you some pom-poms?" I said.

"Would this be for use now or later?"

"Probably later."

"Then yes."

"May have to work late," I said.

"I certainly hope so," she said. "At least the family would know where they stand."

I walked with her through the growing crowd. Kickoff wasn't for another hour, but according to sports radio, attendance promised to be a record day for regular season. I kept on wanting to call it opening day, but I knew that term applied only to baseball. Besides the standard satellite trucks from ESPN, there were droves of news crews, local, national, and cable. The disappearance of Akira Heywood and his famous dad taking the field was too good to pass up.

"So there's no telling how the demands will be issued?" Susan said.

"Nope."

"Do you think the kidnappers would show here?"

"Can't imagine why they would," I said. "It will be a phone call, text, or an e-mail. I don't think these people wish to be infamous. I think they want to get his money and slide into obscurity."

We had our tickets scanned, waited in line at concessions, and found our seats on the club level. They were good seats, almost directly on the fifty-yard line, with a view of the Patriots' bench.

I ate a hot dog and drank some beer. Susan nibbled on fresh fruit. I had been unaware you could buy fruit at any stadium.

After a short while, we stood for the national anthem and watched as the starting players for the Pats were introduced.

The roar from the crowd for Kinjo rattled the stadium seats. He raised a fist as he ran onto midfield and joined his teammates. And after a few more were announced, there was a kickoff and the violence began.

I particularly liked when Kinjo took the field. Not only because he was my client but because I preferred watching defense. I had been a defensive player many moons ago and liked to watch the dismantling of an offensive attack. Kinjo did a lot of dismantling in the first quarter, with five tackles and one sack. He played with a lot of rage, disguised as passion. I drank my beer slowly. If something were to happen, I needed to be alert, focused, and ready.

"Do you think Hawk is cheering?" Susan said.

"Nope."

"Do you think Z is cheering?" she said.

"Nope."

"You're cheering," she said. "Does that mean it's okay for me to cheer?"

"I'm not cheering," I said. "I'm yelling positive encouragement for Kinjo."

"To knock the quarterback's fucking head off?"

"In a matter of speaking?" I said. "Yes."

Susan had her sunglasses down and leaned forward in her seat. Not long into the second quarter, her right leg tapped up and down with excitement. And she stood twice as Kinjo ran after the Bills' quarterback, getting close to a sack. The quarterback let go of the ball just as Kinjo slammed into him, sending him flying. After the play, Kinjo helped him to his feet.

"I never knew you were such a football fan."

"Lot faster than watching baseball," she said.

"True."

"I have to admit, I like the speed."

"Perhaps dealing with some pent-up aggression?" I said.

Susan stayed focused on the game but smiled. The Bills punted and Kinjo trotted off the field. I checked my phone again. Nothing.

With a minute left in the second quarter, Jeff Barnes appeared at the end of the row. He looked at me and crooked a finger toward the aisle. I did not like when anyone crooked a finger at me. In fact, I had broken many fingers that had performed similar actions.

After Brady threw an incompletion, Susan caught me staring.

"Who's that?"

"Head of security."

"Friend?"

"Foe."

"A casualty of your charm?"

"I'm a casualty of his."

"Perhaps he has some news?"

I finished my beer and stowed the cup under my seat. "Perhaps."

I made my way to the steps. I smiled at Barnes and told him what a wonderful surprise it was to see him.

"Cut the shit, Spenser," he said. "Kinjo told me you were coming. That's his business, we can't stop him. But I wanted to let you know my team is aware you're here and to be on your best behavior."

The row was narrow, and a Coke vendor had to do some considerable acrobatics to get past our pissing contest.

"What's the penalty for sticking chewing gum under my seat?"

Barnes flared his nostrils. He was dressed as he'd been dressed every time I'd seen him. Charcoal pin-striped suit, red tie, and a nifty NFL pin on his lapel. I smiled at him some more. His cheek twitched.

"Can you walk up the steps for a moment?" he said.

I turned to Susan. I winked at her and then followed.

We stood out of the sun and in the shadow

of the narrow tunnel leading to the second level. Barnes's steel-gray hair looked as if it had been barbered two hours ago. His face was clean-shaven, with a ruddy glow.

"Listen," he said. "I want you to know I don't give a damn who does what. I just want Heywood to get his kid back."

I nodded.

"So if something happens," he said, "and you can help . . ."

I nodded again.

"It seems Mr. Kraft is friends with an individual you helped out in the past."

"And Mr. Kraft, being Grand Pooh-bah of this organization, has changed your mind about me."

Barnes just stared at me. I smiled. He shook his head and looked away. Something big had happened on the field and the stadium erupted in wild enthusiasm. "The kid used to follow me around at practice," Barnes said. "He pretended like he was a secret agent or something. Thought what I did was cool."

I had a comment for that. But I kept it to myself.

"Okay," I said.

"Six days of this shit," Barnes said. "Silence? I couldn't fucking leave my house. And he's out there playing his guts out."

The first half was almost over and the fans started to fill the tunnel, pouring past us to the bathrooms and concessions. Barnes turned his back and left without another word.

I returned to my seat just in time to see Kinjo knock a short pass from the tight end's hands. He gathered the defense before the next play, calling the shots, seeing what's going to happen before the offense lined up. If only I could do the same.

42

The ransom demands arrived five minutes after the final whistle blew, via Twitter.

FIVE MIL 4 SON. NO COPS, NO TRIX,
NO MARKS MONEY. OR THE KID DEAD.
DETAILS TO COME

Attached to the message was a photo of Akira. The little boy stood against a concrete wall, staring into the camera with very large eyes. Nearly impossible to trace under the handle TRUPATSFAN. Z called me as soon as the message posted. Z being the one with a Twitter account.

Hawk and I were brought down onto the field by two of Barnes's men and then walked into the tunnel and under the north stands. Susan drove back to Cambridge with Z. Most of the players, including Kinjo, had gone into the locker room. A few other players finished up interviews on the field.

There was a lot of standing around, grim talk, and whispers about the news.

"Fucking Twitter?" Hawk said.

"Yep."

"Don't even have the balls to type out a note."

"I don't think kidnappers use typewriters anymore," I said. "Or even craft good ransom notes."

"Lack of professionalism," Hawk said.

I nodded.

The Pats had won by three touchdowns. But none of Kinjo's teammates looked pleased as they passed us, giants with thick necks and limping gaits, bloody knuckles toting their helmets. Heavy cleats echoing through the tunnel. News crews waited like hyenas by the locker room door for Belichick to finish his postgame talk.

"Wanna bet it's another hoax?" Hawk said.

I shook my head. "Nope," I said. "It's time. Same ones from the radio show."

"Paulie and the Gooch."

"Boston's own number-one sports duo."

"And so we wait some more."

"Special Agent Connor won't let us get close to the planning or the drop."

"Ain't up to Connor," Hawk said.

An official-looking guy in a dark suit asked us if we were with the press. Hawk just stared at him.

"Just to let you know, Kinjo Heywood will not be appearing at the press conference or answering any questions," the man said. "We ask that you respect his family's privacy at this time."

His nametag stated his name was Stacy James and that he was vice president of media relations. I told him we weren't media. As he turned and walked away, Hawk grunted.

"Must've mistaken you for a sideline bunny," I said.

"And you an ex-athlete."

I'd been inside a lot of arenas, both as a fighter and on other cases. But I'd never heard a postgame crowd so quiet. The smooth concrete tunnel wrapped around to the office elevators, weight room, and coach's offices. Coaches and players parted the locker room doors and the crowd, heading toward the media room to take questions. Golf carts zoomed past us, loaded down with trainers' supplies, equipment, and buckets and buckets of water and Gatorade.

Hawk leaned against the expansive concrete wall.

After a long while, I leaned on the wall next to Hawk.

Across the hall, there were faint sounds coming from the press conference. Freshly showered and shaved players in expensive tailored clothes hobbled from the double metal doors and walked into the media room. More downcast eyes. More whispers. The postgame started to feel like a wake. The news that Akira really was being held, this wasn't some kind of misunderstanding, seemed to just be dawning on Kinjo's teammates.

Ray Heywood found us before Kinjo walked out.

He was wearing a light gray pin-striped suit, white shirt, no tie. His round face was sweaty and serious when he got to us. Ray was very out of breath.

"Y'all hear that shit?" he said.

Hawk nodded. I nodded.

"Five million," he said. "Five fucking million."

"Can it be raised?" I said.

"Yeah, sure," he said. "But depends on how soon they call it in. It's not like Kinjo stacks it in the freezer or in the trunk of his damn car."

"His bank will open for him," I said. "Even on Sunday."

"Yeah," Ray said. "I guess we been waiting on this. But five million is a lot."

"One year of play," Hawk said.

Ray nodded. He ran his hand over his sweating face. The front of his dress shirt was soaked with sweat. "Kinjo wants y'all with me," he said. "From the bank to the house."

"What about the Feds?" I said.

"Fuck the Feds, man," Ray said. "That's what Kinjo told me and what I'm telling y'all. The Feds officially can't take part in handing over the money. That doesn't mean they won't be around. But they can't be seen."

"And have they gotten any closer?" I said.

"Shit, I don't know," he said. "You?"

"We have a person of interest," I said. "Although calling him a person may be a bit of a stretch."

"Cops know about him?" Ray said.

"Sure," I said. "They brought him in." Hawk pushed off the wall.

We walked to the center of the long tunnel with Ray. Kinjo hadn't come out yet. Maybe sixty reporters had been let into the locker room, with fifty still waiting outside. There were players' wives and coaches' wives. Several kids about Akira's age running in the tunnel, tossing game balls around.

"So y'all come with me," Ray said. "Get

the money. And then watch the money?"

Hawk tilted his head. "Better than watching the action from the stands."

"When?" I said.

But Ray had already turned around to take a cell-phone call, back turned to us, holding up a finger for us to give him just a minute.

"They want me to guard five mil?" Hawk said.

"Ironic," I said. "Isn't it?"

43

As the kind of guy who carried most of his money in his wallet, five million was a little hard to wrap my head around.

Hawk and I had plenty of time to contemplate it on the drive back from Foxboro. Hawk said he'd actually seen four million on a table once. A million bucks made up of hundreds would fit nicely in a shopping bag. According to Hawk, all of it would fit in a couple of large duffel bags or suitcases.

"Tricky for a getaway," I said.

"Could do a wire transfer," Hawk said. "But Feds would cover them like flies on shit."

"Appropriate analogy."

"Ways to reroute that money," Hawk said. "I'd have a pickup man somewhere overseas."

"Given you have those kind of resources."

Hawk nodded. We parked along State Street in front of a bank building with mirrored windows that seemed to continue above the clouds. It was twilight and the day had turned a soft, pinkish gold, with a brisk wind off the harbor. I still had on a blue hunting shirt I'd bought at Ball and Buck, Levi's, and my dress pair of New Balances. I took off my sunglasses in the lobby but kept the vintage Dodgers cap.

All that money might throw a glare in my eyes.

We were met by security, satisfied the security, and made our way up to the twenty-second floor. Kinjo had been given a police escort and had been joined by his brother, Ray, and super-agent Steve Rosen. Kinjo nodded at us. Super-agent Steve ignored us. And Ray Heywood was too busy countersigning on five million to notice.

There were a handful of federal types, Tom Connor not to be found among them. They eyed me and Hawk with admiration, or more likely suspicion. I eyed them back as we waited. It gave me something to do. They wore official badges on their belts and guns in shoulder holsters.

The plan was for Team Kinjo to view the counting of the money, sign the many documents for the money's release, and then Hawk and I would drive the cash back to Chestnut Hill with an escort from the state police and the Feds.

"I just hope they haven't spotted your mug at the post office," I said.

"Babe, my image can't be captured," Hawk said.

The twenty-second floor was soon exchanged for the second floor and the main lobby of the bank. Twelve men and women greeted us in a very large conference room wearing plastic gloves and running used hundred-dollar bills through a dozen high-speed money counters. Two stainless-steel hard-shell suitcases sat on a table in the center of the room. A young woman wearing jeans, a T-shirt, and Ugg boots packed stacks of cash, already prepackaged and sealed in shrink-wrap for the kidnappers' convenience.

Hawk nodded toward the suitcases. With pride, he winked at me.

"You mind me asking when was the time you saw the four mil?" I said.

"There was a general in the Congo Republic," Hawk said. "He liked to buy a lot of weapons, women, and drugs."

"Of course."

There was the constant whir of the money counters. All the tellers were young, quiet, and attentive to the job. All wearing street clothes, brought in late on their days off.

An hour elapsed, and someone sent out for sandwiches and coffee.

Two hours elapsed, and Steve Rosen walked out of the conference room and into the darkened lobby where we sat. He held two clipboards in his hand.

He tried to hand one to each of us.

"Confidentiality agreement," he said. "And that you are responsible if any of the cash goes missing. *Yadda. Yadda.* Typical shit."

We did not reach for the clipboards.

"Bank requires it," Rosen said.

I shrugged.

"Insurance company requires it."

I shrugged even more.

"And I require it," Rosen said.

"We already discussed terms," I said.

"That was a million years back," Rosen said. "This is here and now. This is what I need. Don't be a pain in my ass. Okay, Spenser?"

"We had an agreement," I said. "And this is the same job."

Rosen whipped his head back as if I'd slapped him. "Really? And him? Him I don't know from Adam's fucking housecat."

Hawk grinned.

"He's with me."

"But who the fuck is he?" Rosen said. He

had a great face for smirking, wide and rubbery.

Hawk stood. He did not announce his name. He just looked down at Steve Rosen and studied him with curiosity. Rosen sniffed, his face continuing to go sour.

"I don't need this shit right now," Rosen said. "I've been an agent for fifteen years. I get the respect from my clients because they know I'm an athlete, too. I know the jock code. When I was putting myself through law school, I worked my way up to second-degree black belt in tae kwon do. I still commit myself to the training every day."

Hawk grinned wider. His teeth were very white and perfect.

"Oh, no," Hawk said.

"I'm just saying if you want to fucking get into it," Rosen said, "I'll fucking get into it with you, brother. This isn't the time."

Hawk took a short breath, crooked his head to the right, popping his neck, and hit super-agent Steve Rosen very quick and very hard in the solar plexus.

Rosen landed hard on his knees. He was working on breathing.

Hawk and I walked toward the money-counting room. Ray and Kinjo met us at the door. Most of the money on the table, nearly all of it, had already been shrink-wrapped and loaded into two suitcases.

"I don't give a damn about any of this," Kinjo said. "You hear me? We get the money to these sons a bitches. But I don't want them spooked or scared off. You help me keep the Feds away. I do what these people say and don't want any problems. Akira comes back unharmed."

I nodded.

Ray Heywood was looking over Hawk's shoulder. "Oh, shit," he said. "Something's wrong with Steve. He's having a heart attack or something."

"All that money flying out the door?" Hawk said. "Guess it really do get to a man."

44

We delivered the money without incident to the Heywood house. Since the stone mansion was surrounded by half the cops in Massachusetts, I felt comfortable dropping Hawk at his car and returning to my apartment for a fresh change of clothes.

The kidnappers had contacted Kinjo again. Each time, they had jumped to a new Twitter handle. The Feds pegged that the messages were coming from one of the many thousands who'd used the city's free Wi-Fi that day. A break in the case was as imminent as finding the proverbial needle in the haystack.

I brewed some coffee and pulled out my gun-cleaning kit from my closet. I laid my cell phone on the kitchen table beside my .38 and .357. I unfolded a well-used red cloth on which to rest my .38. I removed the bullets and began to run a brush though each cylinder and then brushed out the barrel. A clean gun is a happy gun.

After the brushing, I changed tools and attached a clean patch to the cloth, spraying a little gun oil on the cloth. I played an old Dave McKenna LP as I worked. Fond memories of Susan and me at the Copley Plaza and days gone by.

I cleaned the .38 more. Fond memories of shooting men who were about to shoot me.

The little patch came out clean each time. But the routine felt right, adding a little oil to the patch, and then spraying some oil into the cylinder. I ran the red rag over the .38 and set it aside, picking up the .357. The .357 needed the cleaning more, as I'd just taken it to the range a few weeks ago with Z.

McKenna played "Fools Rush In (Where Angels Fear to Tread)."

I smiled a bit. I got up, called Susan, and poured some coffee.

When I hung up, it was a little after eleven.

Hawk called. He was headed back to the Heywoods'.

I drank some coffee. I went through the routine on the .357. The patch came out slightly dirty this time. I ran another patch through to make sure it was clean. I added some oil to another and sprayed the cylinder. I spun the cylinder.

McKenna played "Deep in a Dream."

I was back at the old Oak Bar. Susan and I were young, McKenna was alive, and the Sox were still the lovable bums of old. The bar was dark wood panels and leather furniture and familiar bartenders and a genial wave from McKenna, who was known to listen to ballgames while he played. I wondered if I could listen to ballgames while I shot. I decided not, and set the .357 aside. I found a leather rig for the big gun and clipped the .38 to my belt behind my right hip.

Whatever the kidnappers had in mind had been set in motion.

And all we could do was sit and wait.

I removed the needle from the record, locked up my apartment, and drove off along Marlborough Street.

45

Two more photos of Akira were sent from separate Twitter accounts. Both shut down after being sent. One of them showed the child seated in a big, ugly green recliner. His face blank, eyes wide with exhaustion and fear. The next showed the child wearing Kinjo's game jersey, eyes cast downward, and holding up his index finger in the number-one sign. Each shot was very close, impossible to tell much about the location of the photo if the kidnappers were caught.

Kinjo sat alone in his media room while he waited. He watched video from the game. He'd run a play back and forth twenty times before moving on.

It was one o'clock in the morning and the house was very still but alive with federal agents and cops. The two suitcases sat in the center of the living room as if to underscore the waiting.

I was adding sugar to my coffee when Tom

Connor strode into the kitchen, talking on his cell phone. He eyed me, a second of hesitation, but continued toward the big island in the center of the room. He stood across from me and made his own coffee. I did not offer him any sugar or cream.

"What'd you make of that last one?"

"The taunt?" I said.

"Right?"

I nodded. I drank some coffee.

"Why dress up the kid as Kinjo, make him do all that shit?"

"Personal."

"As in Antonio Lima?"

I shrugged. "I haven't dismissed the possibility."

Connor nodded, poured maybe half the sugar container into his coffee. He held the coffee and squinted his eyes in thought, nattily dressed in an official FBI golf shirt and black dress pants. I wanted to ask him if there was a special store catering only to the Feds. But with age comes wisdom. I drank my coffee, curious as to what he wanted.

"One week," Connor said. "And we got nothing."

I nodded, employing an old crime-buster technique — shut your mouth and let the other person keep talking.

"You went to New York," Connor said.

"Yep."

"And talked to Lima's brother?" he said. "Met with the old lady?"

"I did."

"Me, too," he said. "What did you think?"

I shrugged again. I drank some coffee. The kitchen light shone off Connor's helmet of perfect hair.

"And you found out they'd been paid out."

"I did."

"We didn't know that," Connor said. "Kinjo brought it up. Says he's innocent but didn't need the attention."

I nodded.

"You believe that?"

"He said he wasn't involved," I said. "My job is to take him at his word."

"We worked three different cranks," Connor said. "Including those goddamn numbnuts from Charlestown. Jesus H. Those were some whack jobs. That steroid freak? He was the mastermind. Wanted to use the ransom money to open a dog-grooming business."

"We all have a dream."

"But you're onto something," Connor said. He smiled, trying to pull me along. "Right? You go up to New York, work that

276

clusterfuck, and then nothing? I don't believe it. You're holding out."

"I never stopped thinking there was a connection," I said. "But since getting back, I've been a little sidetracked."

I rested my left hand on the kitchen island. A couple more Feds walked into the kitchen, looking for some stray donuts. Connor gave them the stink eye, and they turned on their heels and left. "What is this, Denny's?" he said, grinning more at me. Just a couple of old pals shooting the breeze.

"Why'd you go see Gerry Broz?"

Ah, I thought.

I shrugged, tilted my head. "Catch up on old times," I said. "Offer my condolences on his late dad."

"Joe was a grade-A turd."

"But you worked with him."

"And you don't work with street creeps, hustlers, and pimps when you need it, Spenser?" Connor said. "Don't get all high and mighty on me. We swim in the same fucking ocean."

I took a long breath through my nose and let it out the same way. The coffee had grown cold and I set it in the microwave to reheat. In the living room, Cristal Heywood lay sleeping on the couch. In Akira's bedroom, Nicole Heywood was probably still wide awake and staring at his fish tank.

From the kitchen, you could see Cristal covered in a large blanket, eyes closed, an empty highball glass on the coffee table. Her arm was draped out from under the blanket, long red nails dangling down to touch the perfect white carpet.

"You don't have to tell me jack," Connor said, speaking quietly. "But if you want to help the kid, maybe we should talk."

I waited. The microwave dinged, and I grabbed my coffee. Connor was staring at Cristal.

"Gerry said you wanted to know about Kevin Murphy," Connor said. "You think we hadn't thought about that? We know her background."

"Then what's to discuss?"

"That you know something else," he said. "So what if she liked to show off her goodies on the Internet? Why Murphy?"

"Why not?"

I considered my options. Tom Connor was a distrustful, immoral creep. And I'd rather have my manly parts roasted over an open flame than work with him. But my job wasn't to vet the help. My job was to facilitate the return of an eight-year-old boy to his father. And if working with the devil himself would help, then I'd explore my options.

"An associate of Kevin Murphy followed Kinjo a couple weeks ago," I said. "He drove the same vehicle and all but admitted he'd been nearly shot by my client."

"This was how long before the kidnapping?" Connor said.

I held up all my fingers and exposed my thumbs.

"You follow him?"

"All the way to the depths of Dorchester," I said. "He has a first-class studio over a convenience store near Fields Corner."

"Anything?"

"Business as usual," I said. "Caught Murphy in the act of adding to his oeuvre."

I could tell that Connor was not familiar with the term. Probably not a fan of Godard or Truffaut. Or even Roger Corman.

"I want to pick him up," he said. "You say Kinjo can finger the guy he works with?"

"Yep," I said.

"I want to talk to him."

"You guys have a little more muscle when it comes to gaining warrants," I said. "And getting someone to flip on their employer."

"But you like this guy Murphy for it?"

I shrugged. "Not especially," I said. "But

it's pretty much all we got besides the Lima family."

"You explain the odds to your client?" he said. "About actually ever seeing his son again?"

"I tried."

"Maybe we should both try harder," Connor said. "Everything about this feels wrong."

46

At dawn, Tom Connor and I sat down with Kinjo and Nicole. Neither of them had slept. I worked on a record-setting cup of coffee as the sun rose over their fence and trees, silver and harsh. A bright, winter wind coming way too early for September.

We had gathered in the study after a fourth message had arrived.

BE READY. 2-MINUTE DRILL.

In a new photo, Akira wore an oversized white T-shirt, holding up two fingers. He'd turned his head away from the camera, a postcard-size bandage affixed to his neck. We all saw the blood.

"We just want both of you to be ready when this happens," Connor said. "Mr. Heywood will probably be asked to deliver the money. Or his representative."

He turned to me and nodded. I gave the

old combat-pilot thumbs-up.

"What is that?" Nicole said. "What the hell's wrong with his neck?"

She dropped her forehead into her outstretched hand and closed her eyes. Her chin quivered, but she did not cry. She had nothing left.

"I want to bring it," Kinjo said. "Look them in the eye."

"Probably won't see them," Connor said. "They'll send you an address, you drop the cash, and then leave. They'll have someone watching the drop. And watching it before they tell you, to make sure we don't set up shop. It will be quick and dirty, and you'll have to leave."

Kinjo nodded. "Okay."

"But you both must know something," Connor said, looking to me. I met his eye and nodded.

"No guarantees," I said.

The air very briskly left the room. All of us sat together at a basic grouping in what the realtor had probably called the library. Instead it had been turned into a storeroom of Kinjo Heywood memorabilia. Unhung framed action shots, old trophies, bobble-heads, and boxes of free T-shirts and sporting goods. There was an empty white marble fireplace with unlit gas logs.

The chairs were old and ragged and seemed to have come from Kinjo's previous life. Nicole looked to me and then to Connor and said, "We know what to expect."

"We'll do everything to make sure your child comes home," Connor said. "But I've worked a dozen of these cases before, and often the kidnappers don't keep to the plan."

"What the fuck does that mean?" Kinjo said.

"It means you can't trust what they say."

"And it means they don't like witnesses," I said.

Kinjo was seated but rocked back and forth in his chair. He still had some tears left and started to cry. His face was as solid as granite under the streams, jaw clenching and unclenching. "I want to deliver the god-damn money."

"If that's what they want," Connor said. "But I recommend you stick to the plan, play by the rules, until they change their script."

Kinjo nodded. The library was sealed off from the rest of the house with two French doors, and through the beveled glass we could see more agents had arrived. I spotted at least ten surrounding the big family dining table, laptop computers and cell phones heating up, waiting for the next word.

"How often does that happen?" Nicole said. She had on jeans and a silk top, a small silver cross hanging from her neck.

Connor took in a breath. "More than half."

"In more than half of the kidnappings you've worked on," Kinjo said. "More than half the time, nobody comes back."

Connor nodded. I did not like the son of a bitch, but knew he was telling the truth.

"How often when the money is paid?" Nicole said.

"In every case, the money was paid," Connor said.

"But he's alive now," Kinjo said. "That's what we got to believe."

I nodded. I did not want to tell him that every photo they had could have been taken within hours of his kidnapping and that Akira could very likely be dead. A week was a long while to hold a victim before calling in a ransom. Moving the child around or keeping him hidden would be problematic. When I told Susan about this, she said be positive but honest.

"What if we say they don't get the money unless we see Akira in person," he said. "Get him back right there."

"You can ask that," Connor said. "But they won't go for it."

"Why not?" Kinjo said.

"Because they know we could swoop down on them and grab them all," Connor said. "They want to convince you to give them the money, let them get away, and that Akira will be released once they feel safe."

"And then what?"

"When Akira is back?"

Kinjo nodded. Nicole just stared at Connor. I could tell she disliked him a little more than she disliked me. That was saying something.

"We birddog their asses to the ends of the earth."

"And if he doesn't come back?" Nicole said.

Connor leaned back in the chair. "The same."

Kinjo stood up and walked to the windows. He stared out into the backyard with his back to us. Everyone was quiet for a good long while. The sun rose brighter and higher, bringing long shadows onto the wood floor and up onto the walls. Kinjo illuminated against the glass. "What if I don't pay?"

"Shut up," Nicole said.

"What if I don't give them the money?"

Kinjo said.

"Shut the fuck up, Kinjo," Nicole said. "You will pay it all."

I rubbed my jaw and stood. I was tired of sitting and talking. I was tired of waiting and being pawns of kidnappers with cell phones and all the time in the world.

Connor stared at me, and without breaking the gaze, said what I knew he'd say. "Same odds," Connor said. "Fifty-fifty, whether you give them the five mil or not. These are bad people who want your money and want nothing or nobody to connect them."

Nicole buried her head in her hands. Kinjo was a large darkened shadow against the bright windows. When he turned, something very ugly had happened to his face.

Kinjo did not acknowledge any of us as he bolted from the room, grabbed his car keys, and sped out from his mansion's driveway.

I put my hand on Nicole's shoulder. She brushed my hand away.

I left the room.

47

Two hours later, there was no word from the kidnappers and no word from Kinjo.

I'd left the Heywood household and walked down the hill, away from the Feds, reporters, cameramen, and anonymous weirdos, and returned to my Explorer. A few minutes later, Z pulled in behind me and crawled into the passenger seat.

He had brought a sack from Dunkin' and two coffees. The bag was heavy. Being a trained detective, I knew something was amiss.

"Breakfast sandwiches," Z said.

"Is this retaliation?"

He shook his head. "Eggs and ham," he said. "Some protein to give you some strength today."

"May not need it," I said. "Our client has flown the coop."

Z reached over and turned on the radio, scanning the dial to the Sports Monstah.

Paulie and the Gooch were on early, talking about the kidnapping. I reached over to turn it off and Z stopped me, telling me to wait. After a few seconds, I heard a third voice in the studio with them. Kinjo Heywood.

I looked to Z.

"Came into the studio about ten minutes ago," Z said. "Said he wanted to reach out to his fans through the show. He said his true fans would look out for him because everyone else had failed him."

"Connor and I had a harsh talk with him and Nicole," I said. "But now they know the odds of getting Akira back."

We sat there and listened to a very talkative Kinjo Heywood chatting with Paulie and the Gooch about Boston being a tough city. He talked about the way the city handled adversity, took care of its own. He talked about growing up in Georgia with nothing, coming here as a rookie, and now being part of the Boston sports family.

"I represent this fucking city," Kinjo said. "With pride."

"The FCC phone bank just exploded," I said.

"Spoken from the heart," Z said.

We opened up our breakfast sandwiches and ate on a fine, chilly fall morning. The sky was thick with gray clouds. Up the hill from us, two Hispanic men with leaf blowers worked to clear the sidewalks. Heywood's neighbors had not been thrilled about the influx of visitors. Many had posted NO PARKING signs on their front lawns.

"I know whoever took my son will be found and confronted by the city I love," Kinjo said.

I drank some coffee. I watched the men in my rearview, cleaning the sidewalks and street of debris. They had parked an old truck nearby, loaded with black plastic bags of leaves. The trees were still full of them, still coming down in piles.

"That's why I need y'all's help," Kinjo said. "I need the people of Boston to help me find my son."

Z and I did not speak. I put down the coffee in the Explorer's nifty holder.

"My son is only eight," he said. "He is a good kid. He loves life. He loves to play and have fun. Who took him ain't even human. Somebody out there knows who's done this. They know the man or men who have broken into my world and did this, don't deserve to live. What they have done to Akira and to my family is sick. It's cowardly and a disgrace to this city."

Z nodded along as Kinjo spoke. I had not

289

said "right on" in many years. I nearly said it.

"That's why I've come here to speak to this city and those who have supported me and my family since coming to Boston," Kinjo said. "Whoever you are out there, you cowards who took my boy, you can e-mail me, tweet to me, write it up in the goddamn sky. But we are done. I am not playing any more games. I'm through. Y'all had my child for a week. I have done everything you said. And now you've gone away. So I guess now it's my move."

I looked to Z. He had quit nodding. The leaf blowers walked closer to my Explorer, making a lot of racket, and I turned up the volume. Two television news trucks passed us in the opposite direction, heading up the hill.

"I have five million dollars cash money in hand," Kinjo said. "It's neatly packed and ready to go. I just posted a picture of all that green onto my Twitter account. I wanted the kidnappers to check it out and see what they're missing. Because this is as close as y'all gonna get to this money."

I realized that I had been holding my breath, and let it out as I listened.

"I am offering five million dollars to anyone in Boston who will take these bastards out," Kinjo said. "One of y'all listening knows who did this. You find them, kill them, and I'll be proud to give up this money. Y'all messed with the wrong man and I've now laid down a bounty on your heads. I will not pay a cent —"

Before Heywood finished his speech, I reached over and turned off the radio. The landscapers had tucked away their leaf blowers and equipment into their old truck. The old truck started with a plume of black smoke and puttered into the driveway and then backed out. Another television truck raced up the hill and nearly hit the truck. It had started to rain.

"This is my fault," I said.

"Kinjo had this in mind," Z said. "The pictures of his child in the jersey? It was too much. Calling him out as a man. You telling him the score just gave him an excuse."

I wasn't so sure. We sat in the car for a long while. Neither of us ate or drank. The rain came on fast and hard, pounding the windshield. I turned on the wipers and sat, waiting for Kinjo to return. Z sprinted out into the weather to his car and back to the gym. He had to work a shift for Henry. Life goes on.

48

Kinjo did not return home.

But he did call me two hours later.

We met at a park bench overlooking the Charles River, within spitting distance of the Hatch Shell. I sat with him, and we did not speak for a long while. We watched the crew teams scull up and back across the river. The coaches yelled. The rowers pulled with great intensity. The day was dark, drizzling, and a little cold. A fine day in Boston.

"I don't regret it," Kinjo said.

"May I ask why?"

"Tired of being pushed around," Kinjo said. "They gonna kill him anyway."

I nodded. The words could not be reversed. My reprimanding him for his decision was pointless. His phone kept chirping until he turned it off. He looked around to see if anyone recognized him.

"Did they contact you again?" I said.

"Nope."

I remained silent. Besides the crew teams, single rowers worked alone, with coaches in nearby boats yelling at them. The boats glided with no effort across the flat, calm water. Soon it would be frozen from here to MIT. Many had tried to walk across the ice, but there were often weak spots. I did not wish to ever try it. The Longfellow Bridge was built for a reason.

"I fucking mean it," Kinjo said. "If whoever took Akira winds up dead, I want you to bring the killer the money."

"What if the killer is part of the group that took him?"

"Does it matter?" he said. "I want the man who set this up, set it in motion."

"Might be hard to tell who's the bad guy from the rest."

"Maybe someone out there knows I mean business and are setting Akira free right now," he said. "That the case, I want every cent in that person's hand."

I rested my hands inside my coat pockets and adjusted my ball cap against the drizzle. A team of eight rowers was close enough for us to hear the coxswain tell them to pick it up some. The rowers were impervious to the cold, their overgrown shoulder muscles and deltoids bursting from tank tops.

"You think I fucked up?" he said.

"Not my call."

"If my boy is dead," Kinjo said, "I'll pay you whatever you want for as long as you want to find out who took him."

"I haven't stopped trying."

"I don't care if it's ten years from now," he said. "I want you to hunt down who did this and kill them. All that money is yours. You hear me?"

I nodded. I stretched my legs out and watched the rowing. I did not want to explain that *assassin* was seldom part of my job description. Hawk wouldn't mind, perhaps. A young couple with a child in a stroller jogged past us. The stroller balanced on three wheels, the kid exhilarated with the fast ride, the couple fit and steadfast at jumping puddles.

"I won't quit," I said.

Kinjo leaned forward and rested his head in his large hands. He wasn't looking at the rowers, he was light-years away, thinking on revenge and killing and dark thoughts about what may have happened to his child.

"My job isn't to doubt you," I said.

Kinjo nodded. A hard wind buffeted along the river.

"But others will," I said. "A lot of your fans will question you. It could get very ugly."

"I don't give two shits," he said. "It's not their kid. I laid it the hell down and we'll see the next play. I'm not going to sit around and wait for Akira to be some kind of game to them."

"What if you don't hear back?"

"I guess I will have to fucking live with what I did."

"You prepared for that?"

Kinjo didn't answer.

"And Nicole?"

"She been trying to call me," he said. "You know as well as I do what she'll say."

"Perhaps you should have spoken to her before laying down the bounty."

Kinjo's eyes turned hard and fast on me. He stared at me for a while, breathing hard and uneasy out of his nose. I thought for a moment he was going to hit me. But he just stood, hands on hips, and looked across the river to MIT.

"I did what I thought was best for Akira," he said. "I made the move. I have to live with it. But I'll tell you something. I don't regret it. It's the right play. You'll see. He'll come back. That boy is tough. Me and him the same. Ain't nothing going to get to my boy. He's coming the hell back home."

I stood with him.

"Goddamn it, Spenser," Kinjo said. He

was crying very softly and quietly.

I put my hand on his shoulder. And he thanked me before walking away, down a very skinny trail toward the Hatch Shell.

The trail was way too small for a guy like Kinjo Heywood. As he walked, he swatted at the overgrown branches that blocked his way.

49

"Did you speak to Kinjo again?" Susan said.

"No."

"Are you the one who advised him this was the best course of action?"

"Of course not."

Susan's last appointment of the day had canceled, so she decided to surprise me at my office. I leaned back in my chair and stared at her as she sat at the corner of my desk. Staring at Susan Silverman was the highlight of some long, dark days.

"But you're still blaming yourself," Susan said.

"What makes you say that?"

She nodded at an open bottle of Bushmills next to my coffee mug. I shrugged and poured out a couple fingers more. It had been two days since the Sports Monstah bounty, and in those very long forty-eight hours, all communication from the kidnappers had ceased. Not a phone call. Not a tweet. Silence. All the talk around the case now focused on Kinjo, not Akira. The blame was harsh and consistent.

"I understand why he did what he did," Susan said. "Given the exact same circumstances, and if Akira had been my child, I may have done the same."

"You are far more tactical than emotional."

"A fifty-fifty chance, either way?" Susan said. "Why not hedge the bet and hope someone turns on the kidnappers?"

"Then he shouldn't have answered their messages," I said. "He didn't just confront them. He put a price on their heads."

Susan pondered, legs crossed, head crooked in thought. Susan, being Susan, looked elegant and smart as hell while pondering in a black dress with tall black heels. She was dressed for dinner at Grill 23. I was in jeans and a T-shirt and looked more appropriate for takeout at Taco Bell.

"Did you try and talk to him?" Susan said. I nodded.

"But he wouldn't see you?"

"He won't see anyone," I said. "Kinjo hasn't gone back to practice or left his house since returning from the radio station. He might not admit it, but I'm sure he's thinking long and hard about the choice he made."

"And what about the other leads?"

"Cristal Heywood's ex?" I said. "I turned over that information to the FBI. He was being grilled by the Feds at the same time Kinjo was getting his final ransom instructions."

"Nothing?"

"Even at his chosen vocation, Kevin Murphy comes up short."

"And nothing more from the FBI or the police?"

"I've spent the last two days going through every interview on the Antonio Lima killing," I said. "I've spoken to the lead investigators, tracked down old witnesses, and located two new ones. I learned the Limas once lived in Boston, that the nightclub fight was over before it started, and that the woman who started it all seems to have vanished off the face of the earth."

"Lela?"

"Lopes," I said. "With an *s.*"

"Strange that they were from Boston?"

"Apparently Boston is where most Cape Verdeans move first," I said. "Didn't make them Pats fans."

"Perhaps you should look at this from another angle," Susan said. "What if Kinjo had done as he was told and paid the ransom?"

"The serial numbers would have been recorded," I said. "Witnesses might have eventually stepped forward."

"And now?"

"Now every lowlife criminal in greater Boston is looking for the kidnappers," I said. "This kidnapper or kidnappers have become a human Powerball ticket."

"So this screws the pooch?"

"I'm glad Pearl isn't here," I said. "She'd find that offensive."

I drank a bit of the Bushmills. I had started to drink early, in an effort to think upon the little I knew about the case. As the shadows fell in my office, I knew it had become more of an escape from how I'd been feeling.

"Can you do any more tonight?" Susan said.

"Nope."

"Tomorrow?"

"Yes."

Susan walked to my hat tree and grabbed my bomber jacket. She tossed the jacket to me, along with my ball cap. "I'm buying you dinner."

"As long as you won't try and take advantage of me later."

"I make no promises." Susan grinned.

I grinned back but wasn't feeling it much. The loss of a child seldom brought out my jovial side.

Long evening shadows crept through my office windows. I stood up, slid into the jacket, and met Susan by the door. We walked down the steps and out onto Berkeley Street, heading away from the river and toward Grill 23.

"How'd you know Grill 23?" she said.

"The shoes," I said. "I can always tell by the shoes."

We walked for a minute, Susan's hand in mine. "Is Kinjo being watched?"

I nodded. "His brother removed all the guns from the house," I said. "There are still some local cops on duty."

"And will he speak to anyone about what's going on?"

"Nope," I said. "And Nicole?"

"Did I mention she is now a patient?"

"I had hoped."

"I can't discuss her state of mind," Susan said. "But she does have the benefit of very solid family support. They've flown in to be with her. She's a very tough, resilient woman."

"Who hasn't given up."

Susan smiled.

"Support is nice," I said.

"Bet your ass," Susan said, squeezing my hand as we continued down Berkeley.

50

Susan had not kept to her word, keeping me out late and thoroughly taking advantage of me after dinner. Feeling rejuvenated, I returned to my apartment the next morning. I showered and dressed, fried bacon and eggs, brewed coffee, and then drove out to Foxboro to meet with Jeff Barnes fresher than a field of daisies.

As I waited in the Pats' front office, I studied a helmet and cleats behind a glass case that had once belonged to Gino Cappelletti. I wondered how long it would've taken Gino to make five mil. When Barnes showed, I decided to ask him.

"About a century," he said.

"Sounds about right," I said.

"Those guys in the old league never got paid," he said. "They played because they loved it."

"And now?"

"Depends on the player."

"Kinjo seems to love it," I said. "Seems like the money is gravy."

"You bet," Barnes said. "Poor guy. Did you know we had six hundred people show up to return Kinjo's game jersey yesterday? People are calling him a killer. Said he might as well been the one who pulled the trigger on his own son."

"Lots of that stuff on the radio," I said. "Reason I turn stations."

"And in the paper and on the TV," Barnes said. "Boston has a new pastime of personally crucifying Kinjo Heywood. Hell, I had a meeting this morning with the league commissioner. He was worried about Heywood's safety when he comes back. Some really nasty stuff online. Lots of it racist. Sometimes it makes you wonder about humanity."

"I have stopped wondering."

Barnes smiled. Perhaps this had nothing to do with the vote of confidence from Robert Kraft. I wanted to believe I had won him over with my wit and charm.

"You were a cop, Spenser?"

"Yep."

"I worked for the Pennsylvania state police before getting into this circus," he said. "Started off with the Eagles and took this job three years ago. I miss the old job, but

304

there are plenty of perks in the NFL."

"All the hot dogs and beer you want."

"And the travel details, the groupies, and endless bullshit, too."

I followed Barnes out of the reception area and along a few hallways and into the stadium itself. He had a key to the side door and carefully locked it before we rounded the upper level and went into the press box facing the end zone. Barnes palmed a handheld radio but turned it off as he stood facing a large glass wall of an empty stadium.

He was dressed as he always dressed, dark suit, white shirt, and red tie. But there was something uncertain and shifting in his eyes. He seemed to have had all the confidence drained from him.

"Have you spoken to Connor?" he said.

"Should I?"

"He won't call me back," he said. "I've called him fifteen, twenty times."

"Maybe he's styling his hair," I said.

A few men worked on the field below, moving large stencils over yard markers and NFL logos. The motor on the sprayer hammering away, a delicate hiss as color was applied onto the artificial grass.

"Connor always called me back."

"Maybe he doesn't have anything to report."

305

"That's what I'm worried about," he said. "That he's given up. Moved on."

I stared at Barnes, appraising his comment. Barnes adjusted the NFL pin on his lapel. He looked away and down at the sprawling field. "They pulled out of Heywood's house this morning."

"Not much to investigate when that cord is severed."

"They could wait and see," he said. "Follow up on every crank and every lead. Giving up is complete absolute bullshit."

"Just because they left doesn't mean they've quit."

"Can you find out?" Barnes said. "Can you let me know if you hear anything? Or know what the hell is going on? There is an additional reward being offered by the team."

"I never left the job," I said. "I still work for Kinjo."

"Good," Barnes said, clasping me on the shoulder. "You need anything checked out or run down, let me know. I will have my people on standby. Whatever you need. Anything."

"By the way, just who said a good word about me to Kraft?"

"Some guy named Hugh Dixon."

"Jesus," I said. "He's still alive?"

306

"Apparently so," he said. "They serve on the same charitable board."

"Wow," I said.

Barnes wasn't listening. He shook his head. "Someone knows something. Someone needs that money."

"Kinjo said dead or alive."

"So do we just wait until someone brings in the head of the kidnapper?"

"That's certainly the idea."

"This whole thing is barbaric as hell."

I agreed with him. He let out a very long, very deep breath and took a seat next to me in the press box. We sat and stared out at the empty stadium for a good long while, until his phone rang and he was urgently needed. He walked me to the parking level and offered his hand. I shook it before driving back to Boston and Government Center to see my old pal Tom Connor.

51

I called Connor and he agreed to meet outside the Federal Building in Government Center. He said he wanted to save me the hassle of going through security. I figured he wanted to ditch me fast, until he invited me for a beer. Being offered a beer by Special Agent in Charge Connor might have made Faust reconsider. But as I wasn't Faust, and a beer was a bonus with information, I agreed. We walked across the street to one of the five thousand Irish pubs around Faneuil Hall. This one was called Paddy O's and situated next door to the Union Oyster House.

There was Irish folk music and Guinness on tap and an Irish flag hanging from the wall. I waited for the leprechaun to tap a shillelagh on the bar and ask our poison. Instead, the bartender turned out to be a tall redhead in a tight T-shirt. I ordered a Sam Adams on tap and Connor got a Tullamore Dew on the rocks. Authentic.

"I apologize that I misread you last time, Spenser," he said. "I was wrong."

"Yes," I said. "You were. About a great many things."

He smiled and laughed as if I'd been joking. His big florid face had a certain hound-dog quality that was difficult to describe. But he definitely had the look of a boozer, broken blood vessels in his cheeks and the whites of his eyes. He had on another Men's Wearhouse special, charcoal pinstripe, and a dress shirt with a very long, unbuttoned collar. His purple and yellow tie was clipped to his shirt with an American flag pin. I resisted the urge to salute.

We drank.

I said, "I heard you've pulled out of the Heywood house."

Connor didn't react. He sipped, elbow on the wooden bar, staring straight ahead. No emotion. Noncommittal. "What else can we do?" he said. "Heywood fucked us."

"Don't take it personally," I said. "If he fucked anyone, it was his own family."

Ice cubes rattled in his glass. He shook it more to chill the whiskey.

"Our talk with him the other night was to explain things," he said. "I wanted him to know the precarious situation, not to go

309

vigilante."

"He interpreted that to mean that he wouldn't see his child again."

"Did we fucking say that?" Connor said. He shook his head. "Jesus H. This fucking guy has gone nuts."

The bar was completely empty at four p.m. If we stuck around until five, drinks were only two bucks each. I hoped I would not be sitting around with Tom Connor an hour from now. I tried to move the conversation along.

"Did you give up on Kevin Murphy?" I said.

"That moron didn't do it."

"My feelings, too," I said. "I guess I had higher hopes for him."

"He was bringing Heywood's wife some blow and she wouldn't pay up for it," he said. "His crazy wife said it was true and I asked her why she hadn't let her husband know about this when he pulled that gun. I mean, he could have killed someone right there."

"How I entered the picture," I said.

"Now we have nothing," he said. "You can't trace the demands. And a paid ransom is always a great starting point. We could have followed the money. Whether the child died or not, we would have had some direct contact. We could stake out the drop without them even knowing."

I nodded.

"It's done," he said. "The kid is dead."

"So you're quitting?"

"We're not quitting, but since our victim's father has put a bounty on the kidnappers, I have to think about the best use of my resources. You know, we do have other major crimes in Boston."

"I have heard as much."

"What about you?" he said, nodding to the bartender. She poured him more whiskey while a sad Irish ballad played from the jukebox. The Irish side of me wanted to join in and sing a few verses, had I known them.

"I'm still on the case."

Connor nodded and smiled to himself. "I grew up in the Old Colony Projects," he said. "When I was a kid, I remember a couple girls from my church just heading home one day from school and disappearing. The police, the church, and even the local hoods looked all over Southie for them. But we never found them. Sometimes people just disappear, Spenser."

"This was an orchestrated business deal," I said. "The kid was taken for money."

Connor nodded. "Not much of this shit anymore," he said. "You really got to be some kind of fucking stupid to pull off a kidnapping like you're Machine Gun Kelly. It's too hard. Nobody can really work a drop anymore. That's the shit of the whole situation. The drop is where we could have had them. Now what they did with the kid in the meantime of catching them was the question. But there was never any fucking doubt that we would've gotten them."

"Probably should have explained it better to Heywood."

"He wants us to hunt them."

"He wants me to hunt them," I said.

"He offer you the five mil?"

"Yep."

"If you get the guy, will you take it?"

"Nope."

Connor tapped at his glass and waited for it to be filled. He smiled to himself some more in that kind of off-kilter, alcohol-infused way. The bartender let us know that happy hour would begin soon. "No, thanks, sweetheart," he said.

Connor laid down enough money to cover us both and a handsome tip.

"You see Kinjo?" he said.

"Right after it happened."

"Have you spoken with him today?"

"Won't talk to me."

"I shouldn't tell you this," Connor said,

draining the rest of the whiskey and patting his lips with a cocktail napkin. "But we have had developments not known outside the Bureau. Certainly by the press. You won't tell the press, will you?"

I made the universal symbol of turning the key in my closed mouth. I stopped just short of throwing the imaginary key over my shoulder.

"We got some clothing sent to Heywood's house," he said. "Kid sizes. Sizes to fit Akira."

I took in some air. I shook my head.

"Clothing was bloody and torn," he said. "We got it at the lab right now to test blood types, hair, and all that CSI shit. But when we showed him the T-shirt, Kinjo broke down. He knew the clothes, IDed it as what the boy had on the day he'd been taken. I've seen a lot of people lose it before. But I've never seen something tear loose in a man like that. His brother and a couple lackeys had to hold him down. Four fucking men to hold one. I think he would have ripped down that mansion brick by brick if he could."

"Jesus," I said.

"Been asking for Jesus a lot around the Heywood house," Connor said, turning to leave. "Looks like he never showed up."

I stayed at the bar and could see Connor dodging cars as he crossed the street to the wide brick expanse of Government Center.

52

When I returned to my office, I was surprised to find Z sitting in my client chair. And I was even more surprised to see Ray Heywood sprawled out asleep on my leather couch. His snoring sounded like the approach of the 20th Century Limited.

I closed the door and walked to the filing cabinets to start to make coffee. I had some Red Barn dark roast. I filled water into the carafe, added several heaping spoonfuls, and then sat at my desk. I leaned back in my chair and crossed my feet at the ankles.

"I still had the GPS on his car," Z said. "Didn't have anything else to do, so I tracked him."

"Initiative."

"Well, you told me to keep an eye on him," Z said. "I found him at a bar in the South End called Slade's."

"And he was well on his way."

"Yep," Z said.

"Talkative?"

"Not much I could understand," Z said. "But he said he wanted to see you. Said he had something important to say."

The coffee made gurgling sounds and filled the office with a pleasant, homey smell. "He give you any hint?"

"Nope," Z said. "I tried. Mainly he talked about Kinjo. He's very upset at Kinjo for what he did. Said Kinjo was going to have to answer for what he'd done."

"He'll have to get in line," I said. "I just came from Foxboro and talked to Barnes. His fan base is diminishing."

"Can't get worse," Z said.

I tilted my head and watched Ray's thick body inflate and deflate. His snoring threatened to disrupt the entire office building. I turned back to Z and took in a breath. "It's gotten worse."

Z looked to me. And I told him what Connor had said about the clothes.

"Explains why Ray went off the rails," Z said. "But he didn't tell me about the clothes. He just kept saying the kid was dead and they were to blame. He was drinking Courvoisier and milk."

"Eek."

"With a Rumple Minze chaser."

"Double eek."

Z nodded. "Had the bartender help me get him into my car," Z said. "Man is a lot heavier than he looks."

Ray Heywood snorted a bit, his red polo shirt untucked, his designer jeans loose and baggy on his stumpy legs. His snoring grew so intense that his breath stopped, and he gurgled awake for a moment. I looked to Z. Z shrugged as Ray went back to sleep.

I kept a medical kit in the bottom-right drawer of my desk for cuts, bruises, snakebites, and the occasional bullet hole. In the kit, I found a handful of smelling salts I'd got from Henry Cimoli in case any female clients were so overcome that they got the vapors. I cracked open one and slid it under Ray Heywood's nose.

He awoke with a start, a wide-eyed and very large, very round flopping fish on the couch. His eyes were bloodshot, and he stared at me as if trying to get me into focus.

"Where the fuck am I?" he said.

Z and I remained silent. He glanced around the room, realizing he was no longer at Slade's in the South End. He pushed himself up on the couch, steadying himself with a thick hand on the leather arm. He hiccupped very loudly.

I walked over to the filing cabinet and poured coffee into a thick ceramic mug from the Agawam Diner.

"How'd I end up here?" Ray said, rubbing his face. He took the coffee.

"You wanted to see me?"

"I didn't say that."

"Yeah," I said. "You did."

Ray turned to Z, who had scooted the client chair around to face him. Z nodded his approval of what I'd said.

"I'm fine," Ray said, trying to stand.

He was very wobbly on his feet and sat back down.

"Drink the coffee," I said. "There's a wash basin in the corner if you don't mind the frilly towels. And a bathroom down the hall."

"I'm fine."

"Why'd you want to see me?"

"I didn't —"

But the statement was cut off when he turned to Z. Z had become very good and very practiced at what we call in the biz the "hard look." Sometimes he made Geronimo look like Norman Vincent Peale.

"I think I'm going to be sick."

Z stood and walked toward my office door and brought back a wastepaper basket. He sat it at Ray's feet and then Z sat back down. He crossed his arms over his chest and waited. Z's eyes were obsidian and flat and hard.

He retched a few times but fortunately did not sully my basket. The basket was mainly used for overdue bills and parking tickets.

"Someone sent Akira's clothes," Ray said. "They had blood on them."

He looked to me as he spoke, seeming to find more understanding. I leaned back and listened. He tried some coffee and made a face as if it were not to his liking. But since this was from a man who drank brandy with milk and a Rumple Minze chaser, I was not offended.

"You know?" he said.

I nodded.

"Jesus God," Ray said. "He's probably dead."

I didn't say anything. The room was very still and very quiet. There were slight traffic sounds, horns and motors, out on Berkeley. The night was coming on, and oblong shadows formed on my desk, stretching into the far corners of the office.

"What did you want to tell me, Ray?" I said.

"Does it matter now?"

"It always matters."

Ray swallowed. He seemed to stifle being sick again. He held the coffee but did not touch it. He nodded along with his thoughts. Z and I stayed silent, eyes on Ray, air seeming to be sucked from the room.

"Okay?" I said.

Ray stared at me.

"You can say what you want to say, or you can continue trying to embalm yourself for as long as it takes."

In such situations, an entire minute of silence was a very long time.

"Okay, okay, okay," Ray said. "Fuck."

"Okay what?" I said.

"Antonio Lima's fucking family," he said. "Rosen thought we could throw some money at them and all this shit would go away. But they never forgave Kinjo. They always believed he killed their son. He never would kill nobody. And now those fucking people have something to do with Akira. It's all gone. It's all over. Everything. Kinjo won't ever come back from this. That boy was his heart, man. He's done."

Ray hiccupped some more. He drank some coffee, but this time did not make a face.

I took my feet off the edge of the desk and leaned forward. I dropped my chin but tilted my eyes upward. I nodded and gave him a reassuring smile. Father Flanagan returns.

Z had not uncrossed his arms. He sat not four feet from Heywood, just staring. I continued to offer warm encouragement.

"There was this woman."

"Lela Lopes?" I said.

"You know, then," Ray said.

I did not answer, as I had no idea what he was talking about.

"That bitch was trying to shake us down two months ago."

"Did you meet with her in New York?"

"Here in Boston," Ray said. "She's back in Boston, man. She and the Lima boys grew up here."

53

"She was here the whole time," Z said.

"Yep."

"Right under our noses."

"But with a different name. A flagrant misstep by the investigator," I said. "I focused on New York."

"If we hadn't kept on Ray."

"You always keep up with someone like Ray Heywood," I said. "Something will break. I think he was with Kinjo two years ago."

Z looked at me.

"Working theory," I said. "He was the third man."

"Why'd he lie?"

"And why did Kinjo and his teammates lie for him?"

We sat in my Explorer on Dudley Street in Roxbury, not far from Blue Hill Avenue. A check for an Eva Lopes, the name Ray had said Lela used now, of approximate age and ethnicity led us to a recently rehabbed two-story house cut into several apartments. The building was light blue, with white window casings. All the windows and front doors had bars, and a chain-link fence surrounded the property. Along Dudley Street, storefronts sat boarded up and shuffled between vacant lots.

After some minutes, a young black man toting a backpack turned up the cracked walkway to the apartments. We followed him to the front door as he tapped in his security code. Z caught the door in hand.

The young man stared at us, waiting to hear an explanation. Neither of us replied, only following him into a central hallway, where he walked up some steps, turning back only once.

We followed the hall and knocked on the door for apartment 1C.

No one answered.

"Have I ever shown you my outstanding technique for removing a door frame and deadbolt without leaving a trace of tampering?" I said.

"You have."

Upstairs, a door opened and closed. The hallway was silent.

"Good." I stepped back two paces and kicked in the door with the heel of my right boot. The door frame around the deadbolt splintered.

"That works," Z said.

I removed the shattered pieces of wood below and closed the door behind us. Once inside, I flipped the switch, but the hall light didn't work. I walked into a narrow hallway, my eyes adjusting to the dim light from a streetlamp outside the window. I turned a corner and tried another switch in a kitchen that lit a hanging lamp over a small table. The hallway led to a modest-sized living room with two closed doors on each side. Two windows offered a spectacular view of the identical-looking apartment building next door, with maybe six feet between the structures.

The living room was a mess. There was a tornado of clothes and other crap spun around the room as if someone had just moved in or was planning on moving out. Half-empty boxes. Clothes still on hangers. Half-packed or unpacked boxes. A hand-knitted blanket covered up an old recliner in a far corner. Bookshelves constructed of plastic milk crates lined one wall. On another, a prefab entertainment center held a small flat-screen television. Z closed the blinds and turned on a table lamp. We walked around the messy piles of clothes, books, and DVDs, most in Portuguese, and searched for a clue.

Lela Lopes had a lot of clothes and, unbelievably, more shoes and boots than Susan Silverman. This, in and of itself, may have been a crime.

A green sleeping bag lay on a couch with an old pillow. In front of the couch was a small table covered in a pizza box from Domino's and an open bottle of Pepsi.

"If you find something," I said, "please tell me the game is afoot."

"Afoot?" Z said.

"Afoot."

Z nodded and picked up a framed photograph from a coffee table. A light-skinned black woman with a lot of black curly hair, huge brown eyes, and a bow-shaped mouth stood with an older woman, possibly her mother. If the younger woman was Lela Lopes, it was easy to see how she might ignite a battle between two men pretty quickly.

"Not bad."

I agreed.

"Not much of a homemaker," Z said.

I picked up an ID badge for Eva Lopes from House of Blues, the kind you wear on a lanyard. We also found four House of Blues T-shirts strewn around the room. "At least she is, or was, employed," I said.

Z opened the door closest to the kitchen and walked inside. I sorted through a few boxes, finding several boxes of perfume, open liquor bottles, and folded underwear and socks. I took the opposite door from where Z had entered and found a bedroom and bath, most of it dismantled, mattress and box springs on the floor and bare of sheets. A large dresser sat with open drawers empty of clothing. Two boxes were sealed with tape, and I slit them open with a pocketknife to find stacks of T-shirts, blue jeans, and designer tops. I was down on my haunches as I searched. The carpet was nondescript beige and probably had never encountered a vacuum cleaner. I stood up, a mild protest in the knees, and checked in and around the bed and in and around the bathroom and behind a big oblong mirror and through a selection of assorted shoeboxes. The shoeboxes, surprisingly, contained shoes.

The room was dark, with a very narrow window holding a very narrow air-conditioning unit. I walked back into the living room and into the kitchen, checking cabinets and a refrigerator. Almost nothing inside, and what was left was hard and moldy. I went through a pile of bills on the counter, going through each section, step by step, not overlooking a scrap, when I heard a doorknob rattle and the scraping of door on busted frame. I stopped riffling through bills and stood very still.

I was not sure Z heard the door, but no noise came from the bedroom.

Footsteps echoed down the little hall, passing the kitchen with me hidden in an alcove.

I could see part of a man from under the hanging cabinets over an open counter to the living room. I stilled my breathing and my feet and anything else that might alert him to my presence. The man was quiet, too, shuffling about the room in a leather jacket, jeans, and sneakers. He made several sighs, searching for something lost in the piles of clothing and assorted junk.

I heard Z flick off the light switch in the bedroom and walk out.

I pulled my .38 but holstered it quickly as the man took off down the hall, flinging open the broken door and running into the building's main hallway. Z ran ahead of me and I followed them down the long open hallway and out through the barred security door, catching sight of both crossing a dusty, weedy lot. The man in the leather jacket, a young black man, hopped a chain-link fence, sailing across with no discernible effort.

It had been a while since I had jumped fences. Z gripped the edge of the chain-link fence with his left hand and sailed his legs over to the right. I had to use both hands and my right knee to get across and find us in back of a three-decker with two home-made laundry lines and plastic kids' toys. The man kept on running, Z making some progress, as they made it to another chain-link fence, both jumping the fence with little effort. The seasoned gumshoe needed a bit more propulsion as we all sailed into a back row of storefronts and a narrow alley of Dumpsters and trash cans and flattened boxes. I was gaining on Z, catching up with him, both of us closing on the guy, when a goldish-brown Pontiac with bright silver rims came whipping around the corner, speeding straight for us. The man ahead of us stopped hard in mid-stride, looking to us and then back to the car, catching his breath as the car skidded to a stop and a passenger door flew open. He looked a final time at us and then jumped into the car, which wasted no time coming right for where we stood. Z and I jumped from the trash cans up to the top of a Dumpster as the car flew past us. There were few things less dignified than using a Dumpster to save your life.

"At least the top was closed," Z said.

"Always an upside."

"But we lost him."

We were both breathing very heavy. I was glad Z was breathing just as heavy.

"But now we know that Victor Lima is in Roxbury," I said. "Now we just need to find out where he's gone."

"That was Lima? You sure?"

I shot Z a look. He grinned and nodded.

"You know the other guy who was with him?" Z said.

I shook my head. We both walked back to the car, opting to forgo the fences and take Blue Hill Avenue by using the sidewalk.

54

It was Friday evening, and I stood outside with Kinjo at Gillette, the team buses chugging diesel into the night. The players were flying out to Denver and Kinjo had no intention of staying behind. The night had grown cold and it had started to rain.

"Cristal is gone," he said.

"You have a fight?"

"Nope," he said. "She was just upset and drinking and drove off about an hour before I left. She said she was going to get Akira back herself."

"Drunk?"

"Hard to get Cristal drunk," Kinjo said.

Water beaded off his black umbrella and across the arm of his black topcoat. It puddled the blacktop of the endless and expansive lot.

"So noted."

"I don't know what else to do but keep playing ball," he said. "I feel like I stop and sit around and I'll go crazy. I either play ball or they might as well drug me up and take me to the psych ward. When they brought me Akira's clothes. Damn."

He took a long breath and wiped his eyes. "He ain't dead."

"I haven't stopped."

"Why'd you want to talk to me about the Limas?" he said. "Thought that was all over."

"Did you know Ray was still paying them off?"

"Nah, man," he said. "Ray wouldn't do that without telling me. He knows how I feel about that. I paid them money for their loss, but I didn't admit nothing. If we kept on paying, that'd make me seem like I'm guilty. I never shot anyone. I never killed anyone. Thought we straight on that."

I nodded.

"Who told you that shit about my brother?"

"Your brother."

Kinjo shook his head. The team was boarding the buses to Logan. The parking lot was filled with many very fast and very expensive cars. The players wore their best, not a tracksuit among them. A lot of camel-hair coats over custom suits and handmade shoes. I noticed a lot of the players wore earrings among a ton of jewelry. The watches were big and shiny, and refracted the parking lights even in the rain.

"Why'd he do that?" Kinjo said.

"You'll have to ask him."

"Shit."

"But it led us to something," I said. "We went to see Lela Lopes and ended up finding Victor Lima."

"In Boston?"

"Yep."

"What's he doing in Boston?"

"Lela Lopes, I assume."

"What'd he say?" Kinjo said.

I shook my head. "He ran and we chased him through a few backyards, but he must have had a buddy with him. Someone picked him up and then tried to run down me and Z."

"You tell the cops?"

I nodded. "Car make, model, and license plate," I said. "Stolen plate. But they're looking for Victor and the car. The Feds, too."

"Fuck the Feds," Kinjo said. "They're quitters."

A thick-bodied man with a shaved head and wearing a tight white polo shirt and khakis called to Kinjo. The bus sat waiting with headlights on and wipers going. The man pointed to his watch and boarded the bus.

"Got to go, man."

"Good luck."

He nodded. "Ain't got nothing else," he said. "I'm wrung up and bled out, man. Nobody can do nothing more to me. They took everything I got."

I reached out and shook his hand. He nodded. The coach called out as the rain continued to beat down on the blacktop.

His eyes were dark and very tired. "Spenser?"

I waited.

"Can you find Cristal?" he said. "I know she's a goddamn mess. But she's my wife and a wreck right now. I know everyone thinks low of her, but she loves me, man, and she thinks she's killed my kid. That's not the truth."

I nodded.

"I think she's lost her shit."

"I can look for her," I said. "Any idea where she might have gone?"

Kinjo lifted up his chin and nodded once. "Kevin Murphy."

"Okay," I said.

Kinjo boarded the bus, and I stood under the umbrella as four big silver buses cut a half-circle and headed north. I walked back to my Explorer, crawled inside, and cranked the ignition.

"And," Hawk said.

"And I don't think he knew about the extra payoffs."

"He say why the brother did it?"

"Nope."

"You ask?"

"You know, I do manage to sleuth without prodding."

"Maybe you benefit from some constructive criticism."

"He asked me for a favor."

Hawk turned to me and I told him about Cristal and Kinjo's suspicions.

"Dorchester again," he said. "Shit."

55

Kevin Murphy didn't live far from his international film studios above the packie in Fields Corner. He had a two-story house with aluminum siding off a street called Toledo Terrace. A small driveway curved behind the house, where we found an open gate and recently added wooden stairs up to a kitchen. It was dark and still raining as we knocked on the back door.

Hawk did not carry an umbrella, as Hawk was impervious to rain.

Murphy opened the door in slippers and boxer shorts.

"Yeah?" he said, looking us over. "What the fuck do you guys want?"

"We came to apologize," I said. "We've come to respect your contribution to the motion-picture arts and want to bestow upon you an honorary Oscar."

Murphy made a face and rubbed his hairless stomach. "Eat me."

Hawk just shook his head, grabbed Murphy's face, and walked him backward into the kitchen. Murphy took wide, looping swings at him, but Hawk had very long arms and seemed uninterested in the resistance. I closed the door behind us; Hawk pushed hard with his right hand and dumped Murphy on his ass.

"Where's Cristal Heywood?" I said.

It was a simple question, but Murphy had considerable trouble following it. He pushed himself up off the floor and scowled at Hawk. Hawk leaned against the kitchen counter and began to whistle the theme to *Jeopardy!*

"Suck it," Murphy said.

I shrugged. "Where's Cristal?"

Murphy spit at Hawk and then lunged for a kitchen knife. Hawk backhanded Murphy and gripped his wrist. As he tore the knife from Murphy's hand there was a very ugly, very audible pop. Murphy, being a man of more pleasure than pain, fell to the ground and began to scream.

"Did you really need me for this?" Hawk said.

"Rainy night," I said. "Nice to have company."

Hawk nodded that that was fine by him. Murphy kept on screaming, and after a few seconds of the wailing, Cristal Heywood came staggering from some dark back room. She wore only a T-shirt, her bleached hair spilling over the front and back of her shoulders. "What the hell? What the hell?"

"Come on," I said.

She stepped into the kitchen and helped Murphy to his feet. He was holding his wrist and crying. If he had not been a pedophile pornographer, I might have even felt sorry for him.

"What?" she said. "What did you do?"

Cristal Heywood's breath smelled of so much alcohol, it might have been considered an accelerant. I took a step back but could still see her pupils were pinpricks, and she wavered on her feet. She was indulging in something beyond vodka.

"Smack," Hawk said. "She's fucked up on smack."

"Go to hell," Cristal said, her arm around Murphy.

I tilted my head to the door. "Kinjo is worried about you."

"Kinjo blames me," she said. "He said I killed his son. I killed him. I fucking killed him."

She was screaming in a most unpleasant way. Hawk stood next to the sink, the faucet dripping every two seconds. The only light

337

in the room spilled from a far back bedroom and over a wide-open living room with wood floors.

"Come on," I said.

"I can't," Cristal said. "Kevin knows. He knows where to find Akira. He's going to help me. He's plugged in to this city. He's important. He has friends in the Mafia, they're going to track down the kidnappers and bring him home. Right, Kevin? Tell them. Tell them so they can leave me the fuck alone."

Murphy looked uncomfortable beyond the sprained wrist. The tap-tapping of the water underscored the silence in the small, darkened kitchen.

"Fuck," he said.

"Where did you learn your oratory skills, Kevin?" I said. "They are stunning."

"Eloquent," Hawk said.

"Yep," I said.

Murphy ran a hand over his very unpleasant face and took in a deep breath, his white, hairless stomach straining at the waistband on his boxer shorts. He would not look at any of us.

"That true?" I said. "Are you going to lead us to Akira through your underworld connections? Because if so, let's go. We would love to get this done right now."

"Takes time," Murphy said.

His voice was low and barely audible. He sounded like a crazy man talking to himself.

"What's that?" Hawk said.

"Takes time," Cristal said. "He has to talk to his people and get the word out. But these fucking people are dead if they did anything to Akira. They're going to be dead."

"And Kevin is going to get that bounty?" Hawk said. "Ah."

"Don't be so quick to judge," I said. "Maybe it will be a generous gift to the Boys and Girls Clubs."

"Screw you," Kevin said. "I got people. I know people. I'm trying to help. More than you're doing. All you're doing is breaking into people's houses and giving them shit."

I tilted my head in a very modest way. He had very compactly and neatly explained my best investigative technique.

"And to motivate Kevin, you fuckin' him," Hawk said.

Cristal crossed her arms over her chest. Her knees tight together as she stood. She wasn't standing so good and had to free an arm to brace herself against the kitchen counter.

"Run home to what you know," Hawk said.

"Screw you," Cristal said.

"Come on," I said. I reached out a hand. "This guy is lying to you."

"He knows," Cristal said. "We'll find Akira alive. We need him."

Hawk turned to Murphy. He took two steps forward, his nose nearly touching Murphy. "Be straight with her."

"She came to me, man."

Hawk raised his hand. Murphy flinched. Hawk and I waited.

"I don't know where he is," Murphy said. Again speaking down low on level one.

"What about the Mob?" Cristal said, wobbling and walking toward him. She slapped him hard across the face. "You told me the Mob. What the fuck, Kevin? What the fuck? I just let you screw me back there. What the hell?"

"True love," Hawk said. He turned and walked back out the door and into the rain.

I reached out my hand.

"Fuck," Cristal said.

"Sometimes words fail us," I said.

She was crying very deep and hard now. She was stoned and drunk and a mess as she recovered her clothes and walked outside with me. Murphy did not move from his place by the sink. He stood flabby and useless, the faucet tapping behind us, unable to lift his eyes as the door closed shut.

56

Bright and early the next morning, Martin Quirk called to tell me that Lela Lopes had been found dead, bound and stuffed into an oil barrel in an Eastie industrial park.

Twenty minutes later, I stood with Quirk at a sprawling complex of oil holding tanks and rusting metal warehouses with a spectacular view of the Mystic River. Frank Belson was there, speaking to some men in coveralls. One of the men was pointing out into the river at a slow-moving tug.

"I had begun to get lonely," Quirk said. "So nice of you to call the other day and ask about Miss Lopes."

"I didn't want you to feel excluded."

"You working with the staties and the Feds, I wasn't so sure you'd even remember your pals at BPD."

" 'I thrust my hoe in the mellow ground,' " I said. " 'Blade-end up and five feet tall.' "

"Do you even know what the fuck you're talking about?"

"Disappointingly, yes."

The complex and much of the access road was now a crime scene, with cops and techs walking along from Route 1 and around the huge holding tanks. Quirk was Quirk, thick-bodied and square-jawed, spotless raincoat over a pressed suit and shined shoes. His eyes registered a trace of annoyance as I recounted our encounter with Victor Lima.

"So the door was busted when you and Tonto got to Roxbury?" Quirk said.

"Yes, sir."

"And without a word, this fucking guy Lima just shagged ass from the apartment?"

"Yep."

"Wouldn't be that he thought you guys broke in and were about to put a gun between his eyes?" Quirk said. "Maybe he was searching for Miss Lopes, too."

"Perhaps."

"So no need to test it for, eh," Quirk said, appraising my footwear, "a pair of eleven-D Red Wings?"

"Twelve," I said. "Don't short me."

"And what does Z wear?" Quirk said.

"Hand-tooled cowboy boots made in Montana," I said. "Buffalo hide."

343

"Of course he does," Quirk said. "Jesus Christ."

"So what do we have?"

"Guy on the late shift tried to ash a fucking cigarette in the barrel and saw the vic wrapped up tight in clear plastic," Quirk said. "We think she was dumped within the last eight to twelve hours. Whoever killed Miss Lopes should get a merit badge in Christmas present wrapping. The woman was wrapped so tight, we had to cut into the plastic with box cutters."

"How was she killed?"

"Extreme trauma to the upper body," Quirk said.

"Shot in the back of the head," I said.

"Yeah, you might say that. Small-caliber weapon. Pro job. Nice and clean. Okay. Now you tell me about this girl's connection to the Heywood case."

I told him about the nightclub shooting, my trip to New York, and ultimately the revelation of Ray Heywood paying off Lela Lopes and Victor coming back into the scene. I left out the part about Cristal Heywood and her film aspirations and taking her home last night. Quirk preferred a linear story without digressions.

"Looks like someone wants to collect some of that NFL cash," Quirk said. "Your client prepared to pay up if the son of a bitch steps forward?"

"He'll need sufficient evidence as to who pulled off the kidnapping of his son," I said. "He'll also want answers about his son's whereabouts."

"You know as well as I," Quirk said.

I nodded.

Quirk took in a long breath, keeping eye contact. He turned his head and spit. "Animals," he said. "And this was going to be the Pats' year, too."

Frank Belson walked away from the two workers, carrying a steno pad and holding an unlit cigar loose in his hand. As he moved through a grouping of techs, workers, cops, and reporters, he lit up the foul brown thing and started to puff.

"What does Lisa say about those things?" I said.

"Lisa believes I've quit," Belson said.

"And you'd risk your marriage and health for a fifty-cent smoke?"

"I'll tell you what, I'll quit with the cigars when you quit with the donuts and beer."

I looked to Belson with wide eyes. "Blasphemy," I said.

Quirk had turned his back to take a call, and when he hung up, he said, "Anyone hear anything?"

Belson shook his head.

"See anything?" Quirk said.

Belson said, "Nope."

"Hell of a nice place to dump a body," Quirk said. "I want to dump a body and I'd come here, too. But I'd put it in one of these fucking tanks. Why not stuff the girl where they keep the oil?"

"Maybe that was the plan," Belson said. "But the tanks are locked tight."

"Lucky for us, she was found," I said.

Belson scratched his neck and puffed on the cigar. "You know this girl is Jesus DeVeiga's half-sister?"

"And that might mean something if I knew who in the hell Jesus DeVeiga was," I said.

Belson looked to Quirk and Quirk to Belson.

"Get with the times," Belson said, blowing smoke from the side of his mouth. "Biggest fucking gangbanger in Roxbury."

57

To get up to speed, Quirk suggested I speak to an officer named Carlos Canuto with the gang unit. The gang unit, or what some called the Youth Violence Strike Force, worked out of District A1 in Charlestown. It was a short drive from the crime scene, and not thirty minutes later, I sat with Canuto in his office on the second floor. He was eating at his desk, a tuna sandwich on wheat, and catching up on the earlier shift's overnight arrests.

"Jesus DeVeiga," I said.

Canuto was a short, stocky black man, not yet thirty. He wore jeans, a black T-shirt, and a backward Chicago White Sox ball cap. The name caught his attention in a big way, although he finished chewing to speak. "You think Jesus DeVeiga kidnapped Heywood's kid?"

"DeVeiga's half-sister was just found in a trash barrel in Eastie," I said. "I'd be a

347

pretty lousy investigator if I didn't try and find him."

"What's her name?"

"Lela Lopes. Also goes by Eva Lopes."

"Don't know her."

"Antonio Lima?" I said. "Victor Lima?"

A smile crossed Canuto's face. His wiped his mouth with a napkin and put down the sandwich. "Now we're talking, man."

"You guys have run-ins?"

"Frequently," Canuto said. "When Antonio got killed in New York, I remember thinking he'd been headed for that bullet his whole damn life. Should have figured he'd be tied in some way with the Heywood kid."

"Me, too," I said. "But it's taken some time to clarify. I kept checking the angles in New York."

"That's how it goes, man."

"I knew Lima had priors. Some drug dealing. Stolen goods."

"His report wasn't nothing," Canuto said. "You probably didn't see his juvie record. He was a name on the street, him and De-Veiga, even before his eighteenth birthday. I'm from the same place in the islands, same neighborhood here. I'd have gone the same way if I hadn't had some people look out for me."

"What about Victor?"

"He's an up-and-comer for sure," Canuto said. "Picked him up a few years ago on outstanding warrants. But I heard he'd moved away with his mother when he turned eighteen. She's a good lady, tried to do whatever it took for her boys."

"I thought I found him living near his mother in New York," I said. "She runs a grocery in Yonkers."

Canuto nodded. He apologized but said he didn't have a lot of time. He picked up the tuna sandwich and took a bite, chewing as he thought. A large picture window behind him had a nice view of Bunker Hill and the obelisk monument.

"This kind of stuff is bad for the whole Cape Verdean community," he said. "Most of us have come here and made good in this country. But it's only the criminals who make the papers. People hear Cape Verdean and instantly think gangbanger."

"This won't help," I said. "You know where I can find DeVeiga?"

"I wish," he said. "We've been looking for him for three months. There was a man shot at a barbershop in Dorchester in June and he was seen walking away. If you get a lead on him, let me know."

"Any idea where to start looking?"

"We have the gang unit and the Fugitive guys looking for DeVeiga," Canuto said, standing. He slipped into a black Kevlar vest and righted his baseball hat with the bill forward. He wiped his mouth again and picked up an energy drink, taking a long swallow.

"But he's mainly Roxbury."

"Some believe he's taken over Roxbury," Canuto said. "Those kids move a lot of drugs and make a lot of money. I do a lot of community outreach, go and give the kids pep talks in the gymnasiums, do fundraisers for the Cape Verdean community. But they see a guy like DeVeiga with all that cash and power. Man. They just want to be him."

I nodded. "Can you check your sources for anything on Victor Lima?"

"Sure," Canuto said. "Let me see what I can do."

We shook hands and walked out of the A1 building together. The building was all sharp angles of concrete and glass, very modern for a police station.

"You're different than Quirk said you'd be," Canuto said.

"More charming?"

"No," Canuto said, smiling.

"More witty?"

"Quirk said you were a real pain in the ass," Canuto said. "And to talk to you or you'd be bugging the shit out of him for days."

"Dogged," I said. "Quirk meant *dogged.*"

58

I returned to my apartment, took a hot shower, and ate a late breakfast of two poached eggs over hash with black coffee. I dressed in a navy button-down, jeans, and lace-up boots. I fitted my .38 on a holster behind my right hip and slipped into my leather jacket and ball cap. It was still raining. It had grown a little cold in the Back Bay. Not cold for Boston but cold for September. When I got to my office, I called Hawk at the Harbor Health Club and told him I needed another favor.

"Of course you do, babe," Hawk said.

And hung up.

I made a few phone calls, including one to Kinjo, letting him know Cristal was back home. I called Susan and left a message about Nicole.

I then read the *Globe* and paid particular interest to the sports columnist's take on the Heywood kidnapping and Kinjo refusing to stop playing. Everyone now knew about the return of Akira's bloody clothes. The writer's stance was contrary to all the sports wackos on the air and on the Web. He believed that Kinjo was doing the right thing and showing his respect and love for his child. Kinjo had not spoken to the press since the kidnapping, but it seemed to me he had spoken to the columnist. The title of the column was called "A Beacon of Light." It was very sad and very powerful, and after reading, I closed the paper and set it aside on my desk.

I made coffee and turned slightly in my chair, to watch the dark skies and grumbling weather over the Back Bay.

I did not like this job or the way it had turned out. I did not like my own performance on letting go of the Limas and the club shooting. I wondered why Victor Lima had been in New York City if he'd been involved in taking Akira in the first place. I needed to find out more about Victor Lima, his time in Boston, and his connection to Jesus DeVeiga. And if I was feeling wildly ambitious, maybe I could find DeVeiga, too.

Before I grew too introspective, Hawk walked in my office door. He removed a black rain slicker and sat down in my client's chair. The chair creaked with

Hawk's weight and heft. The chair was more comfortable with long, lean females with shapely legs.

Hawk leaned forward in his chair and waited. A few raindrops dotted his bald head.

"I need an audience with Tony Marcus," I said.

"Okay."

Hawk leaned forward, picked up the phone on my desk, and dialed a number. He told someone at the other end, presumably Tony Marcus, that we were headed that way.

Hawk stood. I stood. And we drove into the South End and Marcus's club, Buddy's Fox.

Most of the South End had now gone high-end, but Marcus was implacable. Buddy's Fox, with its long, stainless-steel front and elegant red cursive neon, was a beacon to the old South End, gateway to Roxbury. The parking lot was empty, since Buddy's Fox was not a lunchtime spot. A large black man in a white shirt and white pants had set up a barbecue grill outside. He was turning some ribs and the air was rich with smoke.

We walked in the front door to find Ty-Bop sitting in a chair, front legs off the ground, his back leaning against a wall. His satin Pats jacket loose and open, a very large automatic worn below his left arm.

I smiled and shot him with my thumb and forefinger.

Ty-Bop nodded.

A very large black man named Junior stood behind the bar, washing glasses. Junior did not acknowledge us as we walked past the bar and through a door to a hallway and then into Tony's office. Tony was at his desk, ushering us in as if he were a CEO to a Fortune 500 company and not the city's biggest pimp.

"You smell them ribs when you come in?" Tony said.

"Hard to miss," Hawk said.

"Want some?" Tony said. "I'll get him to make up some plates. I'll even make one up for Casper, too."

"After all these years and all we've been through together," I said. "Do you still see color?"

"Oh, please motherfucking forgive me, Spenser. Didn't you put my ass into Walpole some time back? Or is your memory slipping out on your ass?"

"How's your daughter, Tony?" I said.

I looked to Hawk and Hawk shrugged. "Man do have a point," Hawk said.

Tony pursed his lips, put the tips of his fingers up under his flabby chin, and told us to sit. He was wearing a canary-yellow suit with a white shirt and a black tie with a black handkerchief in the pocket. The suit was bold and ugly, but Tony was a pimp, and pimps had certain fashion expectations.

"So," Tony said, lighting up a cigar and placing some equally ugly black shoes on his desk. "What the fuck do you want?"

"What do you know about the Outlaws?"

Tony lifted his chin, studied the end of his cigar, and blew on it, getting the red tip glowing bright. "Hmm," he said.

"You know them?"

"Everybody in Roxbury knows those punks," Marcus said. "They make a lot of trouble for the working man. Make the streets unsafe, gangbang battles. All this shit. Nothing changes. Kids always want to puff themselves up, be men when they ain't nothing but kids."

"Ty-Bop was a kid when he came to you," I said.

"Ty-Bop's a man now," he said. "When he start with me, he a true prodigy. How many teenagers shoot like Ty-Bop?"

I nodded and settled back into my chair. Junior and the black man we'd seen cooking outside walked into Tony's office. They handed Hawk and me two heavy paper plates loaded with ribs, collard greens, and slices of corn bread.

Knowing that it would be rude to turn down a pimp's hospitality, I set the plate in my lap and began to eat. Between mouthfuls, we talked about the Outlaws.

"They all from Cape Verde islands, but don't ask me to find it on a fucking map," Tony said. "Having it out with the Vietnamese kids in Dorchester. Street-corner conquests. Turf battles. Lots of dead kids."

"Ever hear of an Outlaw named Lima?"

"Don't know many names," Tony said. "Just know them on sight, running drugs and shit in Roxbury. Ain't my thing."

"Lucky they don't run girls," I said.

"They do that," Tony said, leaning back into his seat, puffing on the cigar. "Then we going to have some serious goddamn problems."

"What about their main guy?" I said. "DeVeiga?"

Hawk listened while he ate. He ate very carefully, since I knew his jacket cost a few thousand dollars and a sauce stain would mess with his style.

"Jesus DeVeiga?" Tony said. "Shit. Small, quick little punk. Can't be trusted. Mean as hell. Watch your back, he got that crazy look about him."

"Where can we find him?" I said.

"Do I look like goddamn Information to you?"

"For certain professions," I said.

Tony set down the cigar and picked up the phone. As he made some calls, Hawk and I polished off all the ribs, collard greens, and corn bread. Buddy's Fox was on its way up in the world.

Tony set down the phone and picked up his cigar. He started to puff on it again, getting the tip glowing and smoke wafting above our heads.

"If I get to him, he'll want to know what this shit's all about," Tony said.

"Looking for a kid," Hawk said.

"What kid?" Tony said.

I told him it was the Heywood kid and Tony let out a low whistle. "Shit."

"You said it," I said.

"Okay," he said. "You want my Junior and Ty-Bop to come along?"

Hawk set the empty plate on Tony's desk. He stood up. "Appreciate the concern," Hawk said. "But don't need help."

"You sure?" Tony said, eyebrows up, appraising us both.

Hawk didn't answer and walked out of the office. I offered my hand to Tony. He studied it for a moment, reached out for his ashtray, and tapped his cigar.

I shrugged and followed Hawk.

59

Two hours later, we got word from Tony that Jesus DeVeiga would grant us an audience at Franklin Park. We were told to use the Walnut Street entrance into the Long Crouch Woods and follow the northern path up into the old part of the zoo. That part of the park was a lot of green space and walkways and bikeways at the edge of Roxbury. It was a great place to be during daylight hours and not so nice at night.

"Public space," Hawk said. "People will be around."

"Good place to get shot," I said.

"Not perfect," Hawk said. "But good as any."

"There's a rock wall on Columbus Ave," I said. "You could hop the fence. Take the path toward me or frolic through the woods."

"Hard to frolic with a twelve-gauge."

"Or we go in together," I said. "And

impress Jesus with our numbers."

"Gangbangers don't have sense," he said. "He into this kidnapping thing, he'll start to shooting. No conversation. Bam."

"But I so enjoy the conversation," I said.

"Call Z," he said.

I did and we rode around Roxbury a bit. Although we had multiple reasons to suspect Jesus DeVeiga and his people, perhaps he might also supply some answers about Victor Lima and his brother and their connection to his half-sister. I could spend the rest of the day chatting with the de facto head of the Outlaws. I wondered aloud if Jesus had ever seen *West Side Story.*

"Sure," Hawk said. "He start snappin' his fingers. Expect trouble."

I took Columbus to where it connected with Blue Hill and then took Blue Hill south as it circled the park. The park was very big and had a lot of ball fields, a zoo, and a golf course. I cut across on Morton and found my way back again north on Forest Hills. We stopped at a Shell station to use a bathroom and get a couple coffees. There was no sense in going against an entire drug gang uncaffeinated.

We parked at the north entrance. Hawk walked around to the back of the Explorer and removed a Mossberg twelve-gauge. He had a specially made leather rig worn for such occasions and slipped the shotgun onto his side. I knew he had his .44 somewhere, along with a .22 pistol worn on his ankle, should all else fail.

We found the stone gate on Walnut and walked inside the park. The sky was a darker shade of slate and the rain had returned. The rain wasn't awful, but it wasn't exactly wonderful, either. It meant fewer walkers and joggers and people milling about. A decided advantage for the Outlaws.

Hawk and I walked down a narrow path cutting through the center of the Long Crouch Woods. We found the northern path, signs marking the way to the old bear dens, and followed.

"Fucking bears?" Hawk said.

"Old bear dens," I said. "The bears have been moved."

"Closest I ever get to a bear was a married woman's rug," Hawk said. "Her husband liked to shoot dangerous animals."

Hawk wiped the rain from his face, his teeth white and beaming.

No one was in the woods that day. The woods and path were cold and still, bright yellow leaves littering the walkway. A few leaves shook loose in the light wind and rain and twirled down. We walked on. No one came out to us. No one approached us on the path. We kept on walking and moving and watching. In the distance, I spotted the big stone entrance to the old bear cages. I remembered coming here as a teenager with my father and the walkway and the bears. It was pretty much the way I recalled, except overgrown by weeds and ivy.

As we crested the top, three men approached us. They were young, light-skinned blacks, and dressed in traditional gang-banger wear. Low-hanging jeans, team jackets, and ball caps. The ball caps were brand-new Sox game caps, flat-billed and still boasting a 59Fifty sticker. All wore thick chains, gold and silver, and sported simple mustaches. They were hardened men, but not as old as a decent whiskey.

"You Hawk?" said a young guy with shoulder-length cornrows.

Hawk nodded.

"I heard of you," he said.

" 'Course you have."

"I'm DeVeiga," he said, not bothering to introduce his friends. Of course, Hawk didn't introduce me, either.

One of his boys was light-skinned and short. The other was taller and of a darker complexion. The darker one wore earrings in both ears and a very unpleasant scowl as

Hawk spoke to Jesus DeVeiga. I smiled at him, but he acted as if he did not notice.

"Your sister is dead," Hawk said.

DeVeiga nodded.

"She tied in with Victor Lima?"

"Mr. Marcus said you're cool," DeVeiga said.

"Mr. Marcus knows his shit."

"Yeah," DeVeiga said. "Lela and Victor. They were together. Been together for a long time."

Hawk stood there, right foot on the tallest step, back foot behind him, but still taller than DeVeiga and his crew. I stood off to the right, very aware of the gun on my hip and the time it would take to draw.

"Where's the kid, Jesus?" Hawk said, pronouncing the name with a hard *J.*

DeVeiga stood his ground, his ball cap obscuring his eyes like a gunfighter in a Stetson. He nodded in thought and looked to Hawk. I smiled again at DeVeiga's crew. No use in spreading a bad attitude for the day.

"Kid's dead," DeVeiga said.

I swallowed and took in a long breath.

"Who?" Hawk said.

"Like you said, Lima," he said. "Him and his brother were Outlaws. But their mama wanted them out. Moved them to New York, tried to get them out of the life around here. Lela come to be with them. She was with Antonio but then with the brother when Antonio got killed. Then they come back to Boston. But this ain't Outlaw stuff, man. This his own shit he swimming in. This gonna be a problem for us?"

Hawk nodded. "You bet, Jesus. You bet."

I stepped forward. "Where's Lima?" I said.

DeVeiga shook his head.

"Can you find him?"

He shrugged, not once looking at me. "That five mil for real?" he said.

"Kinjo Heywood says so," I said. "You get his kid back."

"Money wasn't for finding the kid," he said. "I heard the money was for killing who took him."

"And that's already started."

"Somebody is hunting," DeVeiga said. "Damn, Lela. She fucked up as soon as she hooked up with those boys. Should have come back home when Antonio was shot."

Up behind DeVeiga and his men sat several large, rusted cages connected to failing brick walls. Beyond the cages was a large stone wall with a frieze of two bears caught on their hind legs in a sort of royal seal. The rain was coming down harder now, pinging off the bill of my ball cap, the gangbangers' ball caps, and Hawk's bald head. No one seemed to want to call it quits on account of the rain.

"You helping them?" Hawk said.

"Outlaws got no fucking business with folks kill a child," DeVeiga said.

Hawk nodded, and DeVeiga turned to me. He stared at me and I stared back.

When the rifle cracked in the woods, I recoiled and ducked and DeVeiga spun and turned and hit the ground, toppling down a couple concrete steps. His boys fanned out, pulling automatics and firing wildly into the woods. Two more rifle shots sounded, and the kid with the double earrings was down, too. A large and ugly wound bloomed in his chest. I hopped the side of the stone steps, seeking cover. I had my .357 out, leveled on the concrete wall and firing toward the shots.

The firing stopped. I heard DeVeiga screaming from the top of the steps. I heard my own breath and the patter of rain from the trees. Hawk called out to me, and I called back. Everything was still and silent. I did not move from the wall. I steadied my breath and eased up along the rock barrier against the staircase and raised the gun.

Two more quick rifle shots. Stone and concrete flew upward. The sound of Hawk's

.44 boomed like a cannon into the woods. I looked up in time to see Hawk pulling Jesus DeVeiga from the top of the steps and behind the wall. I fired to give them cover.

The rifle sounded twice more and then went quiet again.

60

DeVeiga had been shot in the upper chest. Hawk removed his jacket and used it as a compress on the wound. One of DeVeiga's men was dead. The other had run for the woods. I wasn't sure if he'd made it or not.

There seemed to be only one shooter taking careful aim from somewhere in the thick woods below the old stone cages. I could jump up again and fire off a few rounds. But it wouldn't do any good. I had absolutely no idea, beyond the sound of the shot, where the shooter had set up.

If I tried to run from the cover of the stone steps, I'd have a nice big target on my back. I could call the cops and wait. But that would give the shooter time to move through the woods and gain a better position. My best chance was to leave Hawk and DeVeiga and get north, beyond the back of the cages, and circle around to the shooter. The only trouble came from about twenty yards of open ground to the cages. I thought about yelling "time out" but figured the bad guy or guys to be not all that sporting.

Instead I looked to Hawk and nodded to the old cages. He nodded back, pressing the wadded-up jacket into DeVeiga's chest. I made it down onto my belly, and snake-crawled inch by inch on the mud and leaves and trash and debris. The rain came on even harder now, and I continued to crawl, stomach and thighs and chest pressed to the ground. Two shots cracked again from the woods. Still, I was confident I could make it without being seen, until the last eight to ten yards, when my plan was to run like hell to the stone wall.

Inch by inch, mud up under my hands and on my .357 carried in my right hand, I made it close to the wall. And then I ran like hell.

Three shots echoed through the woods. I saw stone chip a few feet away to my right and another chip off the far wall as I dove to the ground and crawled behind the wall. The bear cages were more than ample cover, reaching up fifty feet, built of sturdy stone and concrete. The gun went silent. I ran behind the curvature of the old cages, well protected, and hoped to make it back into the woods before the shooter was gone.

My clothes were soaked, jeans drenched in water and mud, bomber jacket coated and heavy. I dropped the jacket at the far corner of the cages, looking into the depths of the Long Crouch Woods. The thick trees, leaf-covered ground, and the stillness of the rain in the woods made it difficult to believe I was still in Roxbury.

I called 911 and reported a shooting and the need for an ambulance. I quickly reloaded my .357 and checked the load on the .38 from my jacket pocket. I listened and waited. I hoped I'd see a movement, a glint off a scope. But in the rain, I couldn't have spotted a rhino tap-dancing to "Stormy Weather." I just needed to make it far enough behind the shooter and come back on him before he spotted or heard me. I would walk with stealth. The wilderness preservation of my world.

I again took up the old tactic of running like hell. I sprinted far into the woods, following the stone fence around the park until I was confident I was beyond the shooter. I cut back into the woods, water dappling muddy holes and tapping hard off the yellowing leaves. I ducked low branches and jumped over fallen logs until I was far within the park. I breathed quietly and tried to listen, but again heard only the rain. If

Pearl was with me, perhaps she might point to the shooter. But if Pearl had been with me, I'd have been worried about her safety. I kept moving, kept walking, far into the woods, heading back to the stone steps where I'd left Hawk tending to DeVeiga. I could see the steps raising up from the walking path and leading up into the old bear cages. I turned from left to right and saw nothing. I had my .357 held tight and at the ready. At another fallen log, I stopped and scouted the woods before me.

I felt one with the earth and with the woods until I heard a voice behind me. "Don't move a muscle, motherfucker."

Although the slight was not appreciated, I did not move a muscle. And soon hands were on me, pulling the gun from my hand and the .38 from my waist. Someone yanked my arm and I turned to see Victor Lima staring right at me. He cocked me in the temple with my own gun. The feeling was not pleasant, but I kept to my feet.

"Stupid," he said. "Stupid."

"Where's Akira?"

"Why'd you keep fucking with this?" he said. "Heywood had to be the man. Had to lay down a price on our heads."

I touched my temple. It was bleeding badly. I felt sick and spit on the ground.

"Fucking dumb," he said. "Now I got to kill you, too."

"Like you killed Lela?"

"Lela?" he said, wiping water off his face with his free hand. "They killed Lela to get to me."

"Who?"

"DeVeiga."

"DeVeiga says this is all on you."

"Five mil levels things a bit," he said. "Now keep walking. Keep walking to that ditch and then lay down. I'll make it quick and easy for you."

"You're too kind."

"Fuck you," Victor Lima said.

We walked for another twenty feet to a wide ditch brimming with running water. He told me to get into the ditch and place my hands on my head. I could reach for him and take the chance of being shot in a good way. Or I could go into the ditch and keep talking. As talking was my strong suit, I thought I could keep it going.

"Where's Akira?" I said. When you got a good thing, stay with it.

Lima didn't answer. He leveled my .357 at me.

"Did you kill him?" I said.

"Everything would have been cool if Heywood had been a man."

"Is he alive?"

Something flashed in his eyes, a moment of hesitation. But then he gritted his teeth and slowly pulled the trigger. His teeth were clenched tight, jaw tight as the hammer pulled back and cylinder gently started to roll.

And then a large shot as I ducked. As if ducking would do much good.

Lima was down, bleeding and hurt, shot in the back. Another pistol shot rang out as Lima got to his feet and ran fast but ragged and ugly toward the far wall circling the park.

I crawled out of the ditch and ran after him, but he had disappeared. As I reached the park wall, Z came up on me, jogging and out of breath.

"You hurt?" Z said.

"Nope," I said, wiping the blood off my temple. "But Hawk's with a guy who's bad."

Z nodded. Sirens screamed in the distance.

"You did good," I said.

Z looked at me with his black eyes and nodded. "I know."

61

DeVeiga went to the hospital. His pal got a ride with the ME's office and his other pal had disappeared. Z drove Hawk back to the Harbor Health Club and I went to Susan's.

It was Saturday, and she was not in session. Pearl the Wonder Dog greeted me at the front door, paws extended onto my chest, and a giant lick on the chin.

"Why can't you ever greet me like that?" I said.

"Because you're covered head to toe in mud?" Susan said. "Ick."

"Can I borrow your hose?"

"Around back, cowboy."

I walked around to Susan's deck, took off my shoes and socks, and hosed myself off. I tossed my shirt but left on my jeans, knowing Susan's neighbors might object to a large man in his underwear frolicking in the water. But probably nothing new for the Cambridge cops.

I wrung out my shirt and socks. I hosed the mud from my boots and set them on the steps to dry. At the second-floor patio, I handed Susan my jeans and stepped inside. She pointed to the bathroom, and I stood in the shower for a good twenty minutes, stepped into the kitchen in my towel, and searched for a cold beer. I found a six-pack sampler from the Avery Brewing Company I'd left there for emergencies.

"Things getting rough in the Back Bay?" she said.

"Franklin Park," I said. "Hawk and I took a stroll."

"And jumped into the lake?"

"Something like that."

"Are you okay?" she said.

I nodded and walked back into her bedroom, where I kept some spare clothes. I changed into fresh Levi's and a black T-shirt and walked back into the living room. She was perched on the couch with Pearl.

"Two men were shot," I said. "But not by us."

"Who were the men?"

"Upstanding members of the Outlaws street gang."

"And who shot them?" Susan said.

I lifted my beer and took a sip. "Victor Lima."

I told her more about Lela Lopes and the connection through Jesus DeVeiga. I drank some more beer and told her about my adventures through the Long Crouch Woods and my salvation by a young Native American.

"Thank God for Z."

"Yep."

"Lima stole your guns?" she said.

"There is that."

Susan had not been expecting me or anyone on her Saturday off. She wore an oversized gray Harvard sweatshirt and black yoga pants with no shoes. Her hair was twisted up into a bun. Pearl rested her head in Susan's lap and stared up at me with her soulful yellow eyes as if to say, "You wish, buster."

"So you'll go after him," she said.

"Yes," I said. "But I wanted to see you first."

"Why?"

"I think Akira is alive."

Susan turned to me and audibly inhaled. "Are you sure?"

"No," I said. "But I strongly suspect it."

"Don't tell his parents yet," Susan said. "Until you're sure."

I nodded and tipped back the beer. I walked over and scratched Pearl's graying head and ears. She grunted and turned over on her back, legs sticking straight up in the air.

"It's stopped raining," I said. "We could walk down to the Open Market. Have a nice dinner at the Russell House."

"We could," she said. "But you can't."

I nodded.

"Bad guys to catch."

"Yep."

"And a very scared little boy to save," she said.

"Lima has disappeared again."

"Did you call Quirk?"

"Quirk, Lundquist, and even my old pal, Tom Connor," I said. "They're all looking for him."

"If you find him," she said, "I want to be with you when you talk to Nicole. Either way."

I leaned down, kissed Susan, and headed out to continue the search.

62

Hawk called me at midnight.

"I got a lead, babe."

"A lead," I said. "That's part of my lexicon."

"Got word some shitbag want to talk."

"Better."

"Says he knows where to find Lima."

I had gone back to my apartment for my spare gun, an S&W .40-cal, which, for a spare gun, wasn't a bad option. I had a leather rig for it, wore it over my T-shirt and under a workout jacket. My beloved A-2 was still air-drying at Susan's.

"He mention the kid?"

"Nope."

"Where?"

"He wants that money," Hawk said.

"Of course he does," I said. "We get Lima and we'll talk."

"That's what I told him."

I checked my watch. "Where and when?" I said.

"Right now," Hawk said. "Time waits for no man."

"Except us."

Hawk gave a "ha" and told me he'd be around in fifteen.

I finished a cup of coffee and loaded some spare bullets in my jacket before walking down to Marlborough. Hawk pulled around from Arlington and stopped in front of my apartment. I got in and he sped off. We cut up Berkeley to Beacon and then took Clarendon, heading south. "Back to Roxbury," I said.

Hawk just smiled, the bright green instrument panel of the Jag lighting up his face and large hands on the wheel. Clarendon hit Tremont and we took Tremont all the way into the neighborhood.

"You got a name?" I said.

"Nope."

"How'd they find you?"

"DeVeiga," Hawk said. "Reached out to him in the hospital. DeVeiga told this guy we could be trusted."

"Part of the kidnap?" I said.

"Probably."

"Who sold out his partners," I said. "Not exactly someone to trust."

"We be careful," he said. "Kid don't have much time. If Lima still breathing, he's going to be on edge and ready to get out of Boston. He can't take the kid with him."

We didn't speak for a long time until we came into Roxbury. Hawk dialed a number and asked where and then hung up. Hawk shook his head with great disdain. "Man wants to meet at Burger King," he said.

"Did you expect the Four Seasons?" I said.

"Kinjo pay up if the man is right?"

"Up to Kinjo."

"And if the boy is dead?"

I didn't answer. The ethics of laying down a bounty were pretty complex. Hawk drove along Route 28 into Dorchester and crossed over to Washington Street and a late-night Burger King. The restaurant sat on a corner with a large but empty parking lot facing a long row of recently remodeled three-story brick apartments. A large sign boasted this was part of the Codman Square Redevelopment Initiative.

Hawk parked at a crooked angle and we got out of our car.

A few minutes later, a white Crown Vic pulled in beside us. A thick-bodied black man in a white shirt and matching white ball cap crawled out and approached us. He had on dark baggy jeans and running shoes so white they gleamed. He had a mustache and goatee trimmed to a razor's width and a coiled gold chain around his neck. He looked at Hawk and tilted his head in recognition.

We did not shake hands or introduce ourselves.

"Where's the money?" he said.

"Ain't no money," Hawk said. "Money comes when we get Lima and the kid."

"Kid's dead."

"How you know?"

"How you know he ain't?"

"Where?"

"I want my fucking money, man," the man in white said. Hawk looked from left to right and then over his shoulder at the Burger King. I rested my backside against his Jag, careful not to apply any pressure. I smiled good-naturedly at the young thug.

"What's your name?" Hawk said.

"Papa B," the young man said. He tilted his chin up with pride.

"You know who I am?" Hawk said.

"Yeah," he said. "You the Hawk."

"You know about me."

The boy swallowed. His eyes darted away for a moment and then back on Hawk. He crossed his arms over his chest and then nodded a few times.

"Where?" Hawk said.

"I want that money."

"You deliver," Hawk said. "We talk. You fuck us and you get dead quick."

The boy reached into his baggy jeans and gave Hawk a crumpled piece of paper. Hawk read it, turned his head to me, and then nodded. He turned back to Papa B and told him we'd be in touch.

"Come on, man," he said. "I got to get something. I ain't doing this for free."

Hawk walked up so quickly on the boy that the boy flinched. Hawk tilted his head down into the boy's, nearly nose to nose, and said, "You kill that girl?"

Papa B didn't answer.

"You in with them?" Hawk said.

Papa B didn't answer.

"You turn on your pals?"

Nothing.

"If you wastin' our time," Hawk said. "I will be back for your ass."

I looked to Papa B and raised my eyebrows. There was little to add to Hawk's comments. We got into the Jag and pulled away from the Burger King and headed to the address scrawled on the scrap of paper.

63

The address led us back down to Foxboro and an old motel off Route 1 called the Red Fox. The sign was red and neon shining what was probably a permanent vacancy for lodgings that only Norman Bates could love. The Red Fox, no relation to Buddy's, was a one-level layout with all the room doors facing the highway. The walls were brick, the doors once white, and the center of the motel was a faux-Colonial with four large columns over an office. I was delighted to see they offered both color television and electric heat.

The lights were out in room 8, but as we walked past, we noted the dull gray flickering of a television set and the muffled voices of broadcasters calling a ball game. We walked back to Hawk's car, parked nose toward the U-shaped units, and waited for a while. After about an hour, Z showed up. He parked next to us in his Mustang and then got into the back of the Jag. No one had come in or out of the building.

Only six cars had been parked along the units. We did not recognize any of them but took down all the tag numbers in case Lima tried to make a speedy exit. If this was indeed the place Lima had decided to hole up.

"We sure?" Z said.

"Sort of," I said.

"Sort of?" Z said.

"It would behoove the informant not to lie to The Hawk."

"I kind of like *The* in front of my name," Hawk said. "Commands respect."

Z got out of the back of the car and was gone about five minutes and came the long way behind us off Route 1 and back into the car. It was raining again, and he was soaked.

"Small windows in the back," Z said. "Old pebbled glass. I can see the light on in the bathroom but nothing else. I can hear a television on but no voices."

"Can you slip into the window?" I said.

"Nope," Z said.

"Front-door entry," Hawk said.

I nodded.

It was my time to get out into the rain, and I walked to the big columns over the

384

motel office. For the size of the entry, the office was very small. A narrow room with a flat-screen television perched on a coffee table and a couple of old chairs facing forward. There was a desk to the right of the front door and two large display cases loaded down with pamphlets of fun things to do in and around Boston. There was no bell, so I coughed, and a moment later, a tired-looking guy in a Pats T-shirt, khakis, and suspenders walked up and looked me over. He was bald on top but had a prodigious amount of red hair over his ears, giving him the unsubtle look of a circus clown.

"My buddy checked in earlier," I said. "And I don't want to wake him up. He's such a sound sleeper. Room eight."

"What's his name?" the guy said.

"Ben Franklin," I said, and laid down a hundred-dollar bill.

The guy looked at me accusingly for about two seconds and then turned and lifted a key off a gold hook. He sucked on his tooth, swiped the money, and laid down the key.

I took the key and headed out into the rain.

I dangled it in front of the Jag's windshield, and Hawk and Z walked from the car. The asphalt was slick with the rain and red with the neon of the Red Fox sign as we

385

walked to unit number 8. I could still hear the television going, what sounded like a baseball game from the West Coast. I tried to listen for a few hints as to the team while I slipped the key into the lock and turned back to see Hawk and then Z staggered behind me. Both had their guns drawn. Z recently taking up with a Remington 870 pump, just in case we were faced with a zombie apocalypse.

Hawk has his .44, in case we faced a charging elephant.

I turned the key and the doorknob, and we were all inside faster than Usain Bolt.

No one shot at us. Nothing moved.

The television had very poor reception of the Dodgers playing the Giants. The Dodgers were up by three in the top of the eighth as Victor Lima lay dead in a tangle of bloody white sheets. He'd been bleeding for a long while, the white sheets over him more red than anything. He had an open liter bottle of Sprite on the bedside table and some rolls of surgical tape, bandages, and pulls. In his outstretched hand was a .357 Magnum. My gun. It dangled from his life-less fingers, him staring into nothing with lifeless eyes.

Z walked over to the television and turned it off. On the console to the TV, he found my .38. He checked the safety and then tossed it to me.

"Damn, Spenser," Hawk said.

Z went into the bathroom and came out shaking his head. Hawk went looking through drawers and rolling over the dead man and checking in his pockets. The room was silent except for the rain hitting the shingled roof. We needed to move fast; Ben Franklin wouldn't buy us much more time. We searched the room for anything, coming up with a cell phone and some scraps of paper, notes on a map. Hawk held up a set of car keys he found in the man's pocket and we all walked outside to find a blue Ford Taurus.

The three of us stood by the car for a moment, none of us wanting to see what was inside but knowing we had to find out. There could be another phone, an address, or something linking us to Akira. I tossed the keys to Z, and he stared at me a long while. He silently nodded and started to walk toward the trunk.

Hawk and I stood shoulder to shoulder with him. The walk was short but felt long.

Z lifted the key to punch the button as we heard the kicking and muffled yells.

Z popped the trunk.

Akira was bound by hand and foot with

silver duct tape. His mouth had been covered in duct tape as well. He was crying and kicking and rolling.

I reached into the trunk and lifted him out. His pants and shirt were wet and soiled. I held him up in my arms as Hawk gently pulled the tape from his mouth. Z used his pocketknife to cut into the tape, freeing the boy's hands and feet. He was crying, which we took as a good sign.

He took in deep mouthfuls of air as if hyperventilating. Hawk went to the car to grab an unopened Coke.

Akira wrapped his arms around my neck. Z nudged me to look into the trunk. Scrawled into the top of the trunk hatch was the number 57. The boy started to cry very hard and very fast, and I told him I'd take him to his mother.

I called Susan to pass on the news to Nicole. And then we waited for the police.

64

The Foxboro police were overwhelmed with the influx of state cops, Feds, and reporters as word leaked that Akira was alive. At dawn, questions had been asked, statements given, lawyers consulted, and finally Akira could go home. The local cops had brought him a cheeseburger and fries from a local pub. He was so hungry, the cops had to get him another. Lima had not fed him for nearly forty-eight hours, the two of them jumping from apartment to apartment since he'd been taken. The kid didn't know where. He knew there had been three of them, two men and a woman. He had picked Lima and Lela Lopes from a photo pack shown by the police.

I called Kinjo in Denver. Susan picked up Nicole in Medford.

At dawn, they had arrived at the Foxboro police station and walked into the chief's office, where I watched over Akira. After eating, he had fallen asleep.

Nicole saw her child and pressed her hands to her face. She dropped to her knees and cried over him for a long while. The crying woke him, and Akira raised up and wrapped his arms around his mother's neck. I could see his small face over her shoulder, eyes closed and holding on very tight. Nicole rocked him back and forth.

Susan nodded at me. I slipped with her from the room.

We stood in a long hallway with a gray linoleum floor and hard fluorescent lights. The police station was old and very institutional. I leaned against the wall next to the chief's office. Susan had her sunglasses on top of her head and purse thrown over her shoulder. I could tell she'd jumped into her gym clothes and sped off to get Nicole.

"He's going to be all right," I said.

"How was he treated?"

"He wasn't fed for nearly two days," I said. "He spent most of the time with his eyes and mouth taped shut and carried about like a parcel."

"Physical?"

"No."

"Sexual?"

"No," I said. "He was just a bargaining chip. Lima was obsessed with getting Kinjo back for his brother. He lectured a lot to Akira. Telling him his father was a murderer."

"What did Akira say about that?"

"He said Lima was nutso."

Susan shook her head and walked up next to me. She slipped an arm around my waist and tilted her head against my shoulder.

"Maybe totally nuts," Susan said. "But he did keep Akira alive."

"Maybe he wasn't physically able to pull it off," I said. "He did die in the bed with my gun in his hand."

"Or maybe Victor never had any intention of killing the boy," Susan said. "Despite doing some awful things, perhaps Victor Lima still had empathy."

"That kid is going to be messed up for a long time," I said. "I find few things empathetic about Victor Lima."

"Akira is alive."

"Yes."

"And Lima had plenty of chances to let that be his revenge."

I nodded. Susan continued to rest her head on my shoulder. As I set my arm around her, I spotted Steve Rosen barreling around the corner with a rail-thin woman with a lot of blond hair and very large teeth.

Rosen walked up to me and stuck out his

hand. He wore his khaki pants very high and a blue polo shirt at least a size too small. His black hair was slicked back and camera-ready.

"Nice, Spenser," he said. "Nice job."

I shrugged.

He introduced the woman as a very important sports journalist who covered Boston for ESPN. I introduced Susan as a very important shrink who covered Cambridge and greater Boston.

"Is he in there?" Rosen said, nodding to the door reading CHIEF.

"Yep."

Rosen licked his lips and reached for the doorknob. I caught him by his wrist.

"Hey," Rosen said. "Jesus."

"You open that door and I'll break your arm," I said.

"And then I'll kick your ass," Susan said.

"This is a big day," Rosen said, smiling. An old and close friend of the family. "This is happy, huge news. Kinjo has dedicated the game to his son. It's being picked up by CBS now. We have the *Today* show live from Gillette tomorrow. I promised an exclusive here, and to be direct, this doesn't have a fucking thing to do with you, Spenser. So let me in and talk to Nicole. I've known Nicole since she was nineteen years old."

"Hard to sign checks with a broken hand," I said.

"Hard to sit down with a broken ass," Susan said.

I shrugged. "People from Cambridge have fancy ways of speaking."

Rosen snorted. "You want to be paid? Who do you think will write you your check on this thing? Don't be stupid. Open the door. Is your head that freakin' hard?"

Susan stepped up to Rosen. They were about the same height. "You have no idea, buddy," she said.

I tapped my skull with my knuckles.

The blond woman with the big hair and the big teeth kept smiling as if her face had frozen. Her eyes switched from me to Rosen and back.

I pulled Rosen's fingers from the door and moved to block the entrance.

"I'll talk to the cops," he said. "You got no power here. I'll get the chief fucking sideline passes."

"He's downstairs getting ready for a press conference," I said. "Tell him I sent you."

Rosen turned and huffed off. The reporter looked to both of us, openmouthed, but then nodded and smiled and followed.

"Is he just learning you're hardheaded?" Susan said.

"Apparently so."

"Do we have to stay any longer?"

"No."

"Can Nicole take Akira?"

"The Pats sent a private car," I said. "It's waiting out back. I spoke to the driver and told them I'd be walking them out."

"Are you okay?" Susan said.

"Dandy."

"Something's still bothering you about this?"

"A lot."

"Even though Akira is home safe?"

I nodded. We sat in the hall and waited until Nicole and Akira were ready to go home. As we walked out into the daylight, pictures were made and questions shouted. Sometime in the last few hours, the rain had stopped and the sun shone very bright.

65

The next morning, Ray Heywood knocked on my office door and walked inside.

He held a large Nike gym bag in his hand and set it on the floor.

"We need you to deliver this," he said.

"Old jockstraps?"

"A half-million dollars," he said.

"Price has gone up on jockstraps," I said.

"Kinjo is a man of his word," Ray said.

I leaned back in my office chair. "He promised all five million."

"You don't think your guy will be happy with this?" he said, smiling. "Isn't he wanted by the cops?"

"Yep."

"So this should help him get out of town."

"Sure."

Ray was still standing. He shifted from one leg to another. He was wearing a gray rollneck sweater with a matching scally cap.

A large diamond glinted from his right ear-lobe.

"You'll be paid, man," Ray said.

I leaned forward and rested my elbows on my desk. I put my right hand to my face and rubbed my jaw. My contemplative look was stunning.

"We straight?"

I reached out and closed my morning paper. I covered the top of my fresh large coffee with the plastic lid. I looked right up at Ray Heywood and said, "Nope."

"Nope?" he said. "What do you mean fucking 'nope'?"

"I mean I don't deliver bounties," I said. "I agreed to bring back Akira. Akira has been brought back." ·

"To his mother, man," Ray said, snorting. "Shit. You should have waited until Kinjo flew back. Do you work for Nicole or for us?"

"Neither," I said. "Our business is done."

Ray bit in his cheek. He started to turn around and then caught himself. He turned to me with his index finger outstretched. "I see how it is. Now you're through with us. Don't need shit from the Heywood brothers anymore."

I tilted my head and nodded a bit. "Only one thing."

Ray crossed his fat arms across his fat body. "What's that?"

"You were with Kinjo the night Antonio Lima was killed."

Ray's eyes wandered over my face. He stared at me for a while and then broke the glance and shook his head with disgust. "What are you trying to say?"

"Why would you keep on paying Lela Lopes and not tell Kinjo?"

" 'Cause that's what I do," he said. "I look out for my brother so he can keep his head right for the game. And that's all I need you to do, is look out for us and pay off this piece of shit like we agreed."

"You shot Antonio Lima," I said. "Didn't you?"

"Bullshit."

"You never showed up in the reports."

" 'Cause I wasn't there."

"Kinjo had three men with him at the club," I said. "Sometime later, that third man disappeared from the stories of Kinjo and his teammates. A few witnesses remembered but thought you were another player. Why wouldn't he tell police you were with him?"

Ray looked at me for a while. I leaned back in my chair and waited. It was a beautiful day on Berkeley Street, and the sunlight filled all of my office.

"You crazy."

"Sure," I said. "But that's beside the point."

Ray shook his head some more but did not deny it. "Will you take the money?"

"No."

"How will the man get paid?"

"That's your problem," I said.

"Must be nice to be blameless, man," he said. "Spotless and clean."

"Nobody is clean in this," I said.

Ray picked up the Nike bag and left in a huff. He didn't even bother to shut the door behind him.

I reached for my coffee, removed the lid, and watched the steam roll out. I opened the newspaper and resumed reading the argument between *Arlo & Janis.*

66

I never knew, nor ever asked, if the bounty was delivered. It took more than two months for my invoice to be paid in full by Steve Rosen Enterprises. I searched within his envelope for a thank-you card or hair-styling tips but came up empty.

It was late November, Thanksgiving week, and I left my office for the Harbor Health Club. I changed in the locker room and walked out to find Z and Henry Cimoli wearing identical white golf shirts with the club logo.

I smiled.

"Don't say shit, Spenser," Henry said.

I lifted up my hands. I wore an old pair of blue running shorts and a gray sweatshirt cut off at the elbows and neck. "I was about to compliment you both on the professional attire," I said.

"Screw you."

Z was cleaning off a lat pull-down machine

and oiling the chain attached to the weights. He looked up at me and just shook his head.

"Women go crazy for Z in the uniform," Henry said. "I got twenty new members in the last couple months. Housewives and divorcees who act like they don't know how to use the machines. Jesus."

"If he asks you to wear the white satin," I said, turning to Z, "run."

Z continued to clean off and oil the equipment as a handful of people ran on treadmills. Some local businessmen on their lunch break talking more than pumping iron. On the other side of the wide picture window facing the harbor, snow flurries twirled and whirled about, dusting across the wharves and melting on impact.

I made my way to the new-and-improved boxing room and went about wrapping my hands and wrists. The walls were mirrored, and I started off with three rounds of shadow-boxing before sliding into the gloves and attacking the heavy bags. On my third round with the bag, Hawk strolled into the room carrying a paper cup of coffee. He set the coffee on a window ledge and watched as I finished up. I took on the bag with an added ferocity, making the bag dance and jangle on the chains.

"No need to show off," Hawk said.

"Showing you how it's done."

"Ha."

"You want to spar a bit?" I said. "I have time."

Hawk shook his head. He raised his eyebrows. "You remember our pal, Papa B?"

"Sure."

"Motherfucker is dead."

"DeVeiga?"

"My guess," Hawk said. "But DeVeiga the one who told me. Said he'd been looking for Papa B since his sister got killed. Seemed upset that he wasn't the one to finish him off."

"Where?" I said, trying to catch my breath.

"Gone to New York," Hawk said. "Live large."

"What's it to us?"

"DeVeiga wants to talk. He says someone else in on this."

"Does it matter?"

"Matters to DeVeiga," Hawk said. "Might matter to us. Depends on what he's got to say."

"Akira said there were three of them," I said. "All dead. Victor Lima. Lela Lopes and now Papa B."

"Real name is Pasco Barros."

"I like *Papa B* better."

"God rest his soul."

I walked to the corner and found a pair of heavy mitts. I tossed the mitts to Hawk. He removed his black duster but not his sunglasses. He slipped the mitts onto his hands and I practiced combos for the next three three-minute rounds. Hawk told me several times that my left hook needed some work. I was breathing very heavily and sweating when I walked over to the water cooler.

"Okay," I said.

"Figure we at least hear what the man have to say."

"Sure."

"And good to know a man like DeVeiga down in Glocksbury."

"A gangbanging drug dealer?"

"You rather know someone with the Rotary Club?"

I took off my gloves and unwrapped my hands. In fifteen minutes, I was showered and changed back into my street clothes and riding in style with Hawk to meet Jesus De-Veiga.

67

We met DeVeiga at the Jim Rice ball fields in Ramsey Park. Two Outlaws stood watch at the iron gates as we walked inside and started climbing the stands toward De-Veiga. He sat alone up on the top row, staring out at the empty field dusted with snow. Hawk took two steps at a time. I followed suit.

"Took Rice a long time to get in the Hall of Fame," Hawk said.

"Would have won the series in '75 if he hadn't broken his wrist."

"Not bad in '86 against the Mets."

"Why did it take him so long?"

" 'Cause Rice is a surly motherfucker," Hawk said. "Press hated him."

"Reason you like him."

Hawk grinned. We hit the top steps and sat down beside Jesus DeVeiga. DeVeiga was wearing the same flat-billed Sox cap, and this time a navy-blue parka with a fur-trimmed hood.

I looked out onto the empty field. " 'A robin hops along the bench.' "

DeVeiga looked to the field and then back to me. He exchanged glances with Hawk, who simply shook his head. "What you got to say, Jesus?" Hawk said, again pronouncing his name with a hard *J.*

"Wondering what you heard about Papa B," he said.

"We know as much as you," I said.

"I didn't kill him," he said.

"Don't care if you did," Hawk said. "Don't care if you didn't."

DeVeiga nodded. "I been looking for him since he killed Lela," he said. "Even checked NYC. But didn't come up with nothing. I'm now hearing he was down there trying to trade out that cash."

"So the bounty was paid," I said.

The wind was very cold and very brisk and shot through the open field and the wide expanse of the park. I had on a peacoat and kept my hands deep in my pockets. Not only to keep warm but to find comfort in the .38 in my right hand.

"I know people," DeVeiga said.

"Good to know people," Hawk said.

"People I know in New York said Papa B traded out fifty grand for thirty-five clean."

"That money wouldn't have been marked," I said.

"Yeah," DeVeiga said. "Tell that to Papa. But why he only trade a little? I heard he got at least a million."

"Maybe he squirreled it away," I said.

DeVeiga shook his head. "Man wanted to split town," he said. "Ain't the type to plan a future. He'd been talking free and easy down there. If someone hadn't shot him, I was coming up the next day to settle the shit."

"So he had a partner," I said.

"A partner who got most of the cash?" DeVeiga said. "That ain't no partner. That's a goddamn boss."

Hawk leaned in from the stands. He had on a leather jacket with the collar flipped up over his ears and dark shades. "You said you got something to say," Hawk said. "Say it."

DeVeiga nodded. The two Outlaws had come into the stadium and were walking back and forth at the bottom of the stands. They strolled end to end and crossed paths in the center like sentries. Neither of them speaking or looking at each other.

"Papa B was a snitch."

"Okay," I said.

"Never trusted his ass," DeVeiga said.

"Didn't like him around any of my boys. Any my boys talk with him and they gone, too."

"I think it's been firmly established that Papa B was of low moral character," I said.

"Papa B wasn't one of the kidnappers," he said. "I know the boy was working with Victor Lima. And took the kid."

I looked at him.

DeVeiga laughed. "For me to know."

"But you still think Papa B killed Lela?" I said.

DeVeiga nodded. "And Lima," he said. "He on the hunt for that money. But here's the thing about Papa B. I think he got tipped. Man ain't smart enough to track down Lima or Lela. He being played."

"By whom?" I said.

DeVeiga stared at me, tilting his head.

"Man talks funny," Hawk said. "Who's the motherfucker put Papa B on this?"

"A cop," DeVeiga said.

I widened my eyes. Hawk leaned in some more and rubbed his hands together a bit in the cold. He nodded, too.

"What kind of cop?" Hawk said.

"People down here say Papa B made his money from the Feds," DeVeiga said. "He was a goddamn CI for them. How he got his groceries. I think they the ones that planted the seed in that dumb bastard's brain."

Hawk stood and looked to me.

"Hmm," Hawk said.

"You said it."

"We straight?" DeVeiga said, touching the upper part of his chest where he'd been shot.

Hawk nodded. DeVeiga nodded down to his boys. They stopped patrolling and waited for him at the foot of the steps. He gave Hawk a fist bump. He just looked at me and walked down the steps.

"I feel excluded," I said.

"What's that shit you said about a robin?"

"Thinking of empty ball fields."

"Mmm-hmm," Hawk said.

"Connor?"

"Fool me once," Hawk said.

"Connor didn't fool me," I said. "Connor does for Connor."

"Man learned from the best," Hawk said. "Joe Broz and Jumpin' Jack Flynn."

"Hard to prove."

"All but impossible," Hawk said.

68

On Wednesday, Susan threatened to cook a turkey and invite Z and Henry to Thanksgiving dinner. We could have invited Hawk, but Hawk did not do Thanksgiving. I told Z of the invitation when I found him working the door at the Black Rose pub on State Street.

He was seated outside on a barstool, drinking coffee from a ceramic mug. Z listened to the news with great suspicion.

"Haven't my people been through enough?" Z said.

"True," I said. "But I promised to help. I may even buy the turkey from Verrill Farm in Concord. Already stuffed and cooked."

Z nodded. He checked some IDs of some tourists and picked up his coffee.

"Say yes," I said. "You can bring the corn."

"And we exchange the tobacco after," he said.

"Exactly," I said. I patted him on the back.

We watched as two shapely women jogged past in matching black athletic attire. Z drank some coffee. I checked the time.

"Very nice for you to deliver the invitation in person."

"I was taking a walk," I said.

Z looked at me. I pointed toward Faneuil Hall and beyond.

"Government Center?" Z said.

I nodded. Z got off the stool, walked into the bar, and came back a moment later. We walked together side by side outside the Quincy Market and over North Street to Congress. The Custom House Tower loomed large and historic behind us.

I had the number in my phone and dialed Connor. I got voice mail and told him I had a gift for him courtesy of Papa B. I hung up. Within the shadow of the Federal Building, Z grinned.

We waited near the flagpoles in the expansive brick open space before what may be the ugliest building in all of Boston. The architecture seemed inspired by the bunkers of World War II. The flags flew and popped tightly in the wind. The day was very gray and the snow had started up again. Still spitting and fluttering, winter giving us what I considered a very poor effort.

Forty minutes later, Tom Connor crossed

the open area. We stood firm by the steps, waiting for him to come to us. He wore a very large smile on his face. His black suit and yellow tie looked as if they'd been stolen from a corpse.

"Spenser," Connor said, offering his hand. I did not take it.

I handed him a legal-size manila envelope. He looked to and fro and then reached for it, peeking inside. "What the fuck is this?"

"Pasco Barros's phone records from the last year," I said. "You must have had him on speed dial."

"I have no idea who you're talking about."

"I had a tough time tracking your third phone," I said. "But me being a master detective really paid off."

"Who are you talking about?" he said. "I got an extensive network in this city. If you're trying to say I'm involved with criminals because I deal with criminals, that's libelous."

"No," I said. "It's slanderous. Unless I put it in writing."

He looked to Z. And then back to me. Z studied Connor as one would study a museum exhibit of an extinct animal.

"What do you want?" Connor said.

"You couldn't resist," I said.

"What?" he said.

"Kinjo's bounty," I said. "What are you buying with it, a boat? I bet it's a boat."

Connor's tie flew away from his chest and he yanked it down and stuck it under his lapel. He looked around us again. "Shut the hell up."

"Makes you miss Scollay Square," I said. "The criminals were more honest."

"I'm fucking tired of you, Spenser," Connor said, his Irish face turning a bright pink. "I think you've gone fucking mental. I think you were mental over that whack-job whore who got killed in Southie and I think this kidnapping case has made you mental now."

"The conversations were recorded," I said. "Barros had them in safekeeping in case something happened to him. He got fifty grand and you kept the rest."

Connor's face cut into a smile. He jagged a thumb at me and said to Z, "Can you believe this guy."

Neither of us spoke.

"Something happens to me and they go out FedEx to your predecessor, Epstein."

"You're fucking serious?"

"I know you bought me a drink," I said. "But I'm not that cheap."

"The kid's alive," he said. "What the fuck do you care? These people are filth, anyway. What kind of man plays Russian roulette

411

with his own son?"

"I think you forced his bet," I said. "Kinjo said you'd been pushing him all along that he wouldn't see his son again."

"You did the same."

"I never asked him to lay down a bounty."

"This is all bullshit, Spenser, and you fucking well know it," Connor said.

"Shall we listen to the tapes?"

Z tapped at the side of his jacket. Connor's face had now turned scarlet. He turned on his heel and walked back toward the Federal Building, his tie crisscrossing in front of him, his fat hand swatting it down, reaching for his badge to show the security guards.

"You really have recordings?" Z said.

"Nope."

"Phone records?"

"Yes."

"Not enough to prove he got the money?"

"No."

"I thought you told me phone records are tough to come by?"

"They are."

"And even tougher from the private number of a Fed."

"True."

"But sources are everything?"

"Crime-buster tip seventy-seven."

"And the source?"

"Epstein."

Z nodded. We walked. The red taillights and blur of headlights made beautiful patterns against the gray sky and gray buildings. "So they are onto him?"

"Very much so," I said. "And have been for a while."

We walked together across Congress. The snow had picked up to a respectable level. A nice crowd had formed near Faneuil Hall, shoppers bustling about holding many bags, Christmas lights being strung along Quincy Market.

"Is Susan bluffing about cooking?" Z said.

I contemplated his question. "I'm afraid not."

"But you'll try and intervene in that, too."

"I'm a very good meddler."

"A very lucky thing for Heywood," Z said, looking up State Street.

A kid about Akira's age brushed by, walking with his mother and wearing a blue Pats jersey. Number 57. The kid seemed very proud of it.

ABOUT THE AUTHOR

Ace Atkins is the author of fifteen novels, including *New York Times* bestsellers Robert B. Parker's *Wonderland* and *Lullaby*. He was nominated for an Edgar Award for Best Novel in 2012 for *The Ranger*, the first book in his Quinn Colson series, which also includes *The Lost Ones* and *The Broken Places*. Atkins, whom the bestselling author Michael Connelly has called "one of the best crime writers working today," lives on a farm outside Oxford, Mississippi.

CPSIA information can be obtained
at www.ICGtesting.com
Printed in the USA
FFOW02n1707220415

9 781594 138317

5